SAPPHIRE SCARS

UVAROV BRATVA
BOOK 1

NICOLE FOX

Copyright © 2023 by Nicole Fox

All rights reserved.

No part of this book may be reproduced in any form or by any electronic or mechanical means, including information storage and retrieval systems, without written permission from the author, except for the use of brief quotations in a book review.

❦ Created with Vellum

MAILING LIST

Sign up to my mailing list!
New subscribers receive a FREE steamy bad boy romance novel.

Click the link below to join.
https://sendfox.com/nicolefox

Kovalyov Bratva

Gilded Cage

Gilded Tears

Jaded Soul

Jaded Devil

Ripped Veil

Ripped Lace

Mazzeo Mafia Duet

Liar's Lullaby (Book 1)

Sinner's Lullaby (Book 2)

Bratva Crime Syndicate

Can be read in any order!

Lies He Told Me

Scars He Gave Me

Sins He Taught Me

Belluci Mafia Trilogy

Corrupted Angel (Book 1)

Corrupted Queen (Book 2)

Corrupted Empire (Book 3)

De Maggio Mafia Duet

Devil in a Suit (Book 1)

Devil at the Altar (Book 2)

Kornilov Bratva Duet

Married to the Don (Book 1)

Til Death Do Us Part (Book 2)

Heirs to the Bratva Empire

Can be read in any order!

Kostya

Maksim

Andrei

Princes of Ravenlake Academy (Bully Romance)

Can be read as standalones!

Cruel Prep

Cruel Academy

Cruel Elite

Tsezar Bratva

Nightfall (Book 1)

Daybreak (Book 2)

Russian Crime Brotherhood

Can be read in any order!

Owned by the Mob Boss

Unprotected with the Mob Boss

Knocked Up by the Mob Boss

Sold to the Mob Boss

Stolen by the Mob Boss

Trapped with the Mob Boss

Volkov Bratva

Broken Vows (Book 1)

Broken Hope (Book 2)

Broken Sins *(standalone)*

Other Standalones

Vin: A Mafia Romance

Box Sets

Bratva Mob Bosses (Russian Crime Brotherhood Books 1-6)

Tsezar Bratva (Tsezar Bratva Duet Books 1-2)

Heirs to the Bratva Empire

The Mafia Dons Collection

The Don's Corruption

SAPPHIRE SCARS

He's my ex's brother.

A terrifying mob boss with a past too dark to share.

And when he finds out I'm pregnant, he becomes something else, too:

The husband I never asked for.

Kolya Uvarov crashed into my life at a funeral and saved me from a mega-creep.

Classic meet-cute, right?

Not exactly—because it was his brother we were burying.

A.k.a., my ex-boyfriend.

A.k.a., the man who hit me, stormed out the door, then died in a car crash before I could ever tell him about our baby.

But Kolya knows the secrets I'm hiding.

Kolya has a plan for how to handle them.

And Kolya just leaned down, smelling like vanilla and sin, and whispered seven little words in my ear.

From now on, you belong to me.

SAPPHIRE SCARS *is the first book in the Uvarov Bratva duet. Kolya and June's story continues in Book 2,* **SAPPHIRE TEARS.**

1

JUNE

I know something is wrong as soon as I open the door.

"Adrian?"

The house is dark, which usually means he's not home yet. I've lost count of how many times he's stumbled into bed in the middle of the night, seeking me out like a security blanket.

But I can smell him in here tonight. And the fact that I can smell that sickeningly familiar tang has my good mood crumbling to dust.

He promised me this time would be different.

Then again, he promised me the same thing last time, too. We all know how that turned out.

"Adrian?"

It doesn't take long. I find him passed out, face first on the sofa. His drool pools at the edge of his mouth, staining the couch an ugly burgundy like old blood. I bought this couch with my first paycheck as a professional dancer. Back when both knees worked right, not just one of them.

There are no bottles to be seen, but I suppose the stench coming off him is proof enough that he's fallen off the wagon. Again.

How long was this stint of sobriety? Three weeks plus a day, if I'm doing my math right. Shorter even than the last time. At least he was able to collect a one-month chip during the last go-around. I still have that stupid chip. And the one before that, and the one before that.

I don't know why I keep them. At first, it was a gesture of my belief in him. *Look at me, the supportive girlfriend. I'm not gonna cut and run when my boyfriend needs me the most. No-siree, I'm a keeper.*

But at some point over the last two years, it became less about being supportive and more about keeping tabs on his failures. His failure to follow through, his failure to keep his promises, his failure to be the man I had fallen in love with from the moment I heard him strike the first chord on his piano.

Just like that, my disappointment twists and bends and transforms into anger.

I put both my hands on him and rattle him awake. He almost chokes on his own drool. His eyes are bloodshot and dazed when he blinks them open.

"J-June?"

"You're drunk."

"W-what?"

I shove him again, if only because it feels good to do something. "Get up. You're leaving a stain on the sofa."

He doesn't seem to be registering my words. He does manage to sit up, though, just barely. "Is it… is it morning?"

"Are you so piss-drunk that you can't tell the difference between pitch black and sunlight?"

"Stop fucking shouting."

"I'm not shouting. It just feels that way because you're wasted."

"Jesus," he growls, lumbering to his feet. "Always so damn dramatic."

That's the other thing with Adrian: I never know what I'm going to get with him. It's either the mean drunk or the apologetic one. He's been sorry the last two times he fell off the wagon, so I suppose I'm overdue for the former.

"We've been down this road so many times, Adrian," I say, hearing the bitterness in my words and hating it. "Too many times."

His eyes are yellow and slitted. "It was just a couple of beers."

"For an alcoholic, that's a couple of beers too many."

He presses his fists to his face. "June, I just need some quiet—"

"And I need a boyfriend who keeps to his word. Looks like we're both disappointed tonight."

"Why is there a fucking stick up your ass?"

My harsh laugh is drenched with lost hope. "Of course you forgot. Even though it's been all I've talked about the last few weeks. The fundraiser, Adrian. The fucking fundraiser."

"Maybe if you spoke softer, I'd have remembered."

I stare up at him, trying to find all the beauty in him I'd once appreciated. As mad as I am right now, I can't help but acknowledge that yes, he's still beautiful. That raggedy swoop of dark hair, those blue eyes—bloodshot though they may be—that burn like Arctic ice.

But that beauty is marred by the years I've spent waiting.

Waiting for him to change.

Waiting for him to come home.

Waiting for him to realize that I'm worth being sober for. That *we* are worth being sober for.

"It's happened too many times." My anger is softening, mutating into something sadder that doesn't quite have a name. "You promised me. After The Accident, you prom—"

"You're going to bring up The fucking Accident again? *Again?*"

His roar takes me off guard. I stumble backwards and my calves hit the edge of the coffee table hard. He's wild drunk tonight. I've only ever seen that happen once before. It ended with blood and tears.

I recover fast and push at his chest. "You just—"

BAM.

I can't even get the words out before his hand smashes across my face. My ears ring like a gong struck inside my skull. I blink a couple of times, but nothing is clear. Everything looks pixelated, fuzzy, indistinct.

I press my palm to my cheek, and when I pull it back, I see blood smeared across it. He cut me open. Of course he did—he refuses to take that stupid, gaudy ring off his finger.

Even now, the gold insignia embossed there winks mockingly at me.

"You… you hit me," I say in disbelief.

"And I'll do it again if you push me," he growls, slurring his words just enough to let me know that his veins are still thrumming with poison.

This is the beast, I tell myself. *This is not my Adrian.*

This is not him.

This is not him.

This is not him.

But I find that the mantra I started repeating years ago no longer soothes me. Can you separate the man from the beast if they share the same body? Does it even matter where one stops and the other begins? Which one's the lie? Which one is true?

"Get out," I whisper.

He swings his gaze in my direction. One corner of his mouth turns up in a sneer. "Are you forgetting this is my fuckin' house, too?"

"I don't care whose house it is. I want you out of here." I make sure to keep a good distance between us as I say the words with as much venom as I can muster. "This is the last time you break your promise to me."

"You've kicked me out before."

"This time, it's gonna take."

Adrian snorts. Even now—even after The Accident, the endless disappointments, even after tearing open my face with the ring he never takes off—his smirk still carries a hint of the man I'd fallen for. "You're forgetting about one thing, Junepenny," he says, using his old nickname for me. "You love me."

And there it is, the chain that binds me to him. The steel restraints that have pulled us back together despite my best efforts. He doesn't usually lord it over me. But he's too drunk to care about the consequences of his disregard right now. He's too far gone to know that some wounds can't be stitched closed.

"Get. Out."

His blue eyes focus on me for a fraction of a second before they splinter off in a dozen different directions. "You know what? Fuck it. Fine. I'll let you cool down," he says, stumbling to the door. "I'll go… find a… motel…"

Motels. He only ever mentions them like this when he's drunk. When he's sober, every motel is beneath him, cesspools for STDs and bad choices. (His words, not mine.)

But when he's drunk, it's the refuge he seeks out. He told me once that motels raised him. I'd assumed, based on the little he'd told me, that they were just personal containers for bad memories.

But every now and again, I wonder if maybe he's only told me about the bad things that were done *to* him—as opposed to the bad things he's done to others. After all, it's easier to forgive someone broken. Someone who's suffered at another person's hands.

But what if it's his hands that caused the suffering?

I stand at the threshold as Adrian stumbles away from the house and staggers down the street. His silhouette melts into the shadows. Then he's gone.

I close the door and turn to my dark, empty house. It still reeks of booze.

All the pride and accomplishment I'd felt walking home today feels like ancient history. It's funny how the painful emotions always feel so tangible and visceral, whereas the good ones feel like hazy dreams that you can't quite catch hold of.

Here's a memory: we went to New York once. Adrian and I bought one dollar hot dogs from the halal cart and sat under a tree in Central Park. He kissed me and it tasted like mustard. I knew then that I loved him.

Before then, he was just the man behind the piano. He came out of nowhere one day, filling in as a favor to the theater owner when our regular player was out sick. But even then, part of me loved him, even if the rest of me hadn't quite caught up to that realization yet. He played and I danced and it just fit together, it just worked, it was just beautiful.

Whenever I recall those memories, I feel like I'm seeing them through sepia-colored glasses. They're grainy. Blurred. Just faded enough to make me feel like I'm missing essential parts.

Contrast that to the first time I realized Adrian had a drinking problem. Everything about *that* memory feels sharp, like a thorn hiding beneath the petals of a rose, waiting to cut you when you least expect it.

I remember the smell of vomit. I remember the clothes he was wearing. I even remember that feeling of doom that hung in the air like the last ringing note of his piano.

This is the end. Not the one you hoped for, but the one you deserve.

I fall asleep on the brown couch I'd bought with my first paycheck. I fall asleep trying to catch my sepia-tinted memories and the hope of possibility. I fall asleep praying that when I wake up, things will be right.

I fall asleep knowing they won't.

2

JUNE

I wake up to the flashing of a red and blue light right outside my window, a banging on my front door, and a dull pain across the left side of my face. I know I haven't slept for very long because it's still dark outside and I can still smell Adrian's dried drool on the sofa cushion.

BANG-BANG-BANG.

BANG-BANG-BANG.

The noise is loud and insistent. It's enough to make me feel like I'm the one with the hangover.

"Jesus," I groan, forcing myself to my feet. "Adrian, I thought I told you to fu—"

I pull open the door and the expletive on my lips freezes against my tongue. It's not Adrian, that much is certain. For one, it's a woman, and for another, she's dressed in uniform. My eyes go right to the gun holstered on her hip. It catches the red and blue lights whirling on top of her patrol car and swallows them up like it's saving them to unleash later.

"What happened?" I ask.

"Ma'am, I'm very sorry to wake you at this time, but—" She cuts off abruptly. "You're bleeding."

Oh. Duh. The slap. The ring. The cut, right in the same spot and shape as the last one and the one before that. "I, uh… I walked into a wall earlier."

The cop looks perplexed, but she falls back into her script. "Right. Well, ma'am, I'm sorry to have to tell you this, but there's been an accident."

My initial thought is that Adrian got into another fight. It wouldn't be the first time. None of this would be the first time, actually.

But for some reason I can't explain, that story doesn't feel right tonight. The look on the policewoman's face is all wrong.

"What happened?" I croak again. My voice isn't quite as steady as it was when I asked the same question a moment ago.

"Do you know an Adrian Cooper? We found your number on his person."

That's a weird sentence. Why would she say it like that?

"I don't understand."

"There was an accident, ma'am," the cop says, her eyes lighting with sympathy. It's the engineered kind of compassion, though. The kind that's trained into you in the academy. Just another mask to put on to get her through her shift. "Mr. Cooper was involved. I'm afraid you're going to have to come down to the precinct."

I shake my head to get the bizarre pieces of this story to settle into place. "If he got hurt, shouldn't I go straight to the hospital?"

Her eyes gloss over. More of that manufactured sympathy. Double-thick, dense and horrifying, like glue I can't get off my fingers. "Ma'am, I'm afraid Mr. Cooper didn't make it. We're going to need you to identify the body."

I close my eyes as the breath catches in my throat.

There it is again: that visceral sharpness that comes with the bad moments in life. I clock every insignificant detail and know even as I'm doing it that I'll remember these things for the rest of my days.

The gleam of the cop's silver gun.

The impersonal disinfectant tang of her uniform.

The way her eyes keep flitting to the dried blood I can feel caked on my cheek.

"It's not Adrian," I say confidently. "He's not dead."

"Ma'am, I'm sure this must be shocking for you—"

"He can't be dead," I repeat.

"If you would just come down to the precinct with me and identify the—"

"Fine," I spit. I'm being catty, but only because I know she's wrong. They made a mistake somewhere along the way. Adrian isn't dead; he's snoring and drooling on some cheap, scratchy motel bed. Or maybe he didn't even make it that far. Maybe he's curled up in the nearest ditch, behind a godforsaken hedge, in someone's backyard. He'll be back in the morning, repentant as always. I don't know what I'll do then, but I know one thing for sure.

Adrian. Isn't. Dead.

She drives me to the station. It takes exactly thirteen minutes. I watch every single one of those minutes tick past on the clock set in her dash. My knee is bouncing—the hurt one, not the good one—which is strange. I tell myself I'm just tired. It's late and I'm exhausted in the way that only repeating the same cycle again and again can exhaust you.

"I should prepare you," the cop tells me as she walks me through the precinct to a claustrophobic stairwell in the back. "The Accident resulted in a head-on collision that toppled both cars and ignited an explosion. The top half of his body was burned pretty badly."

We go down and enter the morgue. It's freezing cold in here. I wrap my arms around myself, teeth chattering. She's still talking, but I'm barely hearing her. I'm too busy smelling.

I've always been good with smells. But you don't have to be good to recognize the charcoal stench of burned flesh. It clings to the walls of this place. Makes me want to hurl.

"Prepare yourself, ma'am. We'll do this as fast as we can." Then she's pulling the blue sheet off the form stretched across the metal table.

My stomach turns, but it's not a personal kind of horror. It's the human instinct to recoil from something awful, something rotten, something wrong.

But after the initial wave of nausea passes, I can breathe again. Whoever this poor, barbecued soul on the table is, he's not my Adrian.

"Like I was trying to tell you, he can't be—"

The words die on my lips when I see the corpse's hand.

The ring on one finger, to be specific.

It's gold and glistening bright under the cold fluorescent lights overhead. Like it's mocking me. Winking at me one more time from beyond the grave. I touch my cheek, and even though it stings because the wound is still fresh, I let my touch linger. The same smooth curve of the metal is embedded in my face.

I have two choices now, I realize. I can either scream into the void…

Or I can fall into it.

I choose the latter. At least that one comes with blissful oblivion.

3

JUNE

"W-where am I?"

"You're in the hospital, ma'am." The voice is female, bright, and faux-cheery in a briskly professional sort of way. "You fainted."

I honestly kind of wish I was disoriented. But as soon as she says that, I remember exactly where I was when I passed out. I remember exactly what I was doing. Or meant to be doing, anyway. I'm not sure I properly identified my boyfriend's corpse before I hit the ground, though I doubt it matters much. I'm assuming that even New York's finest can put those pieces together.

"I want to go home," I whisper.

"The doctor has to clear you first, darling," the voice explains. "He needs to make sure your little fall didn't hurt the baby."

I blink and crack one eye open. Maybe I *am* disoriented, after all. "What baby?"

"Your baby, dear," the nurse says. Her face hangs over me like a gigantic sun I want to run from.

"I don't have a baby."

Her eyes go wide. They're a pretty brown, aged prematurely with decades of sad stories passing through her ward. "Oh, dear... You didn't know."

"Didn't know what?"

"I'm so sorry, darling. We thought you knew," she says, her eyes softening instantly. Real sympathy, not the engineered kind. "You're pregnant."

4

JUNE

I'm pregnant.

I'm pregnant at a funeral.

I'm pregnant at my baby's father's funeral.

"Hello."

A startled gasp escapes my lips. I've been jumpy for days now. You'd think that being in a crowded funeral hall would eliminate that feeling for a few hours, but apparently not.

"I'm sorry," the man who spoke says from behind a smile that's veering uncomfortably close to creepy. I frown, vaguely recognizing his spindly hunch and his distinctive beaked nose. I'm pretty sure I've been creeped out by that smile before. "I scared you."

"No, it's okay. I'm just… on edge."

"Of course. This can't be easy for you."

He's the first person to speak to me in twenty minutes, since Adrian's old work colleagues all left. It was nice of them to show up, but it made me sad to realize that they came out of a sense of obligation rather than any real affection or lasting friendship.

"We've met before, haven't we?" I ask, hoping he's not offended by the fact that I can't really remember him.

He smells of stale cigarettes and strong mint gum that's failing to cover up the tobacco stench. "Yes, we have. Adrian introduced us at his last recital."

I raise my eyebrows. "Adrian hasn't—*hadn't*—performed in over two years."

"Was it that long ago?" the man muses, still not volunteering his name. "I remember it like it was yesterday."

I wish I could say the same. But that's one of the good memories, so of course it's all hazy and indistinct. Even the image in my mind's eye of his fingers gliding over the piano keys looks like a thousand photographs laid on top of one another.

My eyes glide to the piano forte looming in the corner behind a framed picture of Adrian. Floral arrangements bloom on both sides. Understated, tasteful, elegant—Adrian would've fucking hated them.

Too damn fancy. These people probably think I'm trying to impress them.

His voice sounds off in my head like he's standing right next to me. I actually look to my left, expecting to see that disarming smile of his, his eyes all crinkled-up at the edges. I called them laugh lines. He preferred crow's feet.

"He was the best in the business," the spindly creep says, reminding me that he's still here. "I never knew anyone who could play like he did."

I really need to get off my feet, but I'm afraid if I mention that to him, he'll assume I'm extending an invitation to sit and chat. So I stand, awkwardly twisting in the wind, feeling as though I'm playing a part in a play. *The Dutifully Grieving Girlfriend,* we'd call it. It's the tenth run of this performance, though, and I'm already over it.

Not because I don't care about the play, but because I wasn't ready for *this* play. I needed more time.

"Always thought Adrian was a lucky bastard, ya know. He was a good-looking son of a bitch. He had talent. People liked him. And he always got the prettiest girls. You'd be a prime example of that."

For the first time, my eyes veer to him and stay on his face. I must've misheard him, but there's no mistaking that leering smile. Is he seriously hitting on me at Adrian's funeral?

"Remind me again, you're Adrian's…?"

"Cousin. Second cousin, technically, but who's counting?" He takes a step towards me and his hand lands on my arm. He starts rubbing, sliding his fingers up and down, from my shoulder to my elbow and back up again. "You mustn't mourn him too long, you know. Pretty thing like you is wasted on the dead."

"He hasn't been dead very long." I wish my voice would come out stronger, but it lands flat. It sounds weak, tired, frail. Adrian would be annoyed.

It's my damn funeral and you can't muster up a little hysteria? You're never gonna see or speak to me again, Junepenny. The least you can do is act the part.

I shudder under the pull of his imagined voice, but it works on both levels, considering Adrian's second cousin is still touching me. The shudder takes me back out of the creep's reach.

A smart man would take the hint and give me some space.

This one just doubles down on the smirk that's giving me goosebumps in the first place.

"You know you got a bruise on your cheek, right?" he asks.

I spent a frantic twenty minutes trying to layer foundation and blush over the cut this morning, but I guess I didn't do a good enough job. I can't even blame tears for ruining my makeup, mostly because I can't even bring myself to cry. I don't know why. I'm too broken for tears, if such a thing is possible.

"I walked into a wall."

"Do you do that often?" he asks. If he's trying to be funny, he's way off-target.

"Only when I need a good, hard reality check."

He looks at me like he's not sure if he should laugh or not. "How about I drive you home after this thing is done?"

This thing? That grates on me in a way I can't explain. *Oh yeah, this little shindig. This get-together. This tragic fucking funeral.*

"Maybe we can stop for a bite to eat on the way. I'm sure you haven't eaten anything, and I'm starved. Funerals always make me hungry."

I wonder if I should mention that his breath smells of dead ashes, and if I'd had an appetite, it'd be gone already. "I'll probably be here for a while."

"I can wait."

He touches me again. On my lower back this time. I freeze instantly. His proximity, the way he's touching me—it's all way too intimate. The only man who'd touched me like that in years is six feet in the ground just a few dozen yards away from us.

"Could you excuse me for a moment, please?"

I start to step away without waiting for a response, but before I can take a single step, he hooks that claw around my hip and reels me into him. I smell the smoke again, the mint, and it's nauseating, it's fucking disgusting, actually, I want him to stop touching me, to *stop fucking touching me,* but he's just in my face, still smiling that same dead smile, and I open my mouth to scream, but before I get it out—

"Get your hands off of her."

An unfamiliar voice cracks through the air like thunder against a cloudless sky. I feel myself pale instantly, but my reaction is paltry compared to Adrian's second cousin.

"K-Kolya," the man stammers.

The owner of the booming voice steps between us as the cousin's hand falls lifelessly from my waist. The first thing I notice is the black suit he's wearing. I'd say he looks like a model, which is true in the sense that his cheekbones are high, his gaze searing, his hair perfectly imperfect.

But the real truth is that he doesn't look like a model at all, because there's nothing remotely posed or curated about him. He looks like he's thrown on the suit without a second thought. He looks like the kind of man who doesn't think about what he wears or how he looks—because he knows that he'll get anything he wants regardless.

His dark blue eyes are stormy and fixed unblinkingly on Adrian's cousin. "I'd remove that hand if I were you, Salazar," he says, deadpan. "Unless you want it broken."

Salazar. It suits him. Slimy and repulsive.

Salazar tucks his hands behind his back like hiding them will save him. He's not looking at me anymore. Not so much as a glance. It's as if I've gone invisible all of a sudden.

I'm not upset about it.

"Kolya, h-how are you?" he asks, still tripping over his own words.

"You always were one for stupid questions," Kolya growls, his gaze direct and impatient. "Is there a reason you're here?"

"I… I wanted to pay my respects."

"Did he owe you money?"

Salazar's eyes teeter to me for a moment. His throat bobs sickeningly.

"Look at her again, and you're risking the loss of an eye to go along with those fingers," Kolya warns. He delivers the threat so calmly, without even a hint of inflection. He might as well be exchanging small talk about the weather. *Nice day we're having. Beautiful flowers. I'll fucking kill you.*

When Salazar says nothing, Kolya tsks. "Answer me."

"N-no. Adrian didn't owe me anything."

"Then I'd say your respects are paid. Leave. Now."

I watch in amazement as Salazar turns on the spot and walks away from us at a speed that's almost comical. It reminds me of those old Scooby Doo cartoons, when Shaggy's feet are a blur of motion before he zooms off-screen.

I watch him go.

Kolya watches me.

I turn to him, expecting him to drop the stare. He doesn't do anything of the kind. "You should sit down," he says.

Without waiting for me to reply, he places his hand on my middle back. Much less intimate than Salazar, but unlike the first man, this gesture isn't creepy. It's almost impersonal, if that's a thing.

He steers me towards an armada of empty chairs in one corner of the room. "Sit." There's no concern in his tone, not a trace of warmth. It's a command, through and through.

Weirdly enough, I find myself obeying.

Honestly, as crazy as it sounds, part of me likes it. It's nice to be told what to do in this situation. It makes me feel like I've been standing around for hours waiting for this particular man to arrive and take over.

Now, if only he could tell me how to react, or even how to feel.

Maybe he could help me cry at last.

"Here," he says. I look down dumbly at the glass of water that's materialized in his grasp. When I don't move, he sighs, pulls my hand from my lap, and wraps my fingers around the water. I accept it silently and take a sip. The sip turns into a gulp, and before I know it, I've downed the whole thing.

"Thanks."

"I can get you more."

"I'm okay."

I am. In fact, I feel better than I have in hours. I glance at him. He might be the only person in the world who looks good under fluorescent lights. They enhance his somberness, the melancholy in his features. He looks unspeakably sad, but also stormy, in a way I can't place.

I realize I'm being rude and gawking, so I clear my throat and try to make conversation. "Kolya, was it?"

He nods. "You're June."

"Yes. I'm—I was Adrian's girlfriend. How did you know him?"

He sits down next to me. I notice without even trying that he smells like rich vanilla and oaky musk. The watch on his wrist catches the light. Patek Philippe, I see. Adrian loved those.

"We were… childhood friends."

"Oh. I've never met anyone who knew him when he was a boy. He doesn't—um, he didn't talk very much about his childhood."

"I'm not surprised."

He doesn't offer anything else. I'm left sitting there in an uncomfortable silence. "What was he like?" I ask at last. "As a child, I mean."

"Annoying."

I raise my eyebrows, expecting that answer to be followed up with a smile. But no smile is forthcoming. Somehow, I'm okay with that. I'm not sure a smile would even suit him. Every line on his chiseled face looks like it's been engineered for the sole purpose of conveying maximum broodiness. Smiling might break him, honestly.

One of the funeral home employees shuffles by just then with a bucket and a mop to start cleaning up. I think of asking her to wait, but then the commingled scent of her cloying perfume and the rancid mop water hits my nostrils and I almost vomit.

Kolya notices. "Something wrong?"

"I've always had a good nose," I explain, eyes closed as I fight back the waves of my roiling stomach. "But ever since the pregnancy, it's become a superpower."

He doesn't really react. But in a way, the lack of reaction is the reaction. He goes perfectly still, and the blue of his eyes seem to split and shatter. It would have been scary, if I didn't feel so strangely calm in his presence.

"You're pregnant." It's a question only in theory, not in reality.

I nod. "Yeah, I sort of found out recently. So recent in fact that… Adrian didn't know."

Kolya stands upright so suddenly I almost yelp. "Come with me." He takes my elbow and helps me out of my seat before I realize what's happening.

"Where are we going?"

"Away from the smell."

It's bright outside, but the willow trees dotting the grounds offer pools of violet shade. He leads me to a bench tucked beneath one and we sit. The leaves drape in front of us, pale like wedding veils.

Kolya doesn't let go of me until I'm seated. He arches one eyebrow as if to ask, *Is that better?*

"Much better," I say with a sigh. "Only cut grass and vanilla out here." When his eyebrow stays arched, I blush. "You smell like vanilla. It's a good thing. I like the smell of vanilla."

He nods. "Glad to be of service." Again, he speaks without inflection or a smile. It makes me feel uncertain—of myself, more than anything else.

We sit in silence for a while. Indoors, the shuffling of feet and the whispering of mourners was weirdly grating. Out here, the same kinds of abstract white noises—a distant lawn mower, breeze in the treetops—calm my nerves.

"How'd you get the cut?" he asks abruptly.

It's funny how I keep forgetting I have it until other people mention it. "I walked into a door," I parrot automatically.

"Did the door have a name?"

My eyes dart to his, probably giving myself away. "Yes," I whisper, because I know instinctively that he'll see through the lie. "It was just an accident."

"He—"

"He's dead," I cut in abruptly. The emotion I've been looking for all afternoon rises up in my throat out of nowhere, hot and thick, choking me. I swallow it down by force. "He's dead and it was an accident. Let's leave it there, okay?"

"Okay."

I take a deep breath. "Were you and Adrian close?"

"To an extent," he answers vaguely. "We grew apart as we got older."

"Oh. That's a shame." I look around the lawn, then back at Kolya. His eyes have stayed locked on me from the moment we met. It ought to be unsettling, but for some reason, it's the exact opposite. "Can you tell me something about him?" I ask hopefully. "A story from his childhood, a little anecdote. Anything."

Kolya contemplates that for a moment, idly stroking his chin. "He liked to climb. Trees, buildings, rock faces. I used to tell him that one day, he'd go too high and he'd fall. He had a scar on his left knee—"

"Oh my God, yes!" I gasp, grabbing his arm without thinking about it. The material of his suit is soft as butter. I let go almost immediately. "He told me he slipped while playing around."

"He slipped alright," Kolya chuckles. "From the third floor of The Meriden Motel. Busted right through a lattice and tore his knee to ribbons. He couldn't run for a while. That's when he took up the piano."

My heart twinges. I didn't realize how much I needed this—to know that Adrian was a boy once. A reckless boy, by the sound of it, but a boy nonetheless. Not a drunk or an abuser or a failure. Just a boy.

"I can't believe he never told me about that," I murmur. "There are so many things about him I never got to ask."

Kolya makes a strange sound deep in his chest. Not quite a grunt of disapproval, but something sort of like that. Then he stands and straightens his cuffs. I catch sight of a black tattoo on the back of one wrist before it disappears.

"You're leaving." I'm oddly disappointed.

"I have a meeting to attend. I'm already late." He sighs and looks down at me from his full height. The sun is at his back and filtered through the willow branches, so his face is dappled in shadow. But those blue eyes shine out like beacons from the depths of it. "Goodbye, June."

The way he says it feels so final. I suppose, in the context of today, it's appropriate. "Goodbye, Kolya. Thanks for saving me."

He still doesn't smile—at this point, I'm doubting he's even capable of it—but his features do soften a little. Then he inclines his head ever-so-slightly in a quasi-bow, turns, and walks away.

He leaves me there with a hand resting on my belly and the smell of vanilla in my nose.

It strikes me suddenly that I'm sitting here by myself, but I'm not alone. The whole point of motherhood is that I'll never be alone again, right? I try to find some sort of bittersweet comfort in that, but when I can't, I close my eyes instead.

I dream about being on the stage of a dark auditorium. There's a single light aimed at the stage. Light music plays in the background, violins and the tinkling of a sorrowful piano.

And I'm dancing.

5

JUNE

THREE MONTHS LATER

"Any pain?"

"Does the one in my heart count?"

The doctor looks at me like I just told him I'm going to give birth to a three-headed dragon. My comedic timing has never been great. Of course, Adrian used to say that it had nothing to do with my timing; it was the jokes themselves.

Jokes have to be funny, Junepenny.

"Sorry. That was a joke," I mumble. "A bad one."

Dr. Miller gives me an awkward smile. "You don't have to apologize, June. Everyone has different ways of coping."

Coping. God, I hate that term. It's a word that has failure baked into it already.

"How are you feeling?" he asks. "Physically, I mean."

I swallow. The antiseptic smell of doctors' offices always makes my throat itch. "Physically, I feel fine. But I was wondering…"

I spent the whole morning going back and forth on whether I should bring this up at my appointment today or not. Apparently, indecision is another coping mechanism I've developed as of late.

"Yes?"

"Well, I was wondering if it was normal to develop anxiety during pregnancy," I say. "Anxiety, like... bordering on paranoia?"

Dr. Miller doesn't look disturbed. I take that as a good sign. "It's perfectly normal to have anxiety and stress related to a new pregnancy," he says, adjusting his necktie and leaning back on his stool. "After all, it is a major life change. And you're facing it with some pretty heavy extenuating circumstances. Can I ask what symptoms in particular you're experiencing?"

I laugh nervously to try to undercut just how real this feeling has gotten lately. "Well, sometimes I feel like I'm being... watched," I admit. "And sometimes, I'll get home and it feels like my stuff has been moved around. Like someone's been in my place when I'm not there. Which is impossible because no one else has a key to my place. I mean, Adrian did. But he's clearly not around anymore. Unless of course, his ghost is moseying around while I'm at..."

I trail off when I notice the look on Dr. Miller's face. I wonder when I should have stopped—the morbid line about who might have a key to my house, or the ghost joke?

Jokes have to be funny, Junepenny.

I shudder. Based on how often I still hear his voice, maybe the ghost thing isn't such a joke after all.

I clear my throat. "Anyway. Never mind. It's probably nothing."

But the frown on Dr. Miller's face begs to disagree. "How long have you felt this way, June?"

"It's probably just all in my head," I say with another nervous laugh, even less convincing than the first. "I haven't lived alone for a long time, and I'm just psyching myself out."

His grimace deepens. "June, have you considered talking to a therapist? I could recommend a few good ones," he says. "And if cost is a concern, I know several who charge nominal fees for patients with… special circumstances."

That's not the kind of special I ever aspired to be. I always wanted to be special for what I could do, not for what had been done to me. It's gruesomely funny that Adrian took one kind of specialness away from me, but here he is, giving me back another kind I don't want and didn't ask for.

I force those thoughts aside and smile politely. "Thanks, Doctor. I'll think about it."

He gives me a disappointed smile, but he doesn't push the idea, which I appreciate. Instead, he rolls away on his stool and checks my file.

"Everything else seems to be fine, June. The baby's healthy and so are you. Keep taking your vitamins. And don't neglect your mental health."

"Roger. Thank you."

I swing my legs down and grab my satchel. It still has the lame bumper sticker that I impulsively plastered over the label way back when I first bought it: *DANCE IS LIFE.*

I'm not sure why I never peeled it off. These days, it's just a brutal reminder that, if dance is life, I pretty much lost mine in The Accident two years ago.

I swing the strap of the bag over my shoulder, give Dr. Miller a wave goodbye, and head out of the examination room. My next OBGYN appointment is not for another few weeks, and I'm grateful for the respite from being poked and prodded like an alien abduction.

I'm rounding the corner after leaving the obstetrics wing when I nearly crash into a person-shaped wall. "Argh!" I cry out.

Then the scent of vanilla hits my nose.

I take a slow, cautious step backward. My eyes track upwards. From tailored pant legs in a jet black suit fabric. To the open collar of a snow-white button-down shirt. To the tattooed hollow of a man's throat.

And then up into a pair of icy blue eyes.

My voice, when it comes out, is rasped and croaky. "Kolya?"

He looks completely unsurprised to have run into me. "June," he says simply.

"What are you doing here?"

"I came to see a friend." He arches an eyebrow at me. Another silent question. *What are you doing here?* he asks without asking. It's spooky how he can do that. Whole conversations with just a brow.

I put a hand on my stomach, which is starting to pop a little bit even with clothes on. "Had an appointment with my OBGYN. Routine check-up for the baby."

"Everything okay?"

I blush and glance down at my toes. "Everything's fine. The baby's healthy."

"And you?"

"I'm healthy, too. Physically, at least."

He frowns. "What do you mean?"

I cringe internally. "Nothing. Bad joke. Continuation of a bad joke, really." Forcing myself to look back up at him and smile, I ask, "So, um, you said you were here to see a friend? Nothing too serious, I hope."

His frown doesn't dissipate, but he doesn't press the issue. "He was shot."

I laugh, but my laughter breaks off when his glower remains in place. "Wait. You're not kidding."

Kolya shrugs. "He'll live."

I decide that it would be impolite to point out that he doesn't seem all that concerned with his friend's condition. "Do you mind if I ask how he got shot?"

"Wrong place, wrong time."

"Ah. Right." I start out trying to pretend like I know what he's talking about, but then I realize that I actually *do* know what he's talking about. Hadn't a doctor said those exact words to me two years ago? *You were just in the wrong place at the wrong time, honey. Nothing to be done about it.*

I'd carried those words around with me for months after The Accident, trying to make sense of them. Trying to make them work for me instead of against me. *Coping* with them, you might say.

In the end, they didn't do me much good.

I fidget in place, running the heel of my shoe up and down a groove in the tile. The conversation has reached a dead space, and it'd be perfectly acceptable to say my goodbyes and be on my not-so-merry way.

But I'm staying, and I don't quite know why.

I tell myself it has nothing to do with Kolya specifically; it's about what he represents. He is about my last lifeline to Adrian and all those little secrets, those tucked-away memories that he'd taken to the grave with him.

I'd always taken it for granted that I'd get the answers eventually. After all, we were going to spend the rest of our lives together, right? I didn't need all his secrets right off the bat. They'd come out when the time and place were right.

I open my mouth, let it fall closed, open and shut it again. I feel like a dying fish. I probably look even dumber than that.

Kolya watches me coolly. Then his expression shifts just a little. His eyebrows slant down, along with the corners of his mouth. "You want to talk about Adrian," he rumbles.

I wince. "Is it that obvious? It is, isn't it? And it's selfish. I know you've gotta be so worried about your friend. This was super inappropriate of me to even think of asking, right? Forget it then. I'm sorry. I'll just—"

"Do you always do that?" he asks abruptly.

"Do what?"

"Have conversations with yourself."

I let my shoulders sag forward. "I need a cup of coffee. Do you need a cup of coffee?"

"You're pregnant."

I raise my eyebrows, my cheeks reddening with embarrassment. "Oh, wow. I am. Duh. This makes me sound like a horrible mother, but honestly, I really do forget sometimes."

He gazes down at me for a moment longer. Then he lets a soft, minty exhale pass between his lips before he turns and starts to walk down the hall. "Come on," he calls back over his shoulder. "I'm sure the cafeteria will have some non-toxic swill you can imbibe."

He takes long, confident strides and I have to jog to keep up. By the time we get to the cafeteria, I'm winded.

I choose the closest table and sink down into the uncomfortable gray chair. "I'll get you something to drink," he says, walking off before I can tell him what I'd like.

Sighing, I sit there, scratching at my cuticles, wondering what on earth I'm doing here.

I'm lost in thought when I hear a metallic plunk and look up to see him setting a can of lemon soda down on the table in front of me. My one weakness.

"Oh my God," I breathe. "This is lemon soda. How did you… How did you know?"

He sits down in the chair opposite, looking as impassive as ever. "Lucky guess."

Eerie, I think to myself.

"Thank you," I say.

He responds to that with a tiny quirk of his brow. I realize that he's not going to just supply me with information. I'm going to have to ask him what I want to know. Which is a little tricky, since what I want to know is everything.

"When was the last time you spoke to Adrian?" I ask, figuring I can start off easy and work my way up to the harder questions.

"A while ago," he replies vaguely.

"A while as in months or a while as in years?"

"The former."

I frown. "Adrian never mentioned meeting you."

"We didn't always get along."

"Still…" I trail off into silence. Kolya wouldn't be the first thing Adrian neglected to mention to me. I never really pushed him for certain answers. My thinking was that if I gave him space, he would eventually come to me.

I was trying to earn his trust, when it should have been the other way around. Not that he'd ever really needed to try to earn mine. I'd given it to him like a cheap prize at a carnival.

"To be fair, he didn't get along with most people. At least in the last couple of years."

Kolya doesn't offer anything, so I sit there, nursing my lemon soda between both hands, watching the cold beads of condensation sweat onto my thighs.

"The Accident changed everything," I say softly. "Did he tell you about what happened?"

"Yes."

There's a lot contained in that one little word, though it's packed up tightly and locked. I look up, wondering what he's thinking. It's unnerving not having the faintest clue what's going on in his head. Is he humoring me? Is he killing time? Is he just bored?

"I like to blame The Accident," I say. "But the truth is, he was struggling long before then. He didn't have any family… But then, you probably know that already. I was his whole family, and sometimes… Sometimes, I don't think I was enough."

When I look up, Kolya's eyes are fixed on me. His blue irises look like ice, but they're not what I would describe as cold. Just… neutral.

Maybe that's why I feel like I can tell him these things: because I don't think he's going to judge me.

I don't think he cares enough to judge me.

"He liked drinking." My forehead wrinkles as I remember just how much. "At first, I barely even noticed. When we first started dating, it was just social drinking, you know? But then I realized that it didn't matter if we went out or not—he needed to have a drink every day. He said it calmed his nerves. I never asked what he had to be so nervous about."

It's rude of me to blabber. But Kolya seems content to just sit there and listen.

"One drink a day turned into two. Two became three. Then the nightcap became the five o'clock drink and the five o'clock drink became the way he started his mornings. I came downstairs to make some breakfast one day and he was sitting at the kitchen table with a six pack of beer and a plate of eggs." I stop short and take a deep breath. "I knew he had a problem long before I admitted it to myself."

"It had nothing to do with you," Kolya intones. It feels like the first time he's spoken today. His voice has a rough-hewn, just-got-out-of-bed quality that makes me shiver. "His disease was not your fault."

I feel my breath catch at the word. *Disease.* It sounds so, I don't know... binding, I guess. I don't know why it's a shock hearing him say it, when I've known as much for a long time now. "How do you know?"

"It started long before you came into the picture." He toys with the clasp on his watch. Open and shut, open and shut. *Click. Clack. Click. Clack.* Then his eyes find mine again. "He thought music could save him. He was wrong."

My breath catches and releases in my chest with every click of Kolya's watch clasp. "Save him... from what?"

He lets his hand fall idle and fixes me with that unapologetic gaze. "From himself."

I drag my index finger through the puddle of condensation streaking my leg. "He wasn't all bad, you know," I say softly, face aimed down at my lap. "There's a reason I fell in love with him in the first place."

"Which was?"

Strange as it may seem, I didn't expect him to be curious about that. It takes me off-guard, leaves me floundering for an answer. Which of course makes me look insincere. Like I'm trying to change the reality of who he was so that I can mourn him in peace.

"Well..."

I close my eyes for a moment and remember how it began. He came to fill in for a performance of *Swan Lake* when the Duval Theater's usual piano player was home sick with a cold. I was dancing. He was playing. He looked at me and he struck the first note and I looked at him and took the first step and something started. A spark was lit.

"He was an artist," I say simply. "We understood each other."

I'm growing used to Kolya's gaze. It's so penetrating. Invasive, almost. But I like the lack of bullshit, the straight-laced, what-you-see-is-what-you-get kind of attitude. For three months, everyone has come to me cloaked in sympathy, and what I'm learning about myself is that I fucking hate sympathy. I'll take the unflinching truth over sweet lies any day.

"Thanks for talking to me," I say before I drain the last few sips of my lemon soda. "And for the soda."

He nods. Says nothing.

"I should get going. I have to make the house presentable. I'm interviewing potential roommates today."

At that, his eyes flash with a sudden blue fire like the hottest part of a blaze. "Roommates?" he says in a low, dangerous growl.

I laugh nervously. "Well, I can't afford to stay in that house on my own. Especially with a baby on the way. The only way around it is to find a roommate who'll help with half the rent. So yeah, roommates."

His eyes do that weird splitting thing. It's as if the ice is cracking, breaking off like calving glaciers in the Arctic.

"Live with me," he says abruptly.

I blink at him in confusion. I must've misheard. "Uh, what?"

Sapphire Scars

He stands to meet me. "You're pregnant. You've just lost the father of your child. You should be living somewhere comfortable. Not with… *roommates.*"

"Oh, that's sweet of you, but my house is comfortable. It's just—"

"I can have you moved in by the end of the week."

I stare at him with my mouth hanging open. "You're serious."

He just raises an eyebrow. A silent *Yes*. It's eerie how much he can communicate without opening his mouth.

"Kolya, that's… Listen, that's—It's very kind of you. But I couldn't possibly—"

"You don't need to live with a random fucking stranger." It's the harshest I've ever heard him sound, and I don't care for it. It reminds me of all those times that I'd come home from work, only to find Adrian stalking around the house, spoiling for a fight.

"You're a random stranger, too," I point out. "You may have been friends with Adrian once upon a time, but I didn't know that. Adrian never even mentioned you to me. So, yeah. Generous as the offer is, I'd prefer to stay in my own space. It's no mansion, but it's my home."

With every passing second, I like the fire in his eyes less and less. Our once-pleasant conversation has taken a sharp left into uncharted territory, and I'm ready to bolt.

I set the empty can down on the table. "Thanks for the drink," I say. "I've got to be going."

I start walking away, feeling my heart thud painfully against my chest. For a few wild moments, I half-expect him to chase me to the parking lot of the hospital, but when I turn the corner and check over my shoulder, he's nowhere to be seen.

Sighing with relief, I slow down a little and let myself breathe again. I reach my little Honda with the busted fender and unlock it.

I'm just about to open the door when I see his reflection in the window.

The gasp freezes on my tongue as I whirl around. He's twice as big suddenly, twice as tall, and ten times as terrifying. Those eyes are an alien blue. Hot and cold at the same time. He hems me in against my car, smelling like vanilla and charcoal.

"W-what are you doing?" I stammer.

"I'm taking you home," he says brusquely.

"I don't need a ride—"

"Not your home," he growls. "Mine."

6

KOLYA

Beep. Beep. Beep.

"This is insane," June whispers as I get behind the wheel and pull out of the parking spot. Her bright hazel eyes are limpid with shock. "You can't do this. You realize there's a name for this, right? It's called kidnapping. It's illegal. And considering I'm pregnant, you're kidnapping my baby as well."

I sigh. She let me put her into my car so easily that for a moment, I thought she might not fight at all. Pity I was wrong.

"Put your seatbelt on," I tell her as I accelerate. "The car won't stop bleating until you do."

Beep. Beep. Beep. Every tone is an icepick in my temple.

"I'm not doing a damn thing until you stop this car and let me out," she snaps.

I promptly slam the brakes. June screams and braces herself against the dashboard, apparently surprised by how quickly she's getting what she asked for.

Or so she thought.

I reach over, snag the seatbelt, and buckle her into place. Angry horns blare from behind me, but June's stare is death itself. It makes me chuckle.

Once she's secured, I hit the gas and take off, leaving the pissed-off traffic in my wake.

"You're driving too fast," she mutters, white-knuckling the edges of her seat.

"Hence the seatbelt."

"Stop it. You're going to get us killed."

"I'm an excellent driver."

"You'd have to be, wouldn't you?" she snaps. "Most criminals need to be good at driving the getaway car."

"I've got news for you, *medoviy*: no one's following us. And no one's looking for you."

"Not true. My brother is coming over today. He's a big guy, very protective of me, and—"

"Cut the shit," I growl. "You don't have a brother."

June freezes in place as she starts to understand that I know far more about her than she realized. The epiphany seems to shut her up, but I'm not fooled. She may be quiet for the time being, but her eyes remain flush with friction. They keep darting around the car like they're looking for a weapon.

I'm impressed, to be honest. I didn't actually expect Adrian's little kitten to have claws.

Ping. I grab my phone and check the text.

MILANA: *We found the traitor. You were right.*

I close the thread without replying and glance at June. She's pale and trembling and she seems to be ripping her nail beds to shreds. A nervous habit I'd noticed at the funeral.

"Do you want some water?"

She nods silently. I grab the bottle tucked into the side door pocket and offer it to her. As soon as I'm within reach, though, she lunges forward and sinks her teeth right into my outstretched hand.

I curse in Russian, drop the bottle, whip the car to the side of the road, and slam on the brakes for the second time in as many minutes. Once again, the surrounding traffic goes berserk.

But I don't give a fuck. My focus is on June.

I grab her by the throat and pin her against the passenger door. She gasps as my fingers tighten around her windpipe. The fear in her bright hazel eyes—that's what I was looking for. The realization that there are things happening here at a level far beyond her understanding. That the game is so much bigger than she's ever grasped before.

But as soon as the sight of that fear satisfies, it gives me pause, for one reason and one reason only.

She's pregnant.

Fuck.

That's the only thing that could make my fingers loosen. My hand falls slack and she breathes in desperate sucks of air. But the fear remains, simmering and toxic. That's good. She needs to be scared. Fear is the strongest motivator. The most efficient, too.

"If you insist on acting like a wild animal, I'm going to treat you like one."

Her eyes widen, even as her irises darken. "Or what?"

She must be a slow learner. Either that or she's much braver than I've given her credit for. I'm inclined to be tolerant of bravery, but only to an extent. There's a point at which it crosses over to stupidity.

"Or I'm going to give you another reason to mourn."

I don't have anything specific in mind when those words pass my lips. In my experience, open-ended threats are the most effective. The nightmares we conjure for ourselves are a thousand times more terrifying than anything someone else could craft for us.

But whatever she assumes is clearly far worse than I intended. She pales instantaneously. She goes limp all at once, too, as though my words have managed to kill the last vestige of fight left in her.

There's something about her desperate expression that makes me feel uncertain. And I *never* feel uncertain.

Asking her to explain what's happening in her mind would only defeat the progress I've made, though. Like it or not, this is where we are. Regret is for the weak and the dead. I am neither.

So instead, I take my hand from her lap and re-grip the steering wheel. "Are you going to cooperate?"

"You're not giving me much of a choice," she spits.

I nod. "Glad you understand the situation."

"Why are you doing this?" she asks. "I thought you were Adrian's friend."

"Maybe I was overstating things a little," I say with an uncaring shrug. "He's not so much a friend as an acquaintance from my past. If Adrian were around for you to ask, he might even call me his enemy."

I should turn back onto the road, but I want to make sure that the little minx has truly sheathed her fangs. She's looking docile at the moment, but I'm not prepared to risk another accident on the road. Not in her condition. Not with what's at stake here.

"Adrian didn't have enemies."

"If you really believe that, then you didn't know him as well as you thought you did."

"People in real life don't have enemies," she asserts. If only she knew how foolish that makes her sound. "Everyone has people they don't like, but no one has *enemies*. That's... that's comic book stuff."

"What word would you use to describe the man who killed your father?"

Her jaw falls to the floor. "I'm sorry, is that a... like, a figure of speech or something?"

"You tell me."

She swallows hard and her eyes slide away as though she can't bear to look at me anymore. "You're not kidding. You're really not."

Her fear is tangible in the confined space of the car, slick on my skin like spilled oil. It's taken mere seconds and I've completely destroyed the innocent little snow globe model of the world she had in her head.

It's not all sunshine and roses out there. It's ugly and it's violent. She's just now starting to learn that, and if she's a little late to the party… well, that's not my fault. I'd go so far as to say it's Adrian's, actually.

Naivete may be useless, but there's a kind of beauty in it nonetheless.

And he always did like finding beautiful things just so that he could destroy them.

"Y-you're really taking me to your place?" she stammers after a silent minute has passed. "Why?"

"Because you're not capable of taking care of yourself."

"Who are you to judge anything about me?" she demands. A flash of that fire peeks through again.

Oh, little lamb. You should be very, very careful how you talk to me.

"You'll find out soon enough."

She settles back in her seat and watches the road with razor sharp alertness. Her neck cranes after every sign we pass and every notable landmark that zips by. I can practically hear the gears in her head churning.

"Adrian is gone," she says in a small voice after some time has passed. "What could you possibly want with me?"

If I explained it to her, she wouldn't believe me. So I don't bother. I'm not in the habit of explaining things anyway. Whether she believes my intentions or not is immaterial. The bottom line is that I preserve what needs preserving.

When we reach my compound, she leans forward to stare up through the windshield at the spires and turrets rising up over the black studded gates.

"This is where you live?" She turns to eye me, half-amazed and half-repulsed. "It's a freaking castle."

"Are all artists prone to hyperbole?"

Her forehead wrinkles. "I'm not an artist."

"You were a dancer."

The frown deepens. "The operative word being 'was.' I'm not a dancer anymore." Her voice is bitter, salted through with old pain.

The gates unfurl inward, and we take the limestone drive up to the gravel-strewn circle resting in front of the house. My mood is bleak today, and the house suits it perfectly. All dark stone and stark lines, without much in the way of embellishments aside from gargoyles leering above the entryway. I've always been partial to gargoyles.

The moment the car is in park, my men erupt out of the woodwork as though I've triggered some silent alarm. June's eyes dart from side to side in panic.

"Wh-what's going on?"

"Calm down. Get out of the car."

She doesn't do either thing. Instead, she turns to me, defiance battling with self-preservation in her eyes. "Who the hell are you?"

I don't bother answering her. Instead, I give my men the order with a nod of my head. June's door is pulled open and she's ripped out of the car.

"No!" she screams. The girl's got some lungs on her. "Let me go! Kolya, come back! You can't do this! *Kolya!*"

I get out of the car, stand in place, and watch her go. I want so badly to intervene, to calm her fears—which is exactly why I don't. I can't let something as mundane as sentiment get in the way of my better judgment.

Adrian did that, and look at where it got him.

I walk into the house, pretending as though I don't hear her screams echoing down the corridors. If I can't hear them, then they can't bother me—or so I tell myself. I head to my office and shut the door.

In there, the heavy oak drowns out all traces of June. It's a relief. Sometimes, pretending is exhausting. Sometimes, it takes more effort than I'm willing to give.

But it's the hand I was dealt. It's the hand Adrian ran from. Thus, here we are.

He's six feet under…

And I've got his pregnant girlfriend under my roof.

7

JUNE
THREE DAYS LATER

"I just want to stretch my legs," I insist to the new maid, projecting innocence as hard as I possibly can.

This one isn't like the others, I can tell. She's almost six feet tall and built like a lumberjack. Which only makes the powder blue maid's uniform she's wearing all the more ridiculous. Her hair is tied at the back of her head into a bun so tight it's a miracle her forehead hasn't split wide open at the seams. If the phrase "No Bullshit" had a mascot, she'd be it.

"No."

"I've been allowed out of this room before, though."

As prisons go, this has been a fairly pleasant one. My gilded cage is at least five hundred square feet, a space that includes a massive bathroom, a drool-worthy walk-in closet, a sitting area, and a glistening kitchenette.

I hate all of it.

"You have," the maid agrees dourly. "And you tried to run. Therefore, you have lost the right to leave again."

I swing my legs down off the sofa and grab a cushion. I desperately want to fling it at her, but something tells me that this maid will fling it right back and it will hurt way more than I bargained for. Even if I wasn't pregnant, this wildebeest of a woman would eat me alive.

"Please?" I ask sweetly, attempting a different tack. "I'm feeling so nauseous up here. The air's stale."

She's unmoved. "Your room was cleaned this morning. And you finished two trays of food. You can hardly be nauseous."

My fingers tighten around the cushion. "Just one walk around the house?"

"I am not authorized to allow that."

"Authorized by who?"

"The master of the house."

"The master of the house," I mutter darkly under my breath. "Can you give him a message from me?"

"Certainly."

"Tell him to go fuck himself."

If she's surprised by the venom in my voice, the only sign of it is one slow, placid blink. Then she sighs. "Perhaps, madam, you would like to watch something? There's a selection of—"

"I don't want to watch anything. I want to go home."

"If you want something to eat, I can—"

"No," I snap. "I'm not hungry. As you just so politely pointed out, I had two trays of food this morning."

Weirdly enough, despite the still-too-overwhelming-for-me-to-fully-process-it horror of my circumstances, my appetite has been healthier than it's ever been. Apparently, I'm well and truly out of the first trimester morning sickness phase, because I'm starving from dawn 'til dusk without fail.

I came in here planning to launch a hunger strike to earn back my freedom. That plan went kaput on the first day when a different, less curmudgeonly maid had walked into my room pushing a serving cart filled with the most delicious things I've ever put in my mouth.

Blackened salmon drenched in a lemon garlic sauce. The silkiest pasta I've ever eaten. Flaky pastries bleeding raspberry filling. The list goes on: shrimp cocktails, buttery ribeyes, scalloped potatoes dusted with luscious parmesan cheese.

It was like I'd died and gone to culinary heaven.

Only problem is, I'm still trapped in culinary heaven with no lifeline to the outside world. The deliciousness of the food I'm constantly being served isn't enough to make up for the fact that I'm a caged bird.

The worst part: I don't know why.

I don't know much, in fact, other than that Kolya is not who he claimed to be. But still, there's a reason he's locked me up here. There's a reason he wants me to stay.

And apparently, it's not because he wants to talk to me. I've been here for three freaking days and there's been no sign of him. No courtesy visit. Not so much as a simple inquiry into my well-being.

Oh hey, June, it's Kolya. Just wanted to check in and see how the abduction was going for you. Comfortable? Good, I'm glad to hear it. We here at Asshole Enterprises work our little fannies off to make sure our guests are pleased. Leave us five stars!

"I want to see your boss," I tell She-Thor.

"He is unavailable at the moment."

I roll my eyes. "'At the moment'? He's been MIA for days. The least he can do is come up here and speak to his prisoner."

She doesn't respond to that. "If there is nothing else, madam, then I will excuse myself." She-Thor backs out of the room, her feet shuffling over the lush carpet, then stomps off down the hallway.

But there was something missing from that little production. One tiny, telltale sign.

She didn't lock the door.

I wait with bated breath until I'm sure her footsteps are fully gone. Then I race over to the door and stand in front of it, mind racing.

It seems like a strange oversight from a woman who takes her job a trillion times too seriously, but I can't afford to look a gift horse in the mouth. Cautiously, I crank open the handle and pull the door open.

I poke my head out and look both ways. All seems clear.

I slip into the hallway, painfully aware that I'm wearing a pair of silk pajama shorts that barely cover my ass. Not exactly the outfit of my jailbreaking dreams.

But there's no time to go back and pick fresh clothes out of the absurdly stocked walk-in closet in my quarters. It's now or never.

I'm almost at the spartan staircase that leads down to the second floor when I hear the sound of more footsteps. I duck through the first door I see and find myself in a room that's mostly mirrors, fine pieces of framed art, and a Turkish carpet covering most of the marbled floor.

"Lost, are you?"

I gasp and turn on the spot. I was so preoccupied with the decor that I didn't even notice the well-dressed woman standing by the windows.

She's wearing pants so white they're almost blinding. Her black tank top is tight-fitted but modest and her long blonde hair spills down her arms with waterfall-like elegance. She'd be tall enough without them, but her high heels have her towering over me. She looks like if the goddess Venus stepped right off her shell in that famous painting and went shopping at Prada. I'm intimidated, to say the least.

"Who are you?" I croak.

She cocks her head to the side. "I think the better question here is, who are you?"

She's playing hard ball, I decide. Which means I'll have to do the same. Whoever this woman is, she clearly doesn't live here. She's dressed too much like a guest paying a visit. She's either a friend of Kolya's or his girlfriend. My money's on the latter.

I feel a little tug of annoyance at the realization. Of course he would be with someone like her—glamorous, chic, imperious. It's boring how predictable it is.

"I'm a guest of Kolya's," I say vaguely.

"A guest of Kolya's?" One eyebrow rises delicately. It's perfectly plucked, of course.

"Right. June. I'm June."

The woman smiles. "I'm Milana. Those are beautiful pajamas, June."

I'm not sure if she's making fun of me or giving me a genuine compliment. "Oh. Uh, thank you. I overslept this morning and decided to just keep them on."

"So you spent the night here then?"

If she really is his girlfriend, will she take my presence as a threat? I certainly hope so. This might be my best chance of getting out of here. If she raises a fuss, maybe I can slip out in the chaos.

"I did. In fact, I've spent the last few nights here." I eye her as I'm talking, but I can't really tell what she's thinking. *Guess they're a match made in heaven,* I think bitterly. "Kolya has been so generous to me. But I'm not sure I can take advantage of his hospitality for much longer. In fact, I was just about to leave."

"What a coincidence. So was I."

I feel my heart beat a little faster as I sense an opportunity within reach. "How about we walk down together?"

Milana looks bemused. "In your pajamas?"

I force out a tinkling laugh. "Of course not. I'm going to change first. Will you give me a few minutes?"

"I'll wait for you by the staircase," she says, looking down at her phone.

It takes all my willpower not to sprint out of the room. The moment she can't see me anymore however, I make like the wind. I need to swap out my clothes and meet her by the staircase before She-Thor returns to glower at me some more.

I trade the silk pajamas for a pair of black jeans and a white blouse. Then I walk quickly back to the staircase, where Milana is standing by the banister, waiting for me.

She turns as I approach. Her blonde hair ripples gold, a perfect little Barbie.

"Um, I think Kolya's busy today," I say, trying to sound casual and breezy. "I don't want to disturb him, so why don't we just slip out?"

She shrugs. "If you prefer."

I've really hit the jackpot here. She's much more accommodating than her piercing eyes would suggest. Every time I hear a sound though, I jump.

"Everything all right?" Milana asks as we descend the staircase.

"Yeah, yeah, of course. I just don't want to bother the staff, either."

Milana doesn't even crack a frown. She accepts my half-assed explanation with ease. Figures that she's empty underneath that pretty little head of hers. The realization gives me a surge of cruel, petty satisfaction. I don't bother trying to decipher why that is.

I'm ten steps shy of the towering set of fashionably corrugated iron double doors that leads to freedom when Milana clears her throat. "I believe Kolya has men repairing the doors right now, actually. We'll need to leave through the side entrance."

Fuck. My face burns. "Oh, of course," I say, swallowing down my nerves. "He did mention that. Well, lead the way then!" I punctuate it with another badly faked laugh. My heart is thumping hard enough against my ribs to crack something.

I fall in line behind her as we wind down a hallway. It's hard not to be awestruck. Her hair flutters behind her like there's a film crew lighting her way at all times and she smells like Chanel No. 5 straight out of the bottle.

She leads me to a nondescript door that opens out onto a cobblestone path. The path conveys us through exquisitely manicured gardens. Not a single leaf on a single hedge out of place, and every strand of ivy goes exactly where it's told to go.

The air smells like flowers, too. It's heartbreakingly beautiful out here. There's something else, too, another scent lingering on the edge of the summery breeze. A scent like…

Oh, fuck.

Vanilla.

I grind to a horrified halt. Kolya is leaning against the brick wall that lines the periphery of the garden, observing us casually, his blue eyes already splintered in anticipation. "Going for a little walk, are we?"

"How did you—"

I glance towards Milana, who's giving me an apologetic smile that doesn't quite reach her eyes. "Just for the record, I didn't want to do this. But Kolya likes to play games when he's bored."

"What makes you think I was bored?" he drawls.

She rolls her eyes. "I know your bored face. It's very similar to your *I'm-going-to-kill-you* face."

I look between them, feeling the disappointment sink into my pores like dry heat. "You… work for him?"

"I work *with* him," she corrects pridefully. "I'm his right-hand woman."

And to think I was just starting to like her…

I draw myself up tall. These two are like lions playing with their food, but I won't go down that easy. "So you're complicit in my abduction?"

Kolya pushes himself off the wall and takes a sauntering step towards me. "What did I tell you?" he says to Milana. "She has a flair for the dramatics."

"You did pluck her out of her life and force her into your little cage," Milana reminds him in a measured voice. "Some dramatics are the least you can expect."

His eyes flash. "I thought you were supposed to be on my side."

"I am. And part of my responsibility to you is honesty. A man would kiss your ass. I'm not interested in puckering my lips, babe. No matter how pretty you may be."

My eyes ping-pong between the two of them. Their easy banter throws me off-kilter. Along with, y'know… everything else that's happening to me.

"How about we table the flirting for later?" I snap. "And concentrate on the fact that I have a fucking life I need to get back to."

"It's not much of one if you ask me," Kolya remarks. He looks unimpressed with my fire. "Guards," he says, barely raising his voice. Just like when he first brought me to this godforsaken castle, two of his men materialize instantly.

They each grab hold of me, but my eyes are trained on Kolya and Milana. "You can't keep me here forever," I hiss, trying my best not to show fear.

He seems to sense the challenge in my eyes. He moves forward, stopping only when his face is inches from mine. "Tell me, June. Are you scared of me?"

"No."

He smiles. The titillating scent of vanilla makes me want to lean in. The sinister promise in his smile makes me want to run away screaming.

"That'll change," he promises. "That'll all change soon enough."

8

JUNE

Hours pass in my room. I lie on my back and stare at the ceiling until the beams start to shimmer and move like they're alive. A lone tear escapes and tracks down my cheek.

I'd probably lie there forever if I didn't hear a knock on my door.

I prop myself up on my elbows and watch. The lock turns and it opens. More maids coming, I'm sure, to clean or force food down my throat.

But it's not maids.

It's him.

Truth be told, Kolya was the last person I expected to see. He's never once come to the room since the moment I was dragged here. The fact that he's here now fills me with dread.

I leap off the bed and eye him warily, fists knotted at my sides. "What are you doing here?"

"I came to invite you to dinner."

He shifts to the side and I notice a cut running down the left side of his face. It's fresh, bruises spreading from it on either side like blossoming petals.

"What happened to you?"

"I walked into a wall," he drawls, recycling the lame excuse I'd given him not long ago.

I roll my eyes. "Fine. Don't tell me."

"I wasn't planning to." He adjusts the collar of his pristine white shirt. "Dinner will be served in twenty minutes."

"Pass. I'll eat in here like I always do."

"I figured you'd appreciate some company."

"If the company includes you, I'd rather not."

If he hears me, he shows no sign of it. "As comfortable as those sweatpants undoubtedly are, you might want to wear something a little more presentable for the meal."

"I might, if I were coming to dinner. Which I'm not."

A vein in his forehead pulses, the only sign that this robot monster has anything resembling human emotions. "Suit yourself. Unfortunately, the kitchen will be occupied, so you'll have to go without food for the evening if that's your choice."

Right on cue, my stomach rumbles and my nose kicks into overdrive. His scent radiates toward me, much as I'd like it not to.

"Why do you always smell like vanilla?" I ask abruptly.

He sighs and picks at a piece of lint on his cuff. "I dab a little on my cheeks every morning as aftershave. Keeps the skin fresh and youthful."

I gawk at him for a few seconds before I realize that he is in fact joking. "I thought you didn't kid."

He shrugs. "I have my moments."

"Are you going to answer the question?"

"Are you going to join me for dinner?"

"No."

"Very well then. Goodnight, June."

He's halfway to leaving before I come to my senses and yell out his name. He pauses at the threshold, one hand on the door, and looks back at me over his shoulder, eyebrow arched, asking the question without having to ask it.

"Starving a pregnant woman is cruel and unusual," I spit.

"At the rate you've been eating, I'd say missing one meal won't hurt you."

Bastard! Much as I want to spit in his smug fucking face, though, my stomach chooses that moment to growl again, accompanied this time by a wave of nausea and hunger pains.

Looks like dinner is in order.

"I'll be down in ten minutes," I hiss through gritted teeth.

He nods like this all went exactly as he foresaw. Then, without another word, he steps through the door and pulls it closed behind him.

I'm muttering all kinds of obscene curses under my breath as I march to the walk-in closet to search for something suitable to wear. I have no idea how I'm supposed to be dressing, but I decide it doesn't matter anyway. What does it matter if I impress him? What does it matter if I embarrass him?

He's my captor, not my host. All the luxury in the world isn't going to convince me otherwise.

I riffle through the dresses hanging from one of the racks on the left hand side of my closet. I'm not really paying attention until I catch a glimpse of a dark burgundy fabric and I tune back in.

I wore a similar dress, not too long ago. Well, not *that* long ago, strictly speaking, but it feels like centuries since I was on stage in that wine-colored gown, in those tense, breathless moments before the curtains open and the music starts.

Come to think of it, that's how this feels. These last few minutes before I venture downstairs and see what Kolya has planned for me next.

Like I'm about to begin the performance of a lifetime.

I take the burgundy dress off the hanger and walk it over to the full-length mirror in the corner of the closet. Lights warm to life as I approach without me having to flip a switch.

I hold the garment up to my neck. It's a darker burgundy than the one I wore that night at the Duval. It's also a little longer, a little more modest, and the fabric is heavier. Meant to hide rather than reveal.

Fine by me.

Without thinking about it too much, I strip off my sweats and t-shirt and step into the garment. The neckline is scooped, just low enough to reveal some of my newfound pregnancy cleavage. The sleeves are non-existent. Just two thin straps that hold it up over my shoulders.

It's not the same dress, but it's close enough that I feel sad and listless for a moment. Which should probably be my first and second reasons for taking it off.

But I've always been a sucker for pain. Maybe that's why I stayed with Adrian for as long as I did.

I feel guilty on the heels of that thought. It's not as though it isn't true; it just feels like a petty potshot at a man who left behind the best part of himself inside of me.

My hand floats down to my stomach. "He wasn't all bad, all the time, you know," I whisper to my unborn child. "He was just a little lost."

KNOCK-KNOCK-KNOCK.

Sighing, I put on the closest shoes I can find, a pair of pale-colored ballet flats. Weirdly fitting. Then I head to the door, bracing myself for God knows what's to come.

I have no idea what to expect. I'm not even sure who to expect. Will it be Kolya and me? Or will Milana be joining us? Her name comes out sounding snotty in my head. It's just a juvenile outlet for my resentment about her part in the little farce in the gardens.

She-Thor is on the other side of the door waiting for me. "The master is expecting you downstairs."

"Well, we don't want to keep him waiting, do we?" I say sarcastically.

She doesn't respond. Just escorts me downstairs with a firm grip on my elbow like I'm not capable of traversing steps by myself. Maybe Kolya is concerned I'll make a run for it again.

I've given up on another escape attempt, though. The last one was embarrassing enough that it managed to kill my determination to run. If I'm going to make it out of this gilded cage, I'll have to convince him to let me go.

How I'm going to do that is another question entirely.

She-Thor leads me to a formal dining room lit up with black lamps and more lighting recessed into the walls. The ivory wallpaper and thick blush curtains are warm in a way that is somehow unsettling.

But as I enter the space, I feel that imagined warmth crackle on my skin for just a moment before it turns ice-cold.

The circular dining table feels oddly placed in the rectangular room. So does the collection of men sitting around it.

None of them seem to belong to what I would call "polite society." One is wearing a stained wifebeater and half a dozen gold chains. Another one has a diamond set in his front tooth that catches the light and a leer that makes Adrian's cousin Salazar look like the Pope. The man sitting on Kolya's right has only one arm, with the other cruelly severed at the elbow. The smells of this motley crew come fast and furious, too: marijuana, cigarette smoke, stale body odor, and cheap cologne.

I linger at the entrance of the room, regretting my decision to venture downstairs.

"June," Kolya says. "Welcome. Come, take a seat."

There's only one seat left vacant, the one directly to his left. It's the last place on earth I want to go, but I find myself walking meekly over to his side anyway.

He looks perfectly at ease as he gets to his feet to pull out my chair for me. He's the only one who gets up. None of the other men seem remotely interested in making the gesture. I'm not sure some of them know there's a gesture to make in the first place.

"What is this?" I whisper under my breath as Kolya sits down. "Why am I here?"

He looks at me with all the innocence in the world. "To eat of course."

Then he turns his attention to the men at the table and promptly forgets I exist. I don't get the same feeling from the other men, though. They're painfully aware of my presence, and not in a good way. None of them seem too thrilled that I'm joining them.

The man sitting directly opposite me has the lightest blue eyes I've ever seen, like spoiled milk—and they're trained directly on me. His tongue flicks over his bottom lip every few seconds, snakelike and disturbing.

Kolya starts talking, but I have no idea what he's saying. His accent is smooth, but the words are foreign to me. German? Russian, maybe?

The men's eyes slowly shift from me to Kolya. I sit there silently, feeling completely self-conscious and completely out of my depth, as the conversation crackles around me like heat lightning.

About fifteen minutes in, the doors open and the waiters swoop in with armfuls of food. Each person gets a dish set down in front of them. Mine is a sizzling steak, cooked medium rare, surrounded with roasted vegetables, a leek and potato puree, and individual pots of jus. The jus is so thick and red that it looks like blood.

But I'm hungry enough that even that thought doesn't put me off my appetite.

"Let's eat," Kolya says, raising his wine glass.

My glass is filled with lemon soda. Part of me wants to be flattered. Part of me just wants to scream.

In the end, I split the difference: I keep my head down and eat my food quietly. For a few minutes, there's nothing but the sounds of cutlery scraping over ceramic. It's almost comforting. The food is good enough that everyone's focus is off me.

Then that pleasant little oasis of time dries up.

"So," Kolya says in a tone that suggests the social aspect of the evening is at an end. I notice that he's barely touched his food, but his hand is still grasping the steak knife.

He's got a scar snaking down between his first two knuckles. Next to them, in the meat of his fist, he's also got some pretty noticeable bite marks.

I smile inwardly. I did that. It makes me feel powerful for a moment. It's a false, fleeting sense of power, but I cling to it anyway.

It's rare that I feel like this anymore. Dancing was the only thing that made me feel even remotely powerful. I'm sure that this power will get snatched away from me any moment, just like that did.

"Let's talk about the gun shipment."

It can't be a mistake that he switches to English. The other men certainly notice it. They all bristle, a wave of tension running around the round table, and more than one of them casts a frowning glance in my direction.

I clear my throat awkwardly. "I'm tired. I think I'll go—"

"Sit." Kolya's tone cuts like a whip. I fall back into my seat instantly, feeling goosebumps ignite across my skin.

Kolya's eyes scour over each man at the table. " You must be wondering what caused the cut on my face," he says. "You should know what happened. I was ambushed yesterday by some of Ravil's men."

A murmur runs around the perimeter of the table. Some of the men look more outraged than others. The burly man with the diamond tooth hisses—actually hisses, like an alley cat. The skinny man with grotesque scabs running down his neck sits up a little straighter and leans in urgently. The man missing an arm doesn't have much of a reaction, but his eyes darken with promise.

Whoever this Ravil guy is, no one here seems to like him. At least, they're pretending not to. One by one, they all chorus their disapproval.

"Ravil's growing bold. He must be stopped."

"We must put him in his place."

"Say the word, sir, and I will break every fucking bone in the coward's body."

I watch for Kolya's reaction. He looks around at the men, his expression satisfied. "I invited you all here today, because you have been loyal to me, and to my *'krov.'*"

'Krov. I repeat the word a few times in the hopes that I can look it up later and make some sense of whatever the hell is happening here. But I'm tunneling through so much new information that I doubt it'll stick.

The atmosphere in the room has changed considerably ever since Kolya mentioned the name Ravil. It makes me feel strange. Not unsafe, exactly. Just… unmoored.

I'm now weirdly glad that I'm sitting next to Kolya, though I can't quite say why.

"But sometimes," Kolya continues, "loyalty isn't always a permanent state of being."

More shifting. More murmurs. The man without an arm tenses visibly. His eyes dart to and fro, growing frothy with panic. The one with the gold tooth leans back in his seat and cracks his knuckles. It's a sound too close to breaking bones for my liking.

Kostya resumes speaking. "For some, loyalty can be bought. Cheaply, as it turns out. And someone at this table sold theirs for pennies on the dollar."

It's amazing how he manages to whisper and still appear to be shouting. Every word sucks the last vestiges of warmth from the air.

"Someone at this table gave Ravil and his goons my location yesterday. Someone did everything short of cutting my face open themselves."

I watch Kolya. The way his eyes fall on each man in turn. The way each of them either bristle under his gaze or recoil from it. It's like a dance I can't follow, set to a rhythm I can't match.

Then all hell breaks loose.

Kolya flips the blade in his hand, turns, and buries it to the hilt in the throat of the armless man next to him. The poor bastard still has steak juice dripping down his chin, but as I watch, real blood starts to run right along with it.

It feels like there should be more blood. It feels like there should be more noise.

But all I can hear is silence.

The other men at the table seem mostly at ease. Maybe a little taken aback, but not so shocked that they're unable to function. Unlike me, who seems to have forgotten how to use my limbs.

If I remembered, I'd have tried to run by now.

But apparently, I don't need to know how to use my legs, because I feel Kolya's hand on my middle back. With a simple nudge, he has me on my feet and then he's walking me to the door.

I'm not sure if I'm walking or he's carrying me. All I need to know is that I'm leaving behind the dead body sitting at the table with a steak knife sticking out of its throat.

My knees buckle at the staircase, but he holds me upright. I have no choice but to cling to him.

I expect him to push me through my door and leave me alone in there. Abandon me to sift through the horror show I just lived through and make sense of it on my own.

But he walks me right to my bed, scoops me up like I weigh nothing, and lays me down on top of the blankets.

"W-why... why would you do that?" I stammer up at him.

"I've been playing nice, June," he says, standing over me like the flesh-and-blood incarnation of a nightmare. "But what you should know about me is that I will do whatever I have to."

I stare at him, searching for any trace of humanity in those crystal blue eyes. Surely there has to be some humanity there, right? A man without it wouldn't remember to pour me lemon soda.

"I will go above and beyond to make sure you and your baby are… taken care of."

The pause he leaves before the last three words is significant. Like his ever-arching eyebrow, it says everything he needs to say without saying it.

He will protect me—just so long as I dance to his tune.

I find myself nodding, too exhausted to argue, too defeated to think past this night. I just want to lie down and lose myself to unconsciousness. Tomorrow, I'll weed through the chaos of this night. Tomorrow, I'll find my fight again.

Tonight, just give me the mercy of sleep.

I lie back against the bed and close my eyes while he's still in the room. It seems like a stupid move. No sensible person should close their eyes on a man like him.

But I do. Because deep, deep down I don't believe he will hurt me.

Then again, I didn't think Adrian would hurt me, either.

Maybe lightning strikes twice.

9

KOLYA

Milana fixes me with charcoal eyes. "This is the third day in a row that she hasn't eaten a thing. Not even a piece of toast."

"It won't last," I say without looking up from my computer.

"I wouldn't be so sure. Your little stunt the other night robbed her of her appetite. She's refusing everything the maids take up for her. They say she's not looking great, either. I hate to say I told you so—"

"Then don't." I lean back in my seat and glare at my second-in-command. "Take her another tray. Stand there and make sure she eats. Spoon-feed her yourself if you have to."

She shakes her head. "Seeing me will only double her resolve. She won't have forgotten the little part I played in her failed escape attempt." She raps her manicured nails across the gleaming oaken surface of my desk. *Tap-tap-tap. Tap-tap-tap.* "You know what you have to do, Kolya. There's no point in avoiding it. The girl needs to be convinced, and you're the only one who can convince her. You can be very persuasive when you want to be."

"I have better things to do."

Milana raises her eyebrows. "Is that right? Do tell."

I don't rise to the bait. "Any activity on her phone?"

"Not since we took care of everything. Her boss still thinks she's visiting a sick relative, so that's fine. Her landlord has been paid in full, so he has no reason to care where she is. And as for her friends… well, it seems the girl next door didn't have very many of those."

I don't pretend that surprises me. "We can probably credit Adrian with that."

"Maybe she's just a wallflower."

I think back to June sinking her teeth into my hand in the car outside the hospital. "No," I murmur. "I think she's the farthest thing from a wallflower." Grimacing, I rise to my feet. "Fine. I'll go see her."

Milana grins, pleased as can be to get her way with me for once. "Have fun."

"Fun?" I snap. "This is business."

She regards me coolly. "You and I both know this is anything but business, Kolya."

"You've been in the underworld far too long to say something so naïve."

Milana just laughs pleasantly and gets to her feet. "Try to hold back all this charm you're giving off," she suggests with a wink. "Or the girl just might fall head over heels in love with you."

Sapphire Scars

Rolling my eyes, I storm off towards June's room. I hear music when I approach her door. Beethoven. Adrian's favorite.

I use my personal key to open the door that locks only from the outside. It swings inward on silent hinges, to reveal June with her eyes closed and her arms outstretched, fully caught up in the rapture of the orchestra.

The record player in the corner swoons quietly. I stand at the threshold and watch her. She isn't dancing, not quite, but she flows and moves in subtle ways as the music swells up and down, like a flower bobbing in the breeze.

For the first time since I laid eyes on her at the funeral, her face is smoothed free of grief.

Then I shut the door with a *click*, and all that grief comes rushing back into place.

June whirls around and glares daggers at me, her eyes dark with anger. She reaches out to kill the music. The silence that follows is damn near painful.

"What the hell are you doing here?" she rasps.

"You haven't been eating."

Her eyebrows arrow down in a sharp V. "Funny—my appetite kind of deserted me right about the time you put a steak knife in a man's throat."

"I can see how that stopped him from eating. I don't see why it would do the same for you."

She shakes her head in disbelief and sinks into the chair in front of the desk. She's wearing black tights and a black tank top that conforms to her curves. But there's no indication that she's pregnant. Her stomach is still flat, unremarkable.

"You murdered a man in cold blood right in front of me."

I admire that her voice doesn't shake. For a woman who knows just what I'm capable of now, there's still no deference in her posture. No sign of fear, even though I'm positive she's coursing with it.

"What was the goal?" she presses when I say nothing. "You invited me to that dinner for a reason. No other man in that room was comfortable with me being there, but you invited me anyway. Did you want to scare me? Was it a threat? *'Obey me or this is what's coming to you'*? Is that it?"

I lean against the doorjamb, arms folded over my chest. "I protect my people, June. I do what I have to do to keep my people safe."

"That's a hell of a way to keep people safe." She swallows and her throat bobs, which strikes me as strangely delicate. "You're… you're not a businessman, are you? I've been trying to figure out who you are. What you do, at the very least. As far as I can see, you're rich, you're powerful, you're violent. Which means you're…"

She lets her accusation dangle unfinished. She wants my confirmation.

I give her silence. That's good enough.

When the quiet lasts too long, she takes a deep breath. It's more disappointed than anything. "So you're a criminal. Why would Adrian be mixed up with someone like you?"

"There was a lot you didn't know about him."

"God, I'm so sick of you telling me that. I'm—" She lurches up to her feet to give me a piece of her mind, but as she does, she wobbles unsteadily. She has to plant a hand on the desk to stop from tumbling over.

I take a step toward her. "You need to eat. You're weak."

"Don't pretend like you care about how I am," she snaps, eyes fluttering closed.

"If I didn't care, I wouldn't have brought you here. I wouldn't have taken you under my protection."

"'Protection'? We just established that your 'protection' is a little unorthodox, to say the least." She laughs, her eyes flashing with the kind of bitter vigor that her body is lacking. "I need protection *against* you, not from you."

"What you need is to worry about your baby."

"Don't pretend you care about my baby, either," she hisses. "You've got me locked up like a fucking fairytale princess. What happens when I need to see a doctor, huh?"

"You will have an obstetrician. The only difference is that she will come to you."

She shakes her head. "You can't keep me here forever."

"I'll keep you here for as long as I deem it necessary." June recoils, taken aback by the edge in my voice. I sigh and relent. "The man that I killed… He was informing on me. If he had told my enemies about you, about the baby, then both your lives might have been threatened. They still might be."

I tell her all this in the hopes that she understands the gravity of the situation. Adrian left her exposed, vulnerable. Worse, he left her uninformed. He always did have a habit of palming off his dirty work on everyone else.

On me, most of all.

June blinks and furrows her brows. "Okay…? What does any of that have to do with me? I don't have enemies. You do."

"That's where you're wrong."

She drinks that in, still frowning. "Ravil," she murmurs.

I'm mildly impressed. The dinner was no doubt overwhelming for someone unused to wanton violence like that. As dazed as she seemed, she noticed the part that mattered.

"Yes," I echo. "Ravil."

She scrapes at her cuticles, that nervous habit flaring up again. "You know what I don't understand? You keep saying that Adrian was your enemy. So why would you then take in his pregnant girlfriend and offer her your protection? Why would you even care?"

"I never said Adrian was my enemy. I said I was his."

"That doesn't make any—"

"Maybe I'll tell you more one day," I interrupt. "If you agree to stop being stubborn and eat."

She glances at the untouched food tray on the mahogany desk and eyes the avocado toast with regret before wrenching her gaze back to mine. Little by little, I'm getting through to her. She knows it, and she doesn't like it at all.

Right on cue, her stomach growls violently. Her cheeks go bright red.

"Sit," I command her. "Eat."

Defiance flashes across her eyes again. It makes me want to grab her, shove her into that seat, and force some food into her mouth.

But before I'm compelled to resort to that, her shoulders slump and she falls onto the seat. Dispensing with fork and knife, she tears off a hunk of the avocado toast and devours it. I stand silently and watch as she does it again and again until there's nothing left. Her relief afterward is palpable.

"Adrian would never have gotten involved with someone like you," she says abruptly, wiping crumbs from her lips.

I look down on her with pity. "After all this, you really think you knew Adrian at all?"

June bristles. "He was a flawed person. He had secrets, I knew that. But mafia stuff? Murder? That wasn't Adrian."

In many ways, she's not wrong.

The problem is, she's not right, either.

"Your cut has almost healed," I observe, my eyes flickering over her wounded cheek.

She tenses self-consciously. "You won't make me hate him, you know. I know he wasn't perfect, but no one is. He's dead now and for better or worse, he's also the father of my child. You won't make me hate him. You can't."

Again, it doesn't feel like she's talking to me at all. "I'm not trying to make you hate him, June."

"Then what are you trying to do?"

"Prepare you."

She doesn't look at all comforted by my words. The goosebumps rippling over her bare arms are proof enough of that. Her eyes wander from corner to corner, dancing away from me and back again. She's searching for comfort, for reassurance that the world as she once knew it hasn't vanished completely.

But all she finds is an unfamiliar room—and me.

"Do you hate him?" she asks suddenly, as though the thought is just occurring to her.

I'm slow to answer. "No."

"You said you killed his father."

I simply nod.

"Adrian never spoke about his father with me," she continues. "He never spoke about any of this family with me. I'm guessing you know something about that. I'm guessing you won't tell me, either."

"Correct. On both counts."

She looks too exhausted to be angry. Her hazel eyes are bright with sadness, with loss. "You know a lot more about me than you should, don't you?"

I don't bother lying. "I had to make sure you were okay."

She stands tentatively, her legs still regaining their strength, and takes a cautious step toward me. Even from across the room, I can smell her—caramel and lavender.

"I don't understand you," she murmurs, searching my face for answers. "For someone who killed his dad and made an enemy out of him, you still seem to have an awful lot of compassion for him."

I shrug. Her eyes flicker with disillusionment. She's still trying to cling to her good memories of Adrian. I'm not sure why, but that irritates me.

I shouldn't let it. She should be allowed to remember what was good about Adrian. I shouldn't begrudge her that. I *don't* begrudge her that.

I focus on her eyes. From afar, it's unbroken green. But up close, they contain every color in autumn.

"Did he love me?" she asks, almost hopefully.

It's ironic that she assumes that Adrian had confided in me in that regard. I know so much about her, about them. Why shouldn't I know this, too?

Her lips are pursed up, like she's on the verge of prayer. The hope and need in her eyes fill me with a bitterness I can't explain. And before I know it, what's left of my humanity is washed out by ill intentions.

"You were a convenience for him then," I say coldly. "Just as you're an inconvenience for me now."

I stand there long enough to watch her face fall and her dappled eyes pool with tears. Before the first one can fall, I turn for the door. I'm wondering as I go why hurting her hasn't given me the satisfaction I'm after.

Maybe distance will.

10

JUNE

I've been watching him for scarcely half an hour, and in that time, he's managed to put a dozen full-grown men on their backs without breaking a sweat.

One after the next, they all fall. Kolya is not the biggest or the strongest of the bunch fighting in the gardens below my window. But he moves with a lithe grace that none of the others can match. They barrel at him, he becomes a blur of limbs, and a moment later, they're flat on the ground and Kolya is standing tall and victorious over them.

It's weirdly thrilling to watch someone so good at what they do. He sees the angles before they come. Anticipates every twitch of every muscle. I didn't know this before, but it makes sense to me now, that fighting and dancing have the same kind of kinetic beauty.

The only unsettling bit is how much he looks like Adrian. I know I'm just conflating them in my head, drawing a pattern where none exists. But I can't help it. The breadth of those shoulders, that head of dark hair tossing in the evening light —they're one and the same.

Don't compare me to that asshole. I'm nothing like him.

It's weird: the further away I get from Adrian, the clearer his voice in my head becomes. I didn't think it was possible to miss him quite this much.

I miss the oddest things about him, too. I miss the way he would call me Junepenny when he was in a good mood. I miss pressing my finger to the dark birthmark on his chin. I miss the way his eyes would darken on the few occasions I managed to make him laugh.

The Accident made things harder on us. With that pressure ripping him from me and me from him, you'd think I'd have been more prepared for his absence.

But I'm not. It hurts like it's fresh and raw and cruel.

Look at you, getting all sentimental thinking about me. It's almost enough to make me forget that you're ogling another man weeks after my funeral.

"I'm not ogling," I mutter under my breath. "The fighting is impressive, that's all. It's not like I have anything better to do. If you kind of squint, it looks like they're dancing."

Everything is dancing to you.

"You used to hear music in everything," I remind him with a choked laugh. "Even the rain sounded like an aria to you."

Music is one thing. Dance is another.

It doesn't take much to imagine those words coming out of his mouth. He used to say that to me often. Right after The

Accident, when our handicaps were new and we were trying to make sense of a world that terrified us both.

I repeat out loud what I used to say to him back then: "Why? Because music is yours and dance is mine?"

For a change, his voice in my head goes silent. There's a moment of relief, followed by an overwhelming sadness. Things weren't ever perfect between us, nowhere close, but he has been my entire life for so long that I can't remember how it was before him.

After The Accident, when I was lying helpless in that hospital bed, being poked and prodded awake every three hours of the night, I started making lists. Lists of all kinds of things. Objects in the room, colors I could see, dreams I had, foods I loved.

The one I came back to again and again was a list of things I was grateful for. I wrote "dance" and crossed it out so many times that the top line just became a black skid mark on the page.

I didn't have it anymore, not truly. The Accident had taken it from me.

The second line, though, read "Adrian." I still had him.

Now, though, that's a skid mark of its own. So what's left?

My hand floats to my belly. I try to feel the life inside me, but I feel nothing. Ever since the fleeting morning sickness faded away, I've been hard pressed to remember that I'm pregnant at all. I almost miss the nausea.

Sometimes, though, it's easier to forget. Funny how fucked-up that is—I prayed for a baby for so long and now I have one, and all I want to do is go to sleep so I don't have to remember that fact.

"You were always meant to be here for it, though," I whisper to an unseen Adrian.

This time, his voice says nothing.

Kolya is still in the garden down below, sparring with another shirtless man who's half a foot taller and fifty pounds heavier. It goes the same way as all the others: a roar, a tangle of arms and legs, the grunting of men at war. Seconds later, the hulk is eating grass.

I tear myself from the window ledge and drift to the bed. My stomach is full now, and ironically, that's freed up extra brain space in my head. Space for nasty thoughts to take root and fester.

I keep reliving the last few days, starting with that godawful dinner with Kolya's unsavory goons. No matter what he tells me, I can't take him at his word. That dinner was about intimidation and manipulation. He wants me to be so scared of him that I stop resisting his attempts to control me.

Of course, the "why" of that is still in question, but I'm becoming more and more determined to find out.

And then today, when he came to break my hunger strike, he came with ulterior motives, too. The threat laced in his voice. His splintered blue eyes. The way he constantly smells of vanilla and violence.

Everything about him feels like a well-orchestrated ruse to make a fool out of me.

The sad part is how well it's working.

There was a moment there, when we stood inches from each other. He'd stared down at me with the kind of intensity that gathers heat. And I felt… something. I can't be sure of what. But it was powerful enough to make me feel like the proximity between us wasn't so bad after all.

Of course he'd knocked me back to reality with his casually cruel words. Words I can't forget, even now, hours later.

You were a convenience for him back then. Just as you're an inconvenience for me now.

The point of which was… what? To make me feel like a fool? To hurt me? To try and tell me that he knew more about my life with Adrian than even I did?

None of the answers are good ones. None of them make me feel good.

Then again, he never promised to make me feel good. He's promising to keep me safe, offer me protection. Although, he still hasn't told me why I'm in danger in the first place.

So fuck his good intentions. And fuck his mind games. I will not let him destroy what I had with Adrian. It wasn't easy, but it was mine. It was *ours*.

I flop back on the bed, retracing the same mental footsteps again and again. I lie there for an hour, and by the time I'm sick of it, I'm no closer to figuring anything out.

Escaping is no longer an option. I gave that a shot and it went to complete shit. But I figure that if I stay within the perimeters of my cage, I'm free to fly about where I like.

It's not like I have any other great ideas. If I step in this room a second longer, I might blow my brains out.

I get up and pad to the door. When I test the knob, it's unlocked. That's mildly surprising, but I decide to take it in stride. I push it open and peek out into the hallway.

Silence, thick and unrelenting.

I hold my breath and wait. When I'm convinced no one is around, I leave my room and take the stairs down one level.

I smell notes of Lysol hanging underneath the geraniums and roses glistening in vases on the windowsills. Someone's just cleaned this wing of the house.

I slip into the first room I find. This time, I keep my eyes out for a well-dressed blonde with perfectly plucked eyebrows.

What do you think you're gonna find? Adrian scoffs in my head.

"I don't know," I whisper under my breath. "Evidence. He killed a man right in front of me, right? I'm willing to bet there are more skeletons in his closet."

Ever thought about the skeletons in mine, babe?

This room doesn't have any skeletons belonging to anyone, however. It's a guest bedroom, neatly furnished but utterly lifeless. If anyone ever slept here, it was a long, long time ago.

I keep roaming. Every room I enter is sparse and desolate. There are gorgeous paintings on the walls and complex pieces of furniture in every nook and cranny. But each one feels like a display room. A place to look at, not a place to live.

The atmosphere has the stench of false freshness. Cleaning products, floral arrangements changed daily by a dutiful staff. But it only makes it all feel that much deader.

I open every cupboard I find. I snoop through drawers. I even go so far as to get on my hands and knees and check the spaces under things. Under sofas and beds and cabinets standing on four stout feet.

And as I do, I find nothing but bare, polished tile. Bare, shining hardwood. Bare, supple carpet.

I'm starting to feel the uselessness of this dumb little scavenger hunt. If Kolya has gotten away with murder for this long, who am I to think that one evening's investigation can incriminate him? Those splintered blue eyes have looked down on much tougher enemies than me and come away victorious.

You like his eyes, do you, babe?

"Shut up."

I move into another room on the same floor. This one overlooks the garden from a new angle. I still see men swirling around the carpet of lush grass underneath the willow trees where Kolya has been holding court, though I no longer see him among them. In the distance, I spot a tennis facility, a swimming pool, a second one. It feels like his land stretches on forever. Does he have more people like me stashed away, I wonder? A fair maiden trapped in every tower?

I make my way down to the second floor landing without being seen. I can hear sounds coming from somewhere on this wing. Voices chattering, though with the slightest of crackles mixed in. A TV, maybe?

I follow the noise to the source. The sound is coming from behind a black door without a handle. Curiosity gets the better of me. I place my palm on the door and it shifts forward easily and silently. Like it was waiting for me.

I step in. The door floats closed behind me.

When my eyes adjust to the darkness, I realize I'm standing in a home theater. The walls, floors, and ceiling are all pitch black, though skinny strips of lighting mark the path to the handful of seats.

But my attention is caught on the screen.

The footage has the grainy, yellowish tint of a home movie. Two young boys, both eerily familiar, though I'm positive I've never seen either of them before.

They're playfighting like a pair of little pups, pawing and struggling with each other. But whenever the camera catches a glimpse of their faces, there's no joy to be found there. The bigger of the two has a jaw set with grim determination. The younger and smaller one is inexplicably sad.

As I watch, they disentangle. The older boy cracks his knuckles, sets his feet. The younger boy combs his mop of hair out of his eyes and tries to mirror his brother's posture, but he can't match the intensity.

"You are doing him no favors by going easy on him, boy," a voice off-camera growls dangerously. The hair on the back of my neck stands on end. "He's six now, but he will grow. And no one will go easy on him then."

The older boy grimaces. "But, *Otets*—"

"Again. Now."

I watch in horror as the older boy sighs, cracks his neck from side to side, then marches forward and begins to rain blow after blow on the smaller one. At first, the smaller boy holds his hands up to protect himself, but that doesn't last long before he's curled up into a pathetic ball on the ground. Blow after blow lands hard and merciless. The wet, meaty sound of flesh meeting flesh. Whimpers. Cries. A red smear of blood on the older boy's knuckles.

"No!" the child screams. "No, *Otets! Pozhaluysta ostanovis. Pozhaluysta!*"

I don't speak whatever language that is. But *Help me* doesn't need translation.

The older boy's face has turned into an unfeeling mask. There's no emotion there as he rails on the little boy. His eyes are light, hazy, distant. He is not in his body right now— he is somewhere far away, hiding from the pain he himself is causing.

The little boy is still wailing. I want to intervene, but by the looks of the grainy footage, I'm a few decades too late.

The older boy flips over the younger one, and for the first time, I see the child's face clearly. He's got beautiful features, dark hair…

And a dark birthmark on his chin.

I go to gasp, but the air doesn't rush into my lungs nearly fast enough. What comes out is more like a strangled scream.

And suddenly, he's there.

Kolya rises from the darkness like a monster taking shape before me. His splintered blue eyes have never looked so terrifying. Nor have they looked so angry.

And just like that, I realize why the older child on the screen looks so familiar to me.

I never met the boy. But I know the man he became.

The same man who's looking at me now like he's about to devour me whole.

11

KOLYA

"What the fuck are you doing in here?"

June's eyes veer from me to the screen and back again. I grab the remote and kill the film. It gives off an empty blue light that illuminates the horror and disgust on her face.

I can't blame her for hating what she saw. However much she despises it, I despise it a thousand times more.

That's why I make myself watch it again and again.

"I'll ask again: what the fuck are you doing here?"

Her mouth falls open, her eyes turning wide and sad. "Are you… are you Adrian's brother?"

A naive part of me was hoping she wouldn't make the connection. But a different part of me is relieved that she knows now, too. One less secret to keep buried.

"I was, once."

She twitches with confusion. "What does that mean?"

I grab her by the upper arm and drag her into the hallway. After the darkness of the theater, it's blindingly bright out here.

She tears her arm from my grasp. "You're his brother!" she accuses. "Why the hell didn't you tell me?" Her chest is rising and falling fast. Her indignation is battling against her hurt. But neither one is really aimed at me. Not truly.

"I think the better question is, why didn't he tell you?"

"He... he told me he has nothing to do with his family anymore," she says defensively. "Based on what I saw on that video, I can finally understand why."

"You saw two minutes of our lives," I tell her coldly. "Don't presume that you know anything."

"He was six!"

"And I was eight," I reply. "What's your point?"

She draws in a pained, rattling breath and lets it back out. "Who was the bully offscreen?"

"That would be our dearly departed father."

She stops short, her eyes darkening with shock as something registers. "The one you killed? Y-you... Oh, fuck. You killed your own father?"

"He deserved to die."

"And who are you to decide that?" she demands. "Judge, jury, and executioner?"

I meet her gaze. "All of the above."

A shudder runs down her body and she backs away from me. The mark that Adrian had left on her cheek is faint but it's still there. It seems ironic that it remains when he no longer does.

June looks like she's barely registered anything I've said in the last minute. Her eyes keep flitting to the black door of the theater and back to me, over and over again. Wondering how all the pieces of her broken life could ever be put back together.

"Did you find what you were looking for while you were snooping, Junepenny?"

Her face drains of color at the sickeningly familiar nickname. Part of me is savagely pleased. Part of me is disgusted by what I'm doing to her.

The latter part is the one I've spent a lifetime muzzling.

I advance on her, swaggering and all-powerful. She backs up another step, but there's nowhere left to go. I have control of all angles. I have the story in my hands, and I'll unspool it how and when I see fit.

"I d-don't understand…" she stammers. "Why did he never tell me about you?"

"Probably because he was ashamed," I say with a careless shrug. "He cut off his family. He walked away from the life, but he came crawling back whenever he needed something. Whenever he needed *me*."

"Maybe he missed you," June suggests. "Maybe he missed his brother."

"You really believe that?" I laugh harshly. "Do you also believe in fairies and unicorns?"

"You two don't have a monopoly on fucked-up families," she seethes. "I have parents I barely talk to and a sister I barely see. But just because we don't get along doesn't mean I don't sometimes miss them. They're still my family."

"Sounds like masochism to me."

"Says the man watching horrible old movies in the dark by himself." She shakes her head, a spark of vicious satisfaction glowing in those deceptively innocent hazel eyes. "You pretend like you have no morality, no conscience, and no feeling. But if that were true, I wouldn't be here. He may have left the family, but you didn't leave him. Did you, Kolya?"

I freeze. My body knows how to react when someone strikes unexpectedly—I school my face into an iron mask; I keep my fists tight and ready at my sides.

But my heart refuses to obey orders. It's stampeding in my chest, angry and taken aback by the fiery little hellcat in front of me.

June presses in on her advantage. "You cared about Adrian. You *loved* Adrian. You just don't want to admit it, because admitting it would mean that you're not the unfeeling beast you claim to be."

My father's words lash out in my head. *You do her no favors by going easy on her, boy.* So I do what I've spent a lifetime training for: I step into her space and blot out the light, the hope, all of it.

"If you're looking for a heartwarming story, keep looking, Junepenny. You won't find it here. Adrian was *'krov*. Blood. Family. I helped him because the dictates of our shared blood compelled me to. It had nothing to do with sentiment. It sure as fuck had nothing to do with *love*."

I feel like I'm watching a bird die mid-flight. She thought she saw something in me, but I snuffed it out. Clipped her wings right as she aimed herself up to the sky.

And now, she tumbles down to the earth, feathers peeling off one by one.

That's the feeling I was taught to pursue. Not just victory over anyone who dares challenge me, but annihilation of their will to live. For my whole life, that's been my north star.

It's never felt less satisfying than it does now.

"Am I interrupting something?"

June and I turn as one. Milana is standing at the foot of the stairs, her eyes trained on the two of us. June jerks backwards, and I realize just how close together we'd been standing. Her scent dances on the edge of my perception. Caramel and lavender.

I clock the worry on Milana's face instantly. My brow furrows. "What's going on?"

"Ravil is here," she says, lowering her voice. "He's alone and unarmed." She glances back towards the staircase, where I hear footsteps.

I grab hold of June and shove her into the closest room with a door. "You are to stay here silently, until I say so. Is that understood?"

Her eyes narrow, that old spark of defiance flaring hot again. Maybe I didn't fully snuff it out yet, actually.

She opens her mouth, and I realize in the instant before the sound emerges that she intends to scream.

Unfortunately for her, I'm too fast. I clap my hand over her mouth and march her to the rear wall of the room. Her scream is muffled and hot against my palm while I pin her against the bricks.

"You're playing with fire, woman," I snarl down at those gleaming eyes. "That man out there is not the ally you think he is. In fact, he's the very person I'm trying to protect you from."

She tries to say something, but my hand is still pressed against her lips. I can feel her heartbeat against my chest. Her hips flush on mine. Her eyes never yielding, never blinking, not even once.

I break away only because I realize that I like this stance much, much more than I should.

"Why should I believe anything you tell me?" she spits, wiping the back of her hand over her swollen lips. "I don't know this Ravil from Adam."

"You don't have to. Adrian knew him."

"Yeah, and I knew Adrian, and for as many problems as he had, one thing he didn't have was murderous fucking *enemies!*" She throws air-quotes around that word, "enemies," as if her incredulity would stop Ravil from gutting her like a pig, pregnant or not.

"You don't know Adrian half as well as you think you did," I growl. "You don't even know his real name."

The truth of that seems to knock the fight right out of her. She stands there, silent and sullen and confused, looking around the room like she wants to hide.

"You will stay here until I send someone for you," I tell her firmly as I start to leave. "Disobeying me will come with consequences."

"I don't understand why—"

I whirl on her furiously. "You don't have to understand!" I roar. "You just have to fucking listen."

I leave her in the room, shut the door hard behind me, and walk out to find Milana waiting outside. "He's in the blue room," she informs me tensely. "He insists he wants to speak to you. He says it's urgent."

I jut my chin at the door behind me. "Make sure she stays there—*silently*—until he is gone. I don't want him knowing about her existence before he has to."

"You know there's a good possibility that he already knows, right?" she asks, looking at me skeptically.

"For both their sakes, I hope not."

I turn towards the blue room, but Milana pivots with me. "He wouldn't hurt her," she says, but she doesn't sound certain. "She's pregnant with Adrian's baby. Blood is everything. *'Krov,* right?"

"Desperate men are capable of anything," I growl.

"Adrian certainly was."

"Adrian was a fool and a coward," I snap, my resentment bursting out of me unchained. "Ravil is neither. So whatever he's here for… I have a feeling it won't end well."

12

KOLYA

The blue room is exactly what you'd expect. Dappled blue wallpaper, lampshades made of a frosted blue glass, a huge, arcing sofa upholstered in blue velvet.

Ravil is standing by the grand piano when I enter. It too is blue, though it somehow sticks out from the rest of the similarly-hued things in the room. It seems to drink up the light greedily and hide it deep in its own belly.

He pretends not to notice me. The smug bastard keeps his back to me in my own home and runs his finger delicately along the keys, tapping one note to ring out with high, sweet purity.

But I know Ravil. I know all his tells. I see the lines of tension in his shoulders, the caginess in his twitching fingertips.

"You haven't gotten rid of this thing yet?" he asks as he slowly pivots to face me. "Surprising. I sometimes forget how sentimental you can be."

I sigh and take a seat on the sofa. My headache has a name, and it's *June.*

"Is there a reason you decided to pay me this unannounced visit, Ravil?"

"We have business to discuss. You cost me a good man." His lips pull back to bare his teeth. He's never been good at hiding his irritation. Not when he was a little boy and not now that he thinks he's grown enough to go toe to toe with me.

I toy with the clasp of my watch. "You mean the one who I threw into a shallow grave with a steak knife sticking out of his throat? That man?"

"It took me almost a year to turn him."

"Sorry for your loss."

Ravil smiles, though it curdles quickly. "Don't worry, dear cousin. I don't put all my eggs in one basket. Never have."

He's gained weight since I last saw him. He's scrawny by nature, but the extra pounds make him look overstuffed, lumbering.

"Is this the part where you finally spit out the thing you came to tell me?" I drawl, uninterested.

"I know your little secret, cousin." He leaves the piano to saunter over to where I'm sitting. He takes the armchair opposite me and cocks one leg over the other. "I'm a little surprised that you thought you could keep this under wraps. After all, we are talking about a *baby.*"

And just like that, everything gets a hell of a lot more complicated.

But as I did with June just a moment ago, I stick to my training. I make sure my expression and my body language give nothing away. I don't so much as arch an eyebrow.

"A baby?" I repeat, deadpan.

"Please," Ravil says, rolling his eyes. "There's no point in pretending, Kolya. I know about the girl. Pretty thing, and apparently, she can dance, too. Or she could at least. I suppose it doesn't matter anymore as long as she can still fuck, right?"

His leer is enough justification to punch the teeth right out of the gaping hole in his face. But I'm nothing if not disciplined.

"I was a little disappointed, though," he continues. "She's pretty. But… rather common."

My jaw jumps without my permission. Unfortunately, Ravil catches the slip-up.

"Oh dear," he tsks. "Don Uvarov doesn't like that, does he? You must really like this girl. I suppose you would have to, to knock her up in the first place."

And there it is. The hole in his taunting. Which just goes to show: if you stay silent long enough, information comes to you of its own accord. Something Ravil never learned because he was always too busy flapping his gums.

He thinks June's baby is mine.

I refrain from celebrating his idiocy out loud. Better just to let him keep talking.

"You want the Bratva to pass to your son, I assume."

"Which you have a problem with," I guess in a bored voice.

"As a matter of fact, I do. It's *my* Bratva." He leans forward, clenching the arms of the chair, and bares his teeth again. If he thinks he's intimidating me, he's mistaken. "You relinquished your claim to the Uvarov Bratva when you killed my uncle. We do not spill family blood, Kolya. You know this. It's the code we live by. It's the code we've always lived by. Family. *'Krov.* The only thing that matters."

I don't need the history lesson. My father's blood wasn't even cold before the Bratva started splitting down the middle, fracturing off into the men who supported me without question and the men who could not reconcile with the crime I'd committed against their don.

It didn't matter that he was also my father. It didn't matter that he deserved a far worse death than the one I gave him.

All that mattered was *'krov.* And I had spilled blood that I wasn't meant to spill.

"You want what's mine, cousin?" I lean forward, never blinking away from Ravil's bitter, yellow stare. "Come and fucking take it."

Ravil's sneer turns venomous. Those bug-like eyes, protruding from either side of his face, unsettle me as much as they ever have. "I don't want to enter into open warfare with you, cousin," he warns. "But I will if you push me. If you allow the little bastard in that whore's belly to see the light of day, you might as well set your empire on fire."

I tighten my fists out of sight. Blood thrums at my temples, hot and furious. *'Krov* or no, Ravil is dangerously close to getting his throat slit here and now.

"A smart man wouldn't have walked onto my property just to threaten me. I ought to take your head off just for the impudence."

Ravil cackles and leans forward, dragging a taunting finger over his exposed neck. "What was your phrase? *'Come and fucking take it'?* You wouldn't dare, though, would you, Kolya? It's a bit ironic, this whole thing. Spilling Uvarov *'krov* once nearly cost you everything. Doing it a second time would cost you the rest of it."

I clench my teeth hard enough to shatter them like glass. He isn't wrong. What I did was damn near unforgivable in the eyes of many. I've spent years rebuilding the trust that undergirds the Bratva. A single drop of the wrong blood could undo all that work.

But Ravil is a fucking fool if he thinks I'll let him saunter into my house and dictate a single goddamn thing.

"You come into my home, under the goodwill of my protection, my honor, and threaten me? That is reckless, cousin. All it would take is one little slip of a knife, and your line would end forever."

Ravil goes deathly still, his skin turning a sallow yellow that makes him look embalmed.

I give him a careless smile. "You're not the only one with spies, cousin," I tell him, throwing my punches with all the finesse that my father trained into me. "You may think you know my secret. But I know yours, too."

"How did you find out?" he croaks, doing away with the pretense.

"That you're impotent? Not every man who defected to you is actually loyal to you, Ravil. I may have broken a cardinal rule when I killed the old man. But there are still many who see me as the rightful don."

"You were always a cocky little shit," he snarls at me.

I smirk. "And you were always a prickly little bastard with too much pride. Your men are going to find out about your infertility soon enough. That will make things… dicey."

He glares at me with ten years of hatred pent-up behind those yellow eyes. "You don't deserve the throne you stole. Adrian would have made a better leader than you."

"Adrian was a drunkard who kept secrets from the very people he should have been honest with," I snarl. "He was never meant to give orders; he was only ever meant to follow. And even that he couldn't seem to manage very well."

I stand and fix the cuffs of my shirt. I'm done trading words with this fucking worm. I want him out of my sight.

Ravil gets to his feet, though he gives up a good three or four inches to me. "I'll offer my deal one more time: get rid of the baby or I'll do it myself."

I suppress images of bashing Ravil's skull against the floor until the blue carpet turns red with his blood. When my eyes open again, he's still there, bristling with pride and envy and the bitter sting of coming up short.

"I'll offer my deal one more time," I retort. "Get out of my house without saying another word, or I'll—"

Before I can finish my sentence however, the door flies open…

And June runs in.

Her face is flushed, her breathing short, and her eyes pulled tight at the corners with determination. Milana darts in behind June and attempts to drag her back out, but June bats her away with a hiss.

"No!" she screams. "I'm not going anywhere until someone here starts explaining what the fuck is going on!"

I throw Milana a glare so dark that she folds under its weight and looks down at her feet. Ravil, on the other hand, looks like Christmas has come early.

He fixes June with a smile stolen right off Hades's lips. "Hello, dear June. It's about time we were properly introduced."

13

JUNE

That smile.

I didn't know what it meant for my skin to crawl until this moment. Until his dark, misty eyes land on me and his lips pull back to reveal a set of teeth that are too yellow and too jagged to be human.

The structure of his face has shades of Kolya's, but rotten, broken, hollowed-out, malnourished. "My name is Ravil," the man croons. "Ravil Uvarov." His tongue darts out to moisten those thin, chapped lips. "You're even lovelier in person, June Cole. Pregnancy becomes you."

My hand falls instinctively to my stomach and my eyes dart to Kolya. I rushed in here with resolve, but now that I'm here, I'm rethinking my impetuousness. I can feel Milana at my back, waiting to pull me out of the room the moment Kolya orders her to.

But he doesn't. He just sits there, watching me with that unknowable expression on his face.

There are only two things giving me some small measure of comfort at this moment. One is the fresh scent of vanilla in the air. The second is the piano in the corner.

"Who are you?" I ask.

Ravil glances at Kolya with a smile that threatens to make my first trimester nausea resurface. "Tut-tut, Kolya. You should really show her our family tree." He turns his gaze back on me. "I'm Kolya's cousin. Which makes us family."

There it is again—my skin crawling like it's begging me to leave this godforsaken room. Even the air tastes sour and filthy.

"Please sit, June," Ravil encourages, his voice twisting with an oozing charm that I don't trust for a second. "Would you like something to drink?"

It's strange how comfortable he is playing host in Kolya's house. It's almost as if Kolya isn't sitting right there, glowering at him.

"I'm fine." My voice comes out uncertain and croaky. "I'm fine standing."

He gets up, and I instinctively take a step back. Neither Kolya nor Milana make any effort to intercept him as Ravil walks to me and offers me his hand. "No need to be shy. We're all family here, remember?"

I swallow hard, but I let him lead me to the sofa. He smells of black pepper and cloves and his skin feels rough and calloused against mine.

I sit down and he settles down right beside me, much too close for comfort. I look up and catch Kolya's gaze. His expression is less impassive now. There's tension in his eyes and displeasure in the downward tilt of his mouth, but there's also a glimmer of cruel satisfaction.

He's not about to jump in and help me. He's trying to teach me a lesson. *You wanted to be a part of this? Well, this is what you get.*

It reminds me of Adrian. The way he felt the need to "teach me lessons." The slap the night he died was just the grandest and most grotesque in a long line of behavior modifications. Sit up, sit down, say something, say nothing—there was no telling which way the wind blew with him. It was like living with a hurricane.

"You can't be that far along," Ravil murmurs, eyes fixed creepily on my abdomen. "You're not even showing."

"I've barely finished my first trimester."

"I doubt you'll get very big," he says.

"Ravil."

Kolya's voice cracks through the air like a whip. It feels like the first time he's spoken in a long time. I keep my eyes on his face, because it's the only thing that's keeping me from completely freaking out. That steely calm—I need that.

"What's the matter, cousin?" Ravil asks sweetly. "You seem a little put-out."

"Do you think she can't see your smarmy smile? Do you think she can't feel you like slime on her skin?"

"All I'm trying to do is make nice with my cousin's woman—and their future child," Ravil whines. "Family over everything, remember? *'Krov* above all.'"

His phrasing takes me off guard for a moment. It's almost like he's implying that Kolya is the father of my child. Maybe I'm just imagining things though, because Kolya doesn't exactly jump to correct him.

"Ignore my cousin," Ravil says, turning to me. "He's never been very sociable. All I want is for us to be friends."

Even if he had managed to fit a modicum of sincerity in those words, his eyes don't exactly inspire trust. They scale over my body as though he's looking for flaws.

No, not flaws.

Weaknesses.

"He is not your friend, June," Kolya says, his eyes slicing into mine. "He may say all the right things, but you can't trust a single word that comes out of his mouth."

"Like you're any different," I spit.

Ravil's head twists in my direction and his eyes glow with pleasure as he chuckles. "It seems she knows you better than I thought, cousin."

"The problem is, she doesn't know *you*," Kolya snaps. "She wasn't there when I found you with your hands dripping with the blood of that innocent maid. She didn't see that fucking smile on your face. You took such pleasure in it."

Ravil's eyes glow again, but this time, there's an almost radioactive sense of threat in it. Something toxic and deadly. That tongue does its dancing pass over his lips once more.

"Your father needed a favor," he says. "And I am nothing if not helpful."

I stare at him, wondering if he genuinely expects an answer. I lean away from him. From both of them. If this is the family that Adrian ran from, then I can no longer hold his secretiveness against him.

With that, Ravil stands. "I should be going. But, Kolya, I suggest you think on what I said." His eyes find mine and I can't look away no matter how hard I try. "It would be such a shame."

I have no idea what that means, but I don't like how it comes out. Ravil lifts his hand and belatedly, I realize that he's going to touch me. It's like The Accident again, the other car coming up so fast at our windshield, faster and faster, but I can't look away, I can't stop us or them or it, I can't do anything but suck in a breath and get ready to scream—

"Ravil."

Kolya's voice. One word, crisp and dark. But it does what I couldn't do—stops Ravil in his tracks.

Ravil's tongue flashes out and disappears again. He drops his arm, but keeps the smile plastered on his face. "You have a lot to think about, cousin. I'll leave you to it."

Then he's gone, leaving a trail of brimstone and black pepper stinging my nostrils in his wake.

"Kolya," Milana says, breaking the tense silence. "I'm sorry. She broke—"

"Leave us."

Milana bows and retreats out of the room. Kolya doesn't say anything for a long time. I sit in place, too dazed and overwhelmed to do anything but close my eyes and wish I could click my heels like Dorothy to just go back home where I belong. This place, these people… they aren't meant for me, and I'm not meant for them.

I just want out.

I. Just. Want. Out.

"You're a fool for coming in here," he says at last from where he's seated a few yards away. "I told you to stay put."

I grit my teeth. "I don't take orders from you. I don't let violent assholes dictate my life. You want to be a monster? Be a monster. But do it away from me. Do it away from my baby."

He strokes his chin and gazes at the piano for a long time. Then he looks at me and says one word.

"No."

14

KOLYA

"How many is that?" I ask Stanislav as we watch yet another container brimming with weapons get loaded onto the back of another truck.

"That's pallet number... ninety seven," my soldier replies after consulting his list. "Fourteen percent of the warehouse left to go."

"Good. I want it all done before sundown. We don't have time to waste."

"Got it, boss." Stanislav hurries off with his clipboard.

Milana takes his place next to me. "Do you really think all this is necessary, Kolya?"

"Do I ever do anything that's not?"

"I can think of a few things," she murmurs, but even she isn't bold enough to say that straight to my face. June has been a forbidden topic these last few days, ever since the disaster in the blue room. "I do get the logic. I'm just saying, it seems excessive to move every asset in the whole damn warehouse on the off-chance Ravil comes snooping."

I shake my head. "Snake might've fucked up some of the intel he passed to Ravil. But we can't assume he fucked up all of it. So we move this shit now, before Ravil gets his greedy paws on things that belong to me."

"I already said I get the logic," she replies grumpily, folding her arms over her chest. "I don't need a lecture."

"You need a whole remedial course, apparently," I drawl. "Outmaneuvered by a civilian. You should be ashamed of yourself."

She bristles, prideful as ever. "Was I supposed to armbar a pregnant woman?"

"You were supposed to keep her out of sight," I snarl. "Not let her run right into the exact man I'm trying to keep her away from. He put his greedy paws on her, too."

Milana twitches her nose. "You wanna know what I think?"

"Not particularly, no."

"I think you just didn't like him touching her," she says, ignoring me. "You realize that you wouldn't need June at all if you took one for the team, right?"

"Milana—"

"I'm serious. If you produced an heir—"

"Ravil already thinks I've done exactly that."

She is unmoved. "He'll learn the truth eventually. June herself could tell him."

"She wouldn't dare."

"She's dared far more than either you or I thought she was capable of. Underestimating her again would be a mistake. And even if June doesn't tell him, he'll find out some other way. But none of this would even be an issue if you produced an heir. The Sicilians have a princess—"

"I'm not interested."

"In the Sicilians?"

"In any of it," I snap. "I'm not interested in making an heir. I will not subject a child to the indignity of having me as their father."

Her eyes go soft and sympathetic. "You would make a good father, Kolya."

But even I can tell she's just giving me lip service. She has no clue what kind of father I'd be. The odds certainly aren't in my favor.

I look out at the beehive of activity taking place below my feet. I'm on the upper catwalk of one of our warehouses along the river. On the ground floor, dozens of my men zip back and forth like ants, hauling pallets of weapons out of storage and into the bellies of the waiting trucks, to be dispersed to our other secret properties around the city. Every time one of the soldiers catches my eye, they nod respectfully. They know who wears the crown.

Milana sighs melodramatically and leans against the railing. "So you're staking all your hopes on the child in June's belly."

"That child is Adrian's," I remind her. "Bratva blood. Uvarov blood."

"And what if the child is a girl?" she presses. "You think the men down there will accept a queen for a don? Come on, Kolya. You know better."

"We will cross that bridge when we come to it."

Her eyes go wide. I can't exactly blame her. I'm not a cross-the-bridge-when-we-come-to-it kind of man. I move with plans, not predictions. Hope is not a strategy. Nor has it ever been.

My father made sure of that.

"You like her, don't you?"

"I'm honor-bound to protect her," I reply carefully. "For Adrian's sake."

"That's not how you look at her." I narrow my eyes viciously, and Milana holds up her hands in surrender. "Fine, fine, fine. It's brotherly obligation and nothing else. Case closed. Then I have another suggestion—and before you say anything, just hear me out, okay?"

"Fine."

She takes a deep breath before she charges ahead. "Bring back the red trade."

I draw myself up to my full height and look down on her. "That's going too far, Milana. Way too fucking far."

To her credit, she doesn't back down. Not many people still alive can say that. "You said you'd hear me out. Look—we lost a lot of good men to Ravil's cause. Asking them to support a female don or an heir with questionable parentage is just icing on the cake. But if we did it right this time, if we made sure the women were protected, consenting, safe—"

"And after we sell them off to the highest bidder?" I slice in. "What then, Milana? Do we make regular house calls to make sure they're being treated well? Do we set up a hotline? I shut down the red trade because we can't control what happens after the girls are sold off. You think those men buy whores on the black market so they can treat them well? Don't be a fucking fool."

She looks down for a moment, but I can see the resignation in her shoulders. "But—"

Before she can finish her sentence however, I hear a flurry of activity from the south entrance of the warehouse. The stampeding of boots, the crackle of walkie-talkies. A second after that, a barrage of gunfire joins the cacophony.

Milana and I both draw our weapons simultaneously. We don't have to speak or even make eye contact to know what's happening or how we'll respond.

Ravil is here to take what's mine.

We're on our way to make sure that never fucking happens.

∼

An hour later, it's starting to itch where the blood has dried on my skin. Very little of it is mine, though Oleg doesn't know that when I enter the house and he comes running up to take my coat.

"Sir—!"

"I'm fine," I say, holding up a hand. "Have a hot bath prepared in my room. I'm going to make a pitstop before I get up there."

"Right away, sir."

"Anything happen while I was away?"

"Nothing, sir. It's been quiet here all morning."

Of course, I already knew that. The first thing I'd done once the fighting at the warehouse had subsided was call the compound to make sure that no attacks were launched elsewhere while I was busy defending my weapons cache.

My staff had confirmed that June remained in her room all morning. My security had confirmed that no attempts had been made to breach the walls of the compound.

We didn't suffer any casualties on-site. The hit was limited to damaged inventory and minor injuries—for us, at least. Ravil, on the other hand, ended the day with eight fewer men than he began it with.

I had their corpses rounded up. I'd send them back to him for a proper burial—albeit not without a warning sign carved into their chests.

I leave Oleg in the foyer and head up to the blue room. My mother would be horrified to see me sit at her piano in my current state, but she isn't here to admonish me for it anymore.

There's blood and grime caked underneath my fingernails. When I stroke a key, it leaves behind a smear of crimson on the ivory. That's poignant, for reasons I can't quite explain.

I start to play. Note by note, I feel the stress of the fight slide off my shoulders.

I know it's a temporary distraction. The moment I stop playing, the weight will be back. The decisions I'm putting off won't disappear. But for now, I have the keys under my fingers and the conviction of knowing I control the music. I decide where it starts and where it ends. I manipulate every lift and every fall.

Some days, this is the only certainty I have.

15

JUNE

I haven't been able to get the piano out of my head.

I hadn't fully registered the shock of seeing it sitting there in the room the first time I'd stormed in and seen it. I was a little preoccupied with the power struggle playing out on the sofa. But when I finally fell asleep that night, I didn't dream of the yellow-toothed man who touched my skin like he wanted a piece of it for himself, or the splintered blue of Kolya's eyes, or any of the other nightmare fragments that have been floating around my head for the last three months.

I dreamed of the piano.

So when I leave my room for the first time today, I have only one goal in mind: find the blue room with the grand piano.

I'm not totally clear on what I'll do when I find it. I don't have any real use for the thing. Adrian tried to teach me a few chords once, but my fingers were as clumsy as my feet were nimble. Our lesson had ended in a screaming match, a slap, and two days of stone-cold silence.

When we'd finally given up the fight, we'd compensated for our childishness by making love in front of the piano and never speaking of it again. It felt like a good resolution at the time. But looking back on it now, it feels like a prelude to everything that was coming.

We were never very good at communicating the important things. Adrian had an agenda for that. I was just naïve.

I retrace my path back to the room, but when I approach the patterned door, I realize that there's music coming from inside.

Someone's playing.

It makes my heart skip a beat. I'm unfamiliar with the music, but I can appreciate the quality of the playing. Smooth and supple and *pure*, somehow, if music can be pure. I approach the room and gingerly push open the door. The shock that registers feels like an ice bath when you least expect it.

It's Kolya.

I stand at the threshold and watch. Despite how big and bulky his hands are, they move fast and confidently from one side of the keyboard to the other.

Adrian's hands looked exactly the same. Tattooed and scarred, but so lithe and confident. He had the same posture, too—tall and proud, eyes closed, as if the rest of the world had faded away and the only thing left was himself and the music.

I used to know that feeling, though it's been years since I really felt it fully. That's how I felt when I danced. Like nothing else existed. Like I'd entered a world of my own creation, and in it, I was anything I wanted to be.

I want that back. God, I want that back so much, because the world I've been given is nothing like the one that was promised to me when I closed my eyes and danced. Adrian and The Accident took my heart and my knee, respectively, and when they did that, they took away my key to the world I used to dream of.

Without even thinking about it, I reach above my head. One arm stretched high and graceful. I point my toe, long and lean. My bad knee trembles but doesn't give way. Not yet.

I shift my weight, let my eyes flutter closed, and rise up onto one foot as I pirouette. The spin feels good, so I do another.

The music gets louder. Keys crashing together, one chord ramming into the next and splintering apart on impact. I let loose a sigh I've been holding since the day Adrian died and I spin, I spin, I spin, then I—

Fall.

I go too fast. Twist too hard. Bend all wrong. My ruined knee screams in protest and I collapse to the floor, cracking my head against the marble tiling. The tears and the pain are both instant and involuntary.

I roll over with a groan and look up, directly into the lights overhead. Everything is so blue that I feel like I'm underwater. I'm falling deeper and deeper, blackness swimming in from the edges...

Then a silhouette breaks up the light.

It's not until he bends down that I finally realize something is wrong. Kolya's shirt is ripped in half a dozen places. There's blood caked over his face and streaked down his neck. His fingers are drenched in more of the same.

I try to ask what happened, but my lips won't form the words. I get the feeling he wouldn't answer anyway.

My vision is half blue and half black now. I feel myself being lifted into the air. For one crazy, delusional moment, I wonder if I'm dancing again.

Then I realize that the smell of blood has been replaced by the smell of vanilla.

Everything that follows happens in jarring fits and spurts, like a film reel that someone has taken half the frames out of. He's moving so fast through the house that I barely register the pain radiating up my leg and deep into my belly.

"Kolya…" I whisper.

His eyes, the only things I can see clearly, snap down to my face. There's a fresh cut just above his left eyebrow. It's shaped like a half moon. It might have been beautiful if there wasn't so much blood caked around his face.

"I've got you," is all he says. "I've got you."

16

JUNE

When I come to, I'm in some kind of hospital room.

Kolya stands in the corner, arms folded over his chest, face cast in shadow. In front of him is a woman with bright red hair and round glasses. She's dressed in jeans and a striped sweater. No doctor's coat, no medical badge, nothing like that, but she has the walk and assurance of a doctor, and when she smiles at me, I feel a little better.

"Hello, June," she says. "I'm Dr. Sara Calloway. I wish we weren't meeting under these circumstances, but I'm happy to meet you either way. Could you tell me what happened?"

There's something about her I like. She's friendly but matter of fact.

"I, uh… slipped," I say, irrationally ashamed to tell her about the dancing part. "And fell."

"Does it hurt when I do this?" Dr. Calloway asks.

I wince even at her extra-gentle contact. That's when I notice that my leg is already swollen and black and blue, patches of dappled bruising radiating from my knee down my calf.

"Yeah. Ow."

My gaze keeps flitting to Kolya in the back. He hasn't moved. He might as well be a statue carved out of shadows. I notice the blood I saw on his face earlier is gone, and I wonder if I imagined it all in the first place.

"Okay, lie back," Dr. Calloway says. "I'm going to check the fetus first, and once we rule out any danger there, I'll deal with your ankle."

I take a deep breath and do as she says. The world still looks watery and weird through my eyes. Nothing feels quite real. It's nice to be able to just listen to someone else tell me what to do for a change.

She pokes and prods, hems and haws, taps notes periodically into a tablet on her lap. "You have nothing to worry about," she pronounces a few minutes later. "The baby is healthy and safe."

I sigh with relief, not having realized that I was holding my breath this entire time. "Are you sure?"

"A hundred percent," she confirms. "All you need now is a good bandage and some rest. Wouldn't hurt to start you on some vitamins, either. I was going to arrange a full check-up for you tomorrow after we were introduced, but now's as good a time as any."

Kolya steps forward. I blink in surprise. It's like seeing a stone gargoyle come to life. I was starting to think of him as just another fixture in the room.

Dr. Calloway looks at him. "She's fine, and so is the baby," she repeats. "I'll give you two a moment while I fetch some ice."

He nods and she slips out of the room. In the back of my mind, I wonder what kind of hospital has the doctors fetching ice themselves.

"Where are we?" I ask blearily.

"About four doors down from where you fell."

I frown, confused. "Wait, we're still in the house? Why does it look like a hospital room? Come to think of it, why is an OBGYN coaching me on how to ice my ankle?"

"I told you you'd have doctors," he rumbles. "I had an examination room built in the east wing so Dr. Calloway can keep a close eye on you. She'll be here for the duration of your pregnancy."

That's entirely too much information to process at once. He had a *what* built *where* for *how long?* I'm still dazed and possibly concussed, though, so I set those questions aside. Future June will figure out the answers.

"You play the piano," I mumble through fat lips.

"Very perceptive."

"How did you learn?"

"My mother," he says simply, but he doesn't offer me any further information.

"Did she teach both of you?"

He doesn't answer. His eyes are skewering me a little more aggressively than usual. The blue in them is alive, like the face of a melting glacier. His face, though, is perfectly still.

"Well, you play beautifully," I say, focusing on my blotchy ankle. "I didn't recognize the music, though. Who was it?"

The pause right before he answers forces my eyes back to his. "Kolya Uvarov," he says, deadpan.

I stare at him in shock. "You composed that? The… the whole thing?"

"That's generally how compositions go."

I just sit there, gaping at him like a goldfish. I know I must look like an idiot, but I can't seem to change my expression. I detect a smidgen of amusement in the slant of his mouth.

I have a ton of follow-up questions, but they're all cut short when Dr. Calloway walks back in with a medical-grade ice pack. Kolya retreats back to his corner as Dr. Calloway wraps everything up tightly.

"You've aggravated an old injury, it seems," she remarks, casting a critical eye over my leg. Her gaze traces down the scar that snakes from my calf to my knee. "When did that happen?"

I try very hard not to look at Kolya. "Almost two years ago now."

"It must have been a bad accident," she offers delicately.

"It changed my life."

I can feel the lump in my throat, and apparently, Dr. Calloway can too, because she drops the subject there. "Let me give you some painkillers, just for the initial discomfort. It will subside in a day or two."

She hands me a pill and I knock it back gratefully with a little water.

"Excellent. Now, all you need is a little rest."

I'm about to wriggle off the bed when Kolya slips his arms around me and hoists me into his arms. I stifle a gasp while Dr. Calloway holds the door open for us, completely mute.

The walk to my bedroom is silent. I should feel uncomfortable, but the painkillers the good doctor gave me are making me feel a little bit loopy already. The kind of loopy where you start to say things you shouldn't. I bite my tongue, just in case I give in to the lure of the babble.

God, he smells so good, though.

And he feels so strong. A truck could crash right into him, and the truck would be the one that needs attention. I've never met a man so solid before. Not just physically solid, but solid in who he is.

Adrian was the opposite. He made promises he never kept. Told stories that were never true. I never knew if the man I fell in love with was going to show up, or if the other guy would. The mournful drunk, the wild drunk, the silent drunk, the ghost.

"How are you brothers?" I mutter. "You're so different."

He looks down at me, but he doesn't answer. I decide he didn't really hear me. The next second, I find myself sinking into sheets so soft they feel like a hug.

I expect him to leave, but instead, he grabs a pillow and arranges it carefully under my bandaged leg. I feel tears inch their way to my eyes and I have to bite down on my tongue to stop them from surfacing.

I want to cry. Not because of the pain. Not because of the embarrassment of the situation. Not because I'm pregnant and alone, or because I've lost my life partner, or because I'm being held against my will in a strange house by a scary man.

I want to cry because, for the first time in my life, I feel taken care of. I feel looked after.

I feel safe.

17

KOLYA

June's eyes flutter closed. Her breathing is soft and rhythmic and she smells like lavender and caramel. I stand where I am for a long time, pretending I don't notice how one fingertip is still grazing the curve of her calf.

I also pretend I don't notice the way my chest feels somehow denser and tighter, like invisible fishhooks are pulling me toward her.

I pretend I don't notice the thought running through my head on repeat: *What the fuck are you letting her do to you?*

I don't notice that shit because I can't afford to. Because acknowledging it would open doors that I swore I'd never open again.

Just when I was sure she was fast asleep, she murmurs something. "Thank you for taking care of me, Kolya," she says softly. "I can't remember the last time anyone looked after me like this."

I part my lips to say something I shouldn't. To open one of those doors.

Then I do the exact fucking opposite instead.

"I'm not taking care of you," I snap. "I'm taking care of the future don of the Uvarov Bratva."

She blinks her eyes open and recoils sleepily. "Huh? The what of the… huh?"

I glance down at her hand where it's splayed across her belly. "I have no children. Adrian's child is the only one that remains. Which means—"

"It means nothing," she says sharply, her eyes flecking with furious browns. "My child is not going to be the don of anything."

"That's not up to you. This is larger than you. It's larger than both of us."

She looks shocked as she struggles to push herself upright on drugged limbs that don't want to cooperate. "I don't care about your damn—"

Before she can finish her sentence, I push her back down against the pillows. She's soft and pliant under my hands.

I get the result I was after—anger.

But it's less satisfying than I would've expected.

"So make your own damn baby," she tries again, "instead of trying to take mine."

"I don't intend to have children," I say coldly.

"Why not?" she scoffs. "Shooting blanks, are we?"

"Hardly. I just have no desire to procreate."

"So you don't want to make compromises for the future of your Bratva, but you expect me to?"

It's a fair question. In fact, it is *the* question. Unfortunately, I don't deal in justice. I'm not interested in being fair. I'm a selfish, evil bastard and I take what I want.

So I nod.

"That is exactly what I expect."

"And what if I have a girl?" she argues sensibly. "I can't imagine a big, tough guy like you being all that pleased with a little girl."

"A woman still has uses," I say. "Powerful alliances can be made through marriages."

Her hand tightens around her stomach and her eyes widen with horror. "My baby isn't even born yet and you're already planning on marrying her off to some… some… asshole like you?" She shakes her head, like she's trying to wake herself up from a nightmare. "A woman has more value than just being someone's wife. Just because she's—No. Fuck this. Get out of my way."

She starts to struggle upright again. This time, she even manages to swing one bare foot off the bed.

"Where do you think you are going?"

"Away from you."

"You need to rest."

"And you need to leave me alone."

Rolling my eyes, I push her gently but firmly back onto the mattress. She thrashes, but there's no strength behind it. The painkillers are sapping her physical resistance, though God knows it would take a hell of a lot bigger dosage to tamp down her inner fire.

She realizes soon enough that fighting me is a non-starter, and she goes limp on her back. But the anger never leaves her eyes. "Why are you doing this to me?"

I lean in, just so she can see the urgency in my eyes. "Believe it or not, I'm trying to protect you. You met Ravil. Do you think he is the kind of man who plays nice?"

Her eyelids float up and down. Half with sleep and half with confusion. "Ravil…? Why would he…?"

"I told you he wasn't your friend and I meant it. The only reason he's interested in your baby is so he can kill it." Her face goes slack with fear. "You and your baby pose a direct threat to him."

"Why?"

"Because he can't have children of his own. And once his men get wind of that fact, they're going to be significantly less interested in following him."

She frowns. "Wait… does Ravil think that this baby, my baby… is yours?"

"He made an assumption. I didn't think it was necessary to correct him."

"Why?" she asks desperately. "If he knows that I'm carrying Adrian's baby, then—"

"Then he won't care?" I interrupt. "Don't be a fucking fool, June. Adrian's baby, my baby—it won't make a difference. Any grandson of Luka Uvarov is the natural heir to the Uvarov Bratva. He's going to want that risk eliminated."

She shivers. I'd offer her a blanket, but this shiver has nothing to do with the temperature in the room.

"The whole reason you're here," I rasp, "is because I couldn't turn my back on you to let him get his way. If anything happened to you, I wouldn't be able to—"

I freeze. The words wilt on my lips.

If anything happened to you, I wouldn't be able to live with myself.

"I wouldn't be able to honor the promise I made to my brother," I finish.

Before she can drag the real end to that sentence out of me, I jerk back and turn away from her. I need distance from this woman. From her scent, from her eyes, from her fear and her trust and her confusion and her hope.

Everything about her unsettles me.

And a man like me can't afford to be unsettled.

"Get some rest," I tell her gruffly without looking back. Then I storm out of her room.

I run smack into Milana when I open the door. She's slouched against the wall, smirking like the cat that got the canary.

I narrow my eyes. "You were eavesdropping."

She shrugs unapologetically. "I'm your right hand. It's my job to get information."

"Not about me."

She just smiles. "I think you need a drink. Come on."

Sighing, I let myself be convinced and follow her to my office, one floor down. She walks straight to the bar and fixes us a couple of drinks. I drop into the armchair behind my desk.

Milana walks the drinks over and hands the crystal tumbler of whiskey to me. "What shall we toast to?"

"To right-hand women who know when to keep their noses out of my business," I growl, downing half of my drink without bothering to wait for her.

"Grump," Milana sniffles as she sits down on one of the two leather cushioned chairs in front of my desk. She sips daintily at her drink. I fish a cigar from my humidor and light it. Something about the dark sting and tang of the smoke calms my nerves. Maybe because it smells so unlike June.

Milana waits until plumes of smoke are wafting through my office before she speaks. "So…"

"How much did you hear?"

"Enough," she says with an easy grin. "Enough to know that she likes you. Maybe as much as you like her."

"She's… getting attached to me," I say gruffly, quaffing another huge glug of whiskey. It burns on its way down. "She's missing Adrian. It's making her vulnerable."

"Now, now. I wouldn't sell yourself short. You're good-looking, in that cold, scary, brutish way that women seem to like so much. I was a little intrigued when we first met."

I raise an eyebrow. "Just at first?"

"Just at first. Then you started talking and I changed my mind."

"You always were good at listening to your instincts," I point out with a humorless laugh. "June is not. The woman is too generous with her feelings. Too fucking careless with her heart."

"Getting close to her wouldn't be the worst thing, you know," Milana says suggestively. "Winning her loyalty will ensure she's on your side instead of Ravil's."

"She's been manipulated enough. I won't add to it."

Milana's smile gets deeper. "You really expect me to believe that all this protectiveness is for no other reason than a sense of duty towards your dearly departed brother?" She takes a sip of her whiskey. "I call bullshit."

"You can call whatever you want. My answer won't change."

"Stubborn bastard."

"Persistent bitch."

She laughs and finishes her drink. "I'm just telling you to give into what you're feeling. Kill two birds with one stone."

"No," I rumble ominously. "I've had my fill of death for a while."

18

JUNE

I asked my mother once what she'd felt when the doctor told her she was pregnant with me.

She looked at me with a puzzled expression, like she couldn't believe I was asking the question in the first place. Then she replied, "Tired."

I expected her to follow up with something else. Something remotely sentimental. *You were an unexpected gift. I was so excited. I couldn't wait to meet you.*

All I got was *Tired*.

I should have cut my losses and stopped there. But I was ten. I wanted to know that I was loved, wanted, all that good stuff. I should have realized that if I had to ask at all, it's probably because none of those things were true.

"Did you feel the same when Geneva was born?" I asked next.

My mother just looked at me impatiently. "Shouldn't you be practicing your dancing? If you're serious about this, June, you'll need to commit properly."

I'd come around the corner and found Geneva eavesdropping from a seat on the bottom step of the staircase, holding back her laughter. "She was happy to have me," Geneva informed me cruelly. "I was planned. You were just a nasty mistake."

I can't help wondering how my parents would react if I called them now and told them I was pregnant. Would they be happy for me? Horrified? Indifferent?

Or would they just be *tired?*

You know damn well what they'd say, Adrian snarls snidely in my head. *You're just pretending like you don't care so that it'll hurt less when they prove you right and act like they don't give a fuck. Which they won't. Because they don't.*

I hear his phantom laugh in the peripheries of my mind. It makes me want to cry, just as much as it makes me want to laugh. It's just the familiarity of it. Of him. I miss that more than I miss the man himself. I miss knowing the path my life was going to take.

"June?"

I drag myself out of my emotional whirlpool and focus on Dr. Calloway. She moves around the examination room with a practiced ease, as though she's been working from it for years.

She gives me a soft, reassuring smile. Despite my best efforts not to, I actually like her. She's thorough, clearly smart, experienced, and she treats me like a real person, unlike the rest of Kolya's household staff, who treat me like Medusa—look me in the eye and they'll turn to stone. Also unlike Kolya himself, who treats me like a black hole—get too near and I'll destroy him. I'm tempted to tell him the exact opposite is true.

"Sorry."

"Heavy thoughts?"

I blush sheepishly. "I was actually just imagining my parents' reaction to my pregnancy. I haven't told them."

"I'm sure they'll be over the moon."

"Ha. You clearly haven't met my parents." I grimace and rush to correct myself. "They weren't terrible parents or anything. They never, like, beat me, you know. They were just… neglectful. And overbearing."

"How does one manage to be both at the same time?"

I laugh grimly. "You basically stay as far away as possible until it's time for trophies to be handed out, at which point you swoop in and berate your kid for not winning more of them. Other girls used to look forward to recitals. I dreaded them."

"Recitals?"

"Dance recitals," I explain reluctantly. "I'm—I *used* to be a dancer." I hate the way I sound when I'm forced to tell people that. It feels like I'm apologizing for something.

Dr. Calloway glances down at the scar on my leg as she puts the pieces together. "I'm sorry. Losing that can't have been easy."

"You're not going to tell me to be grateful that I can walk?" I ask.

I'd heard that from half a dozen different doctors, back when I was still in denial and convinced that if I found the right one, they'd tell me what I wanted to hear. That my injuries were temporary. That I would be able to dance again. That The Accident was not the end of my career.

Dr. Calloway looks irritated. "I've never understood that school of thought," she says. "Tell a man who's lost his hand that he's lucky he didn't lose the whole arm? It never made much sense to me. You have your arm. What you want are your fingers. That's only human."

I smile. "Thanks, Dr. Calloway. It's nice to not feel crazy for a change."

"Please," she says, waving a hand in my face. "Call me Sara."

"Sara it is." I smile at her. "So, forgive me for asking, but do you live here?"

She laughs pleasantly. "No, no. But Kolya is paying for my accommodation in a lovely little apartment not far from here. I'm supposed to be on call for you twenty-four-seven."

"I apologize," I mutter.

"Don't. He's paying me exorbitantly for my martyrdom."

"I'm sure you're worth every penny."

Sara chuckles. "And then some. Speaking of which, how's the ankle?"

I glance down at the purpled, swollen limb. "It's... alright."

She sinks to a seat on her rolling stool and gives me a half-joking, half-stern glare over the rims of her glasses. "No need to fib to your doctor, June."

I blush and turn my gaze down. "Okay. It hurts. A lot."

"Best not to put pressure on it then," she says, satisfied with my honesty. "You could use a hand when you do stuff like showering, moving around."

"Oh no." I cringe hard. "Is that really necessary?"

"I'd say so, until the ankle has fully healed. It might take a little longer, considering your pre-existing injuries. The body is a little stubborn once we start accumulating miles, unfortunately."

She rolls herself forward to check my blood pressure. A cascade of red hair tumbles over her shoulder and I catch a whiff of coconut. I like that she doesn't tie her hair when she's working, as minor as that seems. It makes her come off as a friend, not a professional.

I need the former way more than I need the latter right now.

"You sure you're okay, June?" Sara asks, unstrapping to the cuff, moving across the room, and taking her coconutty scent with her. "You seem a little preoccupied this morning."

"I guess I'm just a little nervous. I haven't had a proper sonogram since the doctor first told me I was pregnant. And I wasn't really paying a lot of attention back then."

Sara doesn't ask many questions. In fact, she doesn't ask any questions.

"You know the… details, don't you?"

Sara raises her eyes to mine. I appreciate that she doesn't even try to deny it. "I don't know everything. But I know enough."

"I don't want to be here," I tell her.

She nods solemnly. "As I understand it, you're safer here than anywhere else," she says as diplomatically as she possibly can. "You and your baby both."

It seems she's picked her side. I try to swallow my resentment, to remember that I like Sara. More importantly, I'll need her help in the next few months. I'm short on allies and friends alike, so I can't afford to burn bridges.

"How do you know Kolya?" I ask, hoping that's a safe question.

"My father used to work for his."

"Used to?"

"I lost my dad a few years ago. Cancer. Took him quick."

"I'm sorry for your loss," I say automatically, although even as I say it, I remember how much I despised it when people dropped rote lines like that on me after Adrian's death.

I'm sorry for your loss.

How ya holdin' up?

Hang in there—it gets easier.

"Don't be," Sara says breezily. "My father and I weren't what you would call close. He paid for my education, supported me through medical school, made the obligatory Dad calls during birthdays and major holidays. Some might say he did the bare minimum, but he did just enough for me."

"So can I assume that he was Bratva, too?"

Sara nods. "He was. The Bratva was his religion. And Luka Uvarov was his god."

I freeze. Have I made a fool out of myself already in front of someone who's way more loyal to Kolya than they'll ever be to me?

Sara reads my discomfort. "Luka was a god to my father," she clarifies. "Not to me. As far as I was concerned, Luka Uvarov was the man who stole away my father and turned him into a stranger."

"So then why would you want to be a part of this world?" I ask. "If you don't mind me being nosy."

"I'm not a part of it," she says. "I'm here to do a job, and I'm paid handsomely for it. That's all. I don't concern myself with the politics."

A part of me understands where she's coming from. Sometimes, it's easier to have blinders on than admit that what you're doing is morally questionable.

It's the one lesson I learned from Adrian. Nothing is simple. Every choice, every feeling, every fork in the road—it comes with complications. Even something as seemingly simple as love is the farthest thing from it, when you really look close.

You gift someone your heart and they turn it into a weapon.

"You want to leave, Junepenny?" Adrian asked me a year ago, after his third or fourth fall off the wagon. *"Go ahead. See how far you get before you realize I'm the only family you have. I'm not perfect, but I'm here."*

"Here" was a low bar, but no one else in my life was clearing it. I had parents who weren't around and a sister who left home long before she needed to, just to get away. Ex-boyfriends that never lasted and a career that had abandoned me.

But Adrian was there. And underneath his veiled threats, I saw the seal of a promise. He would never, ever leave.

Until he did.

And when he did, he left in the worst way possible. There is no coming back from where he'd gone. No phone calls or letters or hope for an encore. Just eternal silence.

I try to remember his scent. Whiskey, of course. Sweat. The blandness of his cheap laundry detergent.

But he'd had a specific scent before then. In the vast in-betweens of his sobriety journey, there were still moments when he smelled like himself.

What was that scent...?

I can almost pick it out in the fragments of old memories. On the periphery of my feelings. But every time I try to catch it, it springs out of reach like a dream that's fading fast.

How can I have forgotten his scent so fast? So soon?

Maybe because all you're smelling now is vanilla.

Don't.

Am I wrong?

He's not you.

No—he's better isn't he? Taller. Smarter. More confident. Far more handsome.

I sigh so deeply that Sara looks at me, her eyebrows knotting with concern. But she doesn't ask me, and I appreciate that. I'm not sure I can keep up the pretense much longer.

"Well, enough of my boring life story," she says, clapping her hands. "Shall we move onto the sonogram?"

"Yes," I say, desperate for a distraction from my own thoughts.

The machine flickers to life, and Sara pulls out what looks like a metal penis. "I know it looks a little intimidating, but it's just an ultrasound probe. It'll be a touch cold and you'll experience some mild discomfort, but I'll be gentle. You ready?"

"As I'll ever be."

"Okay then. Lie back and part your legs for me, please."

I do as I'm told, the smell of cold metal skimming my nostrils, followed by the acrid prick of sanitizer. Then I feel the probe at my vagina and I suck in a sharp breath.

"Then here we go."

The probe slips inside me and I bite down on my tongue. The pinch of discomfort fades after a moment. I turn my attention to the monitor.

"Okay," Sara says, looking at the screen along with me. "There we go. That's your womb… aaand that's your baby." She points with one gloved finger at a blobby little alien shape rendered in black and gray.

A human being in the making.

"Oh wow," I breathe. "Wow. Wow…"

And then I start crying. It happens so suddenly and so unexpectedly that it takes both me and Sara completely by surprise. I blubber as I stare at the beating heart on the screen, and Sara hands me a tissue.

"I-I'm sorry…"

"Don't be sorry. Just let me know what I can do."

"C-c-can I have j-just a few m-minutes alone?"

She gives me a soft smile, puts the probe away, and disappears without a word.

"You should have been here," I say, whispering out loud to the empty room in the hopes that Adrian's ghost will hear me. "You should have fucking been here. Like you promised me."

All I get in return is silence.

Typical. Fucking typical.

Even if there was such a thing as ghosts, Adrian's wouldn't be sticking around with me. He didn't have the patience for my heartaches or my pain while he was alive.

He sure as hell wouldn't have it now that he's gone.

19

KOLYA

It's been two full days since I last saw her.

I get three reports daily, and they never vary. She eats her meals without complaint now. She takes a walk around the grounds in the mornings after breakfast, and another in the evenings before dinner. Sometimes, she goes to the library to read a book. Other nights, she watches a movie in the home theater.

She goes for her check-ups regularly. I hunt down Sara each time to make sure everything is okay.

"Of course everything's okay," Sara assures me repeatedly. "She just likes talking. She's lonely, and I think she's looking for a friend."

I don't need to know more.

I don't need to know what she's going through or how she's feeling. My concern is her health and the health of her baby. Whether she's happy, whether she's sad, whether she's lonely, whether she's afraid—that shit does not concern me.

"Grisha!" I call out, flexing my fists until the knuckles crack. "You're up."

Grisha steps forward from the circle of bare-chested men ranged around me in the gardens. He's relatively new, though no longer truly a recruit. He wears the brand of the Uvarovs burned into his shoulder, proof that he has passed all the tests that matter. Even if he didn't have that, the scars riddling his body would show that he's fought his fair share of battles.

It won't save him today, though. He bends his neck from side to side, drops into his crouch, and squares up against me.

Over his shoulder, I notice Milana join the throng of Uvarov soldiers waiting their turn to fight. She stands out from the collection of sweaty, scarred torsos in her pale pink heels and her lily-white wraparound dress. She looks delicate, but every man who glances in her direction drops their eyes to the ground just as fast. They've seen what she can do, and they know better than to gawk.

I raise my hands and gesture Grisha forward. "Come."

He has a reputation as a talented fighter. But it's all over far too quickly. He charges, throwing a rapid flurry of punches. I sidestep them all, the rippling of his grunts passing by me, then turn and unleash one succinct blow into his ribs.

Something cracks beneath my fist and he drops to a knee immediately. I could leave him there, but I'm in a mood for blood, and a don showing mercy in front of his men is not worthy of the crown he wears.

So I twist around, hook a forearm under his chin, and drag him down on top of me. He splutters and gasps, trying to wrench me off of him, but it's no use. I take him right to the brink of unconsciousness before I let him loose.

Then I push him off of me and brush the dirt from my clothes.

Standing, I look around at my gathered men. More than half of them are beaten and bruised already, courtesy of yours truly. We've been out here for hours, facing off one by one. Not a single one of them has come close to landing so much as a scratch on me.

They all bow their heads respectfully as I sweep my gaze around the circle. "We're done for now."

But then all eyes flit over my shoulder. Motion from behind.

"No!" Grisha roars. I turn to see him wipe blood from his lips with his fist, then drop into his fighting stance once more. "Again."

"I said we are done," I growl. "Do not make me repeat myself again."

For one moment, I wonder if he'll disobey me and force me to make an example of him. Then it occurs to him who he's talking to. He drops his chin to his chest, humbled. "I apologize, my don. I forgot myself."

I slap a hand on his shoulder as I move past the men towards Milana. She pushes herself off the wall and arches one golden-brown eyebrow. "You're going to run out of foot soldiers if you keep beating them senseless."

"Grisha is still standing."

"Only because I showed up at the right time," she says shrewdly. "I saved the kid's ass. Or is it your ass I'm saving? I can't keep up anymore."

I clench my jaw. "I'm too tired for banter, Milana. What do you want?"

She gives me an innocent smile. "Nothing at all," she says. "I'm just here to talk to you about our dear guest. Apparently, there's new swelling around June's ankle. Sara suspects that June is ignoring her recommendation to accept assistance with her daily activities. Showering, in particular, seems to be hands-off for the maids assigned to care for her."

I grit my teeth. "Of course it is. Stubborn fucking *kiska*."

Milana smiles, as though this whole situation is amusing the shit out of her. When my dark gaze veers towards her however, she tries to wipe the smile off her face.

"Do you want me to go up and talk some sense into her?" Milana asks.

"No. I'll handle it."

I'm distantly aware that I'm using this little hiccup as an excuse to see her. But I figure I've stayed away for two and a half days.

A visit is overdue.

20

KOLYA

I find her lounging on the sofa in her bedroom. She's wearing a thin silver slip and paging through a book in her lap.

She jerks upright when I walk in. The book tumbles to the floor. We just stare at each other for a moment, and the air starts to heat and thrum.

I close the door and walk over to her. She shrinks back into the cushions, her eyes turning small with wariness.

"What are you doing here?" she asks.

"Let me see your ankle."

She instantly throws a blanket over her lower body. "It's fine. It's healing."

Ignoring her, I step forward and rip the blanket away, then kneel and take her leg into my hands. It's not the best move, considering her silver slip slides right up her leg, revealing an expanse of creamy thigh. But I make a decent pretense of keeping my eyes glued to her bandaged ankle.

The swelling is red and angry now. She tries to wrench her foot from my grip, but it must hurt worse than she's letting on, because her lips fall open and her cheeks go pale.

I pretend to examine her leg a little longer, if only to keep my hands on her bare skin. If only to admire the slim beauty of her dancer's muscles.

When I can't justify holding onto her any longer, I place her foot back down on the cushion of the sofa. She seems taken aback with how gentle I'm being.

"You're only hurting yourself with your stubbornness," I say grimly. "Something I'm sure Dr. Calloway has already told you."

"I have to move around. Sara said I don't need crutches if I don't want them. Anyway, why do you care? This has nothing to do with you."

"This has everything to do with me. You're carrying my niece or nephew. My heir."

"My child will *never* be your heir," she spits with conviction.

I almost believe her.

Then I remember that I'm Kolya Uvarov and I have faced much worse than a spitfire dancer with more spirit than strength.

"We'll see about that."

"If those maids come in here, I will fight them both," she warns.

I can't help it: I laugh. She flinches again as though my laugh has the power to hurt her. Instead of cowing, though, she seems to get taller. She pushes herself off the couch and gets to her feet. Wobbly, but ferocious.

"You think I'm joking?" she demands.

"I know you're not. That's why it's funny."

Her forehead wrinkles. Before she can dream up another line of argument, I do what I suspected I'd have to do from the beginning.

She's light as a feather as I hoist her over my shoulder. I expected her to scream, but she doesn't even have the presence of mind to do that quite yet. Her slip flutters over my nose, perfumed with her scent.

We step into the bathroom, but instead of putting her back on her feet, I seat her on the marble countertop, then reach around her to turn the shower on hot. She sucks in a deep breath, her eyes wide with disbelief. I'm sure the fury will follow, but for now, I take advantage of her silence.

"There's no sense troubling the maids for something I can see to myself."

"Y-you… wouldn't."

"Watch me."

She shakes her head. "You can't do this. I'm a grown woman. You can't do this."

"Repeating a thing won't make it true," I tell her harshly as steam starts to fill the bathroom and fog up the mirror. "I gave you several options and several chances to compromise. You've officially used up every single opportunity you've received. I'm done talking. I'm done negotiating. You don't get a say anymore. Now, do you want to take the slip off? Or should I?"

She opens and closes her mouth a few times as the anger builds and builds inside of her. A bead of sweat forms at her temple. I dream of kissing it away.

Instead, I shrug. "So be it."

Done playing nice, I grab her waist with both hands and carry her into the shower.

That's when she finds her voice. "No!" she screams, beating her little fists against my back. "Kolya! Let me go! Stop! Stop!!"

Her yells devolve into unintelligible sounds as the water hits her. You'd think it was ice-cold, the way she's carrying on. But it's searingly hot.

As the water drenches us both, I can feel the slip disintegrating under my hands. At least, that's how it feels. It clings to her body like a second skin, revealing every curve it's been hiding. Every secret dip and bend that I've spent the last several days trying not to notice.

Her nipples are pressed up my shoulder. I set her down and twist her away from me before I do something stupid, but all that does is grind her ass against the hardness behind my zipper.

I falter for a moment. My hands fall off her as I grimace, and when I stumble backwards, the water hits my face, blinding me.

June takes that as an opportunity to attack. Ripping the secondary shower head out of its holster, she spins around and swings it at me.

I consider letting it hit me. Letting her crack my skull open and leave me here to bleed, gibbering and drowning to death on my own blood and water hot enough to surge through hell. I can't say I wouldn't deserve it. From the moment I found her, I've tried to hurt her, if only to keep her at bay. Because letting her too close would be a catastrophe.

At the last second, though, decades of training take over. My body moves without my mind's permission. I pluck her wrist out of the air mid-swing and twist it until she cries out and drops the shower head. It clatters to the floor, then I shove her back up against the tile wall as it cries tears of condensation. The thunder of falling water washes out our mingled, panting breaths.

"Will you fucking stop?" I growl. "I'm trying to help you."

"I don't need your damn help!" Her cheeks are flushed bright pink and the slip is plastered tight to her body.

She shoves at my chest, but I can barely feel it. All I can sense is her minty fresh breath, and her rock-hard nipples, and the pulsing heartbeat filling the space between us.

"I'm not my fucking brother," I hear myself say. "When I tell you I'm going to help you, I will. When I tell you I'm going to protect you, I fucking will."

Why am I separating myself from Adrian? Is it a threat to her? A warning to me? Or is it just a reminder that there are lines we cannot cross?

Because she's got my brother's baby in her belly.

And I have my erection pressed between her thighs.

I stare down at her lost hazel eyes, and I see in them all the complex, twisted grief she's been carrying around with her since Adrian's death. I'm a selfish fuck. Always have been.

But right now, all I want to do is be selfless enough to make her forget she ever loved my brother.

Maybe that is why I kiss her.

To show her that there is another way.

21

JUNE

His kiss is every bit as aggressive as he is. Powerful. Overwhelming. All-consuming.

The water rinses away everything that could stop this, including my own judgment. In here, it's like I can wash away my old skin and take on a new one.

I half-expect to hear Adrian's voice in my head, scorning me for my impulsivity, cursing me for my betrayal, ridiculing me as a whore, a cheater, a tramp.

But in here, I can't hear his voice. In here, I can't hear anything other than the steady beat of water and the sighs flowing from Kolya's lips.

Maybe I'm a sucker for pain. I chose Adrian, after all. And now, here I am, throwing myself at the other brother. The Uvarov sibling with all the influence, all the wealth—and all the tools to ruin my life.

I know all that. God knows he's told me as much and backed up his words plenty of time already.

And yet even in the light of that knowledge, I wind my tongue against his, my fingers raking at his wet shirt, desperate to pull it off him.

When he pulls his lips from mine, I barely see his face before it lands on my neck. His teeth nip at the nape before sliding down to my collarbone. He pulls my strap off my shoulder, freeing my breast, and sucks my nipple into his mouth.

My back arches involuntarily. One of his huge hands paws my hip, pinning me against the wall. The other strokes against my belly, feather-light, as if to remind us both of what lies between us.

His fingers run down my stomach, down between my thighs. He teases and taunts as the water keeps on pouring relentlessly around us. When he finally finds my clit, it tears a heaving breath out of me.

"Oh God…" I gasp. "Kolya…"

And when his fingers slip inside me, I cry out, pain mingling with the pleasure, until the former recedes completely, leaving me with nothing but pure desire coursing through my tired body.

The ache in my ankle is virtually nonexistent now. I can only focus on so many things at once, and so maybe I should let this happen, if only so I can forget about all the pains I've been carrying around with me for so long now.

Our intertwined hands knock over a bottle of something on the recessed shelf behind me. It breaks on the floor at our feet and the scent of honey and hibiscus fills my nostrils.

I bury myself against him and push my hips forward, inviting his fingers in deeper. I want to rip away his shirt, but I can't seem to make my fingers cooperate.

I close my eyes as Kolya's fingers steal more of my resolve, my self-respect, my hope that I'll ever be able to walk away from this gilded prison with my head held high. When he pulls them away for a moment, I'm heartbroken.

Until he replaces them with his hard length, and just like that, I can no longer speak.

The stream of water comes down over my face, rendering me blind for a moment. I don't mind, though. It's enough to feel him, to smell him.

It's enough not to feel so empty for once.

On the heels of that thought is horror. I tell myself that it's okay to want those things. I'm fucking my dead boyfriend's brother, but if it's either that or lose myself to madness, that's okay, right?

Maybe that's a shitty explanation, I don't know. All I know is that it makes sense right now, against the heat of our bodies and the cacophony of the water.

I wrap an arm around Kolya's neck to cling onto for dear life and angle my face up to the ceiling. I can't see anything but steam. Swirling clouds of mist and heat that hold endless hollow promises.

"Forgive me," I whisper as Kolya continues to thrust into me, harder and harder, unwinding every last defense I have left. "Forgive me."

I'm not sure who I'm asking forgiveness from. Adrian? My baby? Myself?

My plea for forgiveness rises up like the mist and I lose it, too. I lose everything as the orgasm finds me.

Sapphire Scars

I feel Kolya come right on my heels. His heat, sticky and unlike all the other heat around us, fills me up. Then his thrusting slows. Eases. Stops.

He reaches out and cuts off the flow of water.

Just like that, a creeping sense of wrongness follows. When it was hot and wet and steamy, this felt okay. Now that the cold is coming, the clarity is coming with it.

So is the shame.

A random man would have been bad enough. But I chose a man who I knew was a murderer. A man without any qualms about killing in cold blood.

Worse still, he's the brother of the man whose baby I'm carrying. Adrian has been buried—what, how many weeks ago now? Time has lost all meaning. Whatever the answer, I know that it's not nearly long enough to warrant sex with another man. Not nearly long enough to justify fucking his brother.

I tell myself it's okay because it meant nothing. I'm not in love with Kolya Uvarov. I'm still in love with Adrian. Kolya is just… second-best. He's the only part of Adrian left that I can still touch, and in some twisted way, maybe that's what I was looking for.

The final piece of the man who abandoned me.

Kolya turns from me. He kept his shirt on the whole time. The fabric of it clings to the muscles of his back.

When he turns back around, he offers me a towel without ever raising his eyes to meet mine.

I take it cautiously and wrap around my body, eyeing him the whole time. Kolya doesn't seem concerned with getting himself dry. He doesn't seem to want to remove his wet clothes, either. It's more like he's waiting for something.

"You should go sit down," he mumbles. "Get off your ankle."

For some reason, that pisses me off. He should at least have the courage to own up to what he just did. What *we* just did.

"You did what you came here to do," I snap. "You can leave."

He's quiet and still for a long moment. He still won't look at me. Goddammit, why won't he *look* at me?

Then he pivots and makes for the door.

"Kolya?" I call just before he can leave.

He pauses but doesn't turn around, doesn't say anything. His back is broad and soaking wet. The white shirt plastered against his back makes him look like a marble statue.

"I will accept help from anyone in this house. But not from you. Not anymore. Not ever again."

He just nods, as though this was his end goal all along. Then he leaves and my door snaps shut, blotting out the light.

22

KOLYA

"Boss," says Samuil at my office door, "there's a woman at the gates, requesting entry."

I wave him off without even looking. "Turn her away. I'm not expecting anyone, and I don't entertain uninvited guests."

I go back to my work. The mess at the warehouse has forced me to get creative with where we're resituating those supplies. I have men all over the city stuffing pallets of high-powered firearms and bricks of pure heroin into every little hole in the wall we can find.

A few minutes later, there's another knock. "Sir…"

I glance up to see Samuil again. I arch one eyebrow, a silent question.

"The woman, sir…" he begins haltingly. "She… she tried to break in."

Gritting my teeth, I drop my pen and snap the file folder in front of me closed. "Who the fuck is this woman and why does she want in my house so badly?"

Samuil pokes the door jamb with one booted toe. "She claims to be Ms. June's sister, sir."

Sister. Fuck me. That's one of the last people on the planet I am interested in talking to right now, for about a thousand different reasons, not least of which is the fact that she's one of the first people on the planet that Ravil would try to use to get to me.

I get to my feet slowly. I can feel a real motherfucker of a headache coming on.

"We have her confined to the inner courtyard," Samuil explains, "but she's struggling. Permission to use force?"

How easy would it be to say yes and turn a blind eye to this. I've got enough problems as it is.

"No," I sigh. "I'll speak with her."

The only sign of Samuil's surprise is a slow blink. Then he nods and holds open the door. "I'll escort you to her location, sir."

When we enter the inner courtyard, I find the woman contained by two more of my household guards. Nikifor has a scratch on his left cheek, fresh and weeping blood.

"Did she get you, Nikifor?" I ask in amusement.

"Only the one time, boss," he says gruffly. "She didn't manage a second swipe."

I turn my attention to the woman between Nikifor and Meric. Hands folded behind my back, I pace in front of her. "And who might you be?"

Sapphire Scars

A curtain of dark hair drapes over her face, mussed from her struggle with my men. She tosses it back with a flick of her head and focuses her glare on me.

There isn't much June in her posture or her facial structure. But her eyes—there's some of June's spice in there.

"Oh, fuck you," she spits. "Don't pretend like you don't know. Men like you always do your research."

I continue pacing like a caged tiger. "Do you have a lot of experience with men like me?"

She bristles as if she's offended, but it's an unconvincing acting job. My suspicions deepen.

"More than most," she says vaguely.

"Interesting."

"You wanna know what I find 'interesting'?" she offers. "I find it 'interesting' that you've had a young woman locked up in this pretentious-ass mansion for weeks and no one's said a word about it."

"I'm not in the habit of locking up young women."

"Then why haven't I seen my sister in over two weeks?"

"Probably because you haven't made the effort to stay in touch. That's really more of a you problem than a me problem."

Her eyes are tight slits, her lips drawn even tighter. She's feisty, this one. A mare who needs breaking.

But I have my hands full already—and even if I didn't, I'm not interested.

"I want to see my sister," she declares.

"I'm afraid that's not possible."

"Juuune!" she screams without warning. "June! June!"

Sighing, I gesture to Samuil over my shoulder. He comes up from behind me with a thick leather gag in hand. The woman sees it while she's sucking in air to start screaming again. Her eyes bulge out of her head and she changes course at the last minute. She goes from thrashing and bucking and wailing to limp and pitiful in the blink of an eye.

"No!" she gasps. "No!"

"Then I suggest you stop screaming," I snarl as I hold up my hand once more to keep Samuil at bay for the time being. "You had the opportunity to speak to me like a human and you wasted it on belligerence. Now, I'm annoyed. Things will go poorly for you if I stay that way."

"I-I'm not scared of you."

"Then you must not be very smart."

"I'm—Fuck." This time, her voice finally breaks. If it weren't for Nikifor and Meric holding her, she'd have collapsed to her knees right now. "I just want to see my sister. I just… I just want to make sure she's okay."

Her eyes are closed as if she's praying. I wait for one long beat to pass, then I shrug. "Very well."

She recoils and looks at me in alarm, then around the courtyard, like this is all the setup to some prank show. "Seriously?" she asks. "You're just… letting me see her. Just like that?"

"If you've changed your mind, I could—"

"No! I mean, yes. Please, I want to see her."

I nod. "Follow me."

Nikifor and Meric let go of the woman's arms. The two of them and Samuil remain in the courtyard, eyes tracking us warily, as she and I mount the stairs. June's sister strokes at her hair nervously with trembling fingers. I hold the door open for her and escort her in.

As she passes me, I tuck a recording device into the back pocket of her Levi's.

I lead the way down the hall, up a floor, around a corner. I don't glance behind me, but I observe her from every hallway mirror and reflective surface we pass. She doesn't have any of June's grace. Even her footsteps are clunky and loud.

Finally, we get to June's door. When I open it, we see June sprawled on the bed, staring at the ceiling. For a moment, it seems like she's talking to someone.

"What are you doing here?" she demands, getting out of the bed as the blush rises hot on her cheeks. "I told you I—" She stops short when her sister walks in behind me. "Oh my God... Genny?"

"Juju!" she crows back. She makes a big show of brushing past me, running towards June, and sweeping her up into a *thank-God-you're-safe* kind of hug more fit for the movies than for real life. Like down in the courtyard, I'm not convinced by the display of emotion. Even June looks a little confused.

When the sisters finally break apart, June stares at her older sister as though she's seeing a ghost. "Wh… what are you doing here, Geneva?"

"I came to see you!"

"How did you even know I was here?" June asks.

Excellent question, but Geneva is in no mood to answer it in my presence. She keeps a hand tightly clasped on June's wrist, even as she turns to face me.

Standing next to one another makes their differences all the more obvious. Geneva is the taller one, more slender, but she has no shape. Just a bunch of straight lines that lack character.

"I'd like to speak to my sister alone," she declares haughtily.

Her snotty tone makes me want to drag her out of here by her mousy brown hair. But I suppress the urge—for June's sake, if nothing else.

"You have an hour."

I glance at June. We haven't had any interaction since our little encounter in the shower. I've tried hard to erase those moments from my memory, but the more I try to forget them, the deeper they take root.

I finally gave up the effort early last night. Instead, I'd stayed in bed, reliving the whole damn thing, minute by minute, breath by breath, touch by touch by searing touch.

Her eyes are trained on me, as green as ever. She looks like she wants to say something, but she bites her bottom lip at the last moment and swallows the words back down.

I walk back towards her door, but I stop at the threshold and turn to face the two sisters. One is looking at me with scorn and disgust. The other just looks lost. Like she's not sure if she wants me to stay or go.

I know what I'd prefer.

Which is why I make myself do the opposite.

"One hour," I remind them both. "And then the uninvited guest is out on her ass."

23

JUNE

I should be relieved.

Isn't this what I've wanted the entire time I've been here? A familiar face, someone I know, someone I'm comfortable with?

But that's the thing: I'm not sure I've ever been comfortable with Geneva. Sister or not, we were never very close. And yet she's here.

Which brings up a lot of questions. Questions like, How? Why? *Huh?*

"Genny," I mumble for the fifth or sixth time, as though saying her name will help me process her appearance a little better. "You look good."

She does. There's a fresh flush on her face that undoes some of the coldness her sunken cheeks give off. She's not wearing any makeup, but I think it suits her better.

"You think so?" she asks skeptically, as though she's searching for the insult underneath the compliment. "Thanks. You look good, too. But then, you always did."

She reaches up and twists a finger through a strand of my hair. She used to do that a lot when we were kids. Back then, though, she used to pull down on the lock of hair so hard that it felt like she was going to rip it off my head from the root. I'm reasonably sure she's not going to do that today.

Not completely sure, but reasonably.

"This is quite the setup you've got here," she remarks, looking around the room while she releases my hair.

I smooth it back behind my ear and observe her a little closer. Her expression is careful, guarded, and she's radiating unease. Plus cheap perfume, of course. She's always radiating cheap perfume.

"I wouldn't say it's mine, exactly."

"Of course not," Geneva says. "It doesn't suit you."

I grit my teeth. She says it like a backhanded insult. *It doesn't suit you*—as though somehow I'm not good enough to belong in a house as luxurious, as opulent as this one. I know from experience that calling her out on it would just lead to a long, drawn-out argument that I don't have the energy for anymore, so I sigh and let it go.

"That brings me to my next question," Geneva continues. "What the hell are you doing here, Juju?"

"I could ask you the same question," I retort. "How did you even know I was here?"

"Nuh-uh. You answer my questions first, and then maybe I'll answer yours."

I bite back my irritation. It's always been like this with Geneva. She always has to have the first and last word. She makes the rules and I'm expected to follow them. She and Kolya have a lot in common.

"Fine," I concede. "What do you want to know?"

"Are you being kept here against your will?"

It's blunt, and it's also the most important question she could have possibly asked me. It's one I've been hoping to be asked from every single person who's walked in here.

But this is not just anyone asking. This is Geneva. My sister. The same sister who used to pull on my hair, and exclude me from her games, and lock me outside the house when she was supposed to be babysitting.

This is the same sister who heckled me at all my dance recitals and stole my first boyfriend just so that she could break his heart three days later. The same sister who told me that Adrian was too damn good for me, right before she pretty much walked out of my life for good.

We've had some contact since then, but nothing meaningful. Mostly just obligatory birthday calls. Short coffee meet-ups, attempts at reconciliation that fizzled as soon as they started.

Even after The Accident, she didn't come to see me. I'd been in the hospital almost a full week before she sent me a bunch of flowers and a cheap card that said *Get Well Soon, Grandma* with the *Grandma* part crossed out.. When she did finally visit in person, almost three months later, she seemed annoyed that I was annoyed with her.

"You look fine," she'd told me when I'd mumbled something under my breath. *"It can't have been that bad an accident."*

"The crash was three months ago, Geneva. I've healed since then."

"Exactly. So what are you so bent out of shape for?"

She isn't an obtuse person by nature. She just chooses to be sometimes, because it's easier than being present. It's easier than caring.

Maybe that's why I lie. Because I don't want her to know how badly derailed my life is right now. I don't want her judgment, and worse still, I don't want to see the satisfaction on her face.

"No," I say firmly. "Who told you that?"

Her brow wrinkles. She's surprised. More than surprised, in fact—she's shocked. In all her life, she's never needed prompting to speak. But now, I have to press. "Geneva?"

"I was working yesterday. Double shift at Athena's," she says at last. "You know the kind of men that come into the club."

"I do."

Men like Kolya.

Men like Ravil.

"Well, there was this one guy who walked in. Tall, handsome, real dangerous-looking." I frown. Those adjectives certainly don't describe Ravil. Not *handsome,* at least. But maybe Genny's tastes are just a little different than mine these days. "He came with like four other guys. They got one of the private rooms and ordered the most expensive things on the menu. At the end of the night, the tall guy invited me to sit with him for a drink."

"What does this have to do with me?"

"Jesus," she says, rolling her eyes, "you are so self-absorbed. I'm getting to that part. Anyway, he asked me my name and—"

"You didn't get his name?" I interrupt.

The annoyance in her eyes deepens. "No."

"You didn't ask?"

"I asked; he just didn't seem very interested in sharing. So I didn't push. Anyway, I told him my name, and he said he'd recently heard of someone with the same last name. He wanted to know if we were related."

My heart is starting to pick up speed in my chest. "Genny, our last name is Cole."

"I'm aware. And?" she asks impatiently.

"And it's a pretty common last name."

"Look, do you want to hear the rest of this story or not?"

I sigh and try not to give away how badly I'm starting to tremble. If Ravil knows who Genny is and he's really as bad as Kolya claims he is… "Go on."

"So yeah, he said that he'd heard of a June Cole who was living with this dude named Kolya Uvarov. And apparently, the Uvarov guy has a horrible reputation. He made it seem like you were here against your will. Like, involuntarily."

I turn my back on her and walk to the opposite end of the room, then back toward her. I repeat the cycle a few times, still saying nothing.

"What the hell are you doing?"

"What does it look like I'm doing?" I retort. "I'm pacing."

"Why?"

"Because I'm frustrated!"

"With me?!" She gapes at me. "I'm sorry, but what have I done to warrant your frustration? I checked in with your work and they told me you'd basically gone silent on them weeks ago after some B.S. excuse about a family emergency. Which I happen to know is horseshit!"

"You can calm down with the dramatics," I snap. "You look stupid when your face is arranged that way."

She narrows her eyes at me, and for a moment, I think things are going to end in a brawl, like they did when we were little girls.

"I'm your sister!"

"Really?" I ask calmly. "You could have fooled me."

"What is that supposed to mean?"

"When was the last time you called, Geneva?" I ask. "When was the last time we so much as met for coffee? I called you three months ago. Do you remember that? I left you a bunch of messages on your machine because you didn't pick up. Ring any bells?"

She has the audacity to frown. "I was gonna call back. I got busy." She brushes her hair out of her eyes. "Did you call to tell me you and Adrian broke up? 'Cause that would explain why you're shacked up with another man."

"Yeah, I guess you could say that Adrian and I broke up," I say, feeling the lump in my throat get bigger. "The breakup happened somewhere in the middle of I-78."

She frowns. "You were driving?"

"We weren't. *He* was. I was at home, sleeping."

"I don't understand."

"That's because you didn't pick up three months ago."

She seems to realize that I'm unraveling, because her expression goes from defensive to concerned. "June…"

"He died, Geneva," I snap. "He fucking died on me. He was driving drunk. He had a head-on collision with a truck and both cars went up in smoke. I was called in to identify his body, and I could barely do it because he was burnt to a crisp. I could actually smell his flesh."

Her hand snaps up to her mouth. "Oh God…"

I start pacing again. Moving feels so much better than standing still and watching my sister's pity float over towards me. If there's one thing I hate more than her ridicule, it's her pity.

"Fuck… June. I didn't think it was—I'm sorry. That must have been hard for you."

"It still is." I stop pacing and face her. "But if you're here to pretend to care, don't bother. I'm fine."

"I didn't mean it that way, June." She gnaws at her bottom lip, a gesture we both inherited from our father. Though I'm not sure if he does it anymore. I haven't seen him in a long time. "I'm just… thrown, okay? I thought you were in trouble."

"I'm not. I'm… I'm pregnant, actually."

Geneva gasps. "You're… Shit, you're serious? You're really pregnant?" She moves forward suddenly and grabs me. For a second, I think she's going to put me in a headlock, but then I realize she's hugging me.

She holds me so long that I get the whiff of spiced cherries coming from her dark hair. The residue of her perfume lingers, too. Sickly sweet and nauseating.

"June?"

"Sorry," I mumble, releasing her and stumbling backwards. "I'm just tired. It's late."

"Right. And our hour's almost up," she says, glancing towards the door. "Listen, before I go I just want you to know that I won't be contactable for the next few days, okay? That guy I told you about, the one who told me about you…"

A sense of unease sweeps up my spine instantly. "Yeah?"

"He offered me a gig. He has this huge event coming up that he's hosting in Mexico, and he wants me to come help throw it. He's cutting me a huge check at the end of it, and covering all my expenses. So I took a couple of days of leave and I told him I'd do it."

"Gen—"

The door bursts open and Kolya stands at the threshold, looking like the devil at the gateway to hell.

"Time's up," he says coldly. "Say your goodbyes."

Geneva turns to me. "I'm gonna call you, okay?" she says. "I know I have no right to ask, but pick up. Please."

She squeezes my hand before she heads for the door. Right in front of Kolya, she pauses. "You better treat her right."

"I treat her better than you do," he answers coolly. Then before she can say anything else, Kolya looks past her at someone outside my line of sight. "Samuil, see that she's off my property in the next five minutes. If she isn't, throw her off."

I expect the door to shut on me. And it does—with Kolya on my side of it. I feel the hairs at the back of my neck stand on end.

He turns to me. The shards of blue in his eyes have never looked more dangerous. "It's time for the two of us to talk."

24

KOLYA

The recording device was effective—up to a point.

It caught most of their conversation, except for a few moments when it stifled out. Sometimes, it sounded like June was pacing. I could hear the thump of her footsteps growing and shrinking, her words coming out breathy and convoluted.

"Had a nice chat with your sister?"

"As nice as can be expected," she retorts. "Given the circumstances." There's worry in her eyes that has nothing to do with me.

"Worried about Mexico, are you?"

She stops short, her eyes going wide with realization. She looks around the room as though she expects someone to jump out of a dark corner.

"You were eavesdropping?"

I shrug. "There is no such thing as a private conversation on my property."

She just stares at me for a moment, but I can tell she's running through the conversation she just had with Geneva. She's trying to remember what she said. What I heard. What bits of it might be used against her.

I can't speak for June, but the part that stuck out to me was when she not-so-subtly let her sister believe she was carrying *my* baby.

Or maybe I can speak for her—because right then, realization tints her cheeks bright scarlet and she's suddenly very interested in the grouting of the tile floor between her feet.

"Something the matter, June?" I ask innocently.

She fidgets but doesn't meet my eye. "It's simpler this way. If she knew the truth…" Her blush deepens. I didn't think it was possible for a person to turn so red. The color is disarmingly attractive on her. Especially against the flecked hazel of her eyes. "It had nothing to do with you, okay? I just don't want Geneva mixed up in this horrible world."

I raise my eyebrows. "It seems it's a little late for that."

The blush recedes as worry takes center stage. "You heard about her new client. The one that somehow magically connected the two of us together based on our very common last name."

"You smelled a rat, too?"

"I think we've already established I have an extremely sensitive sense of smell." That makes me smile. "I was thinking it might be your cousin. But the man she described—"

"Was probably just a decoy," I conclude. "Ravil might have been part of the entourage. Or he might not have been there at all. He used a plant to muddy the waters."

June frowns, but not with surprise. Just disappointment, really. I'm quietly impressed by her ability to connect the dots.

"She's going to Mexico for this job," June murmurs.

"Another giveaway. Ravil has a lot of business in Mexico."

"What kind of business?"

"The kind that involves very bad men with lots of money, lots of drugs, and lots of guns."

June blows out a gust of panicked air. "See? I need to speak to Geneva. I need to tell her to turn down the job, no matter how much money he offers—"

"No."

I don't raise my voice, but she buttons up like I just screamed in her face. "What do you mean, 'no'?"

"There's a reason that Ravil offered her a job," I explain. "He has an ulterior motive here, and I want to know what that is. I won't be able to find out if she declines."

She gawks at me, wide-eyed and still filled with naïve horror. "That's why you walked in when you did," she gasps. "It had nothing to do with our hour being up. You didn't want me to warn her about Mexico."

"Glad to see you're not just a pretty face after all."

"Kolya!" she snaps, frustration and fear convulsing together as she takes a step towards me. "She is my sister."

"I'm aware. And I've got to be honest, I wasn't impressed. I'd assume that you got the looks and she got the brains, but she didn't seem very smart, either."

"This is not funny," she says. "This is not a game."

"Everything is a game," I say harshly. "All that changes are the stakes."

June's eyes harden. A vein in her forehead throbs dangerously. My fingers start to itch with the desire to step close to her, smooth it away, work the tension from her body one muscle at a time. I've seen her fall apart in my arms, and that memory is still burning in my head. Her open mouth. Water cascading down past those soft lips.

I choke all that down and focus on the fire blazing in her eyes.

"I just covered for you tonight. I lied to my own sister for you." I can see the desperation in her eyes. "I can't let her go to Mexico. Not when I know that your psycho cousin is the one who's lured her there. I can't…" Her voice wobbles, but she refuses to let it break. Dragging her eyes up to meet mine, she finishes, "I can't stand the thought of losing someone else."

June's chest rises and falls. I watch it, watch her, wondering when the tears of someone I barely know began to mean so goddamn much to me.

"I will make sure nothing happens to your sister," I tell her grudgingly. "But she's still going to Mexico."

"But—"

"So am I. I'll ensure that Ravil can't hurt her."

June looks skeptical for a moment. Then her jaw sets with that feisty determination I love and hate so much. "Then I'm coming with you."

"Not a fucking chance."

"Kol—"

"I'm not negotiating with you, June. I told you once already: if I let something happen…"

For the second time, I fall silent. I can't finish that sentence. I *won't* finish that sentence.

I clear my throat and glare down at her. "End of discussion."

"No," she snaps, folding her arms across her breasts. "Not even close to it. You're being short-sighted. This is all a power struggle for optics, right? Tug of war between the two big bad wolves? So how do you think it'll look to everyone who's on the fence if you show up to Ravil's party like it means nothing—with your pregnant woman in tow?"

I open my mouth to retort, but the words curdle on my lips. She has a point. An irritatingly good one. This is a game of heirs, of sons and fathers—and I have a trump card standing right in front of me.

I'm playing with fire. But fuck it—let's burn.

She sees the war on my face and knows what it means. A smile stretches her lips and relaxes the clench in her jaw. "So is that a…?"

"Fine," I snarl. "But there will be conditions. You will stay with me at all times. You will *listen* to me at all times. This is dangerous territory we're entering, June. One wrong move, and it'll cost us our lives."

"Done."

She doesn't seem deterred. In fact, if I'm not mistaken, I actually detect a hint of excitement on her face.

"I won't be disobeyed, June." My cock aches as I survey her. Hip jutted at an insolent angle, eyes bright, hair wild. She looks good like this. It'd be so easy to…

No. Keep your hands to your fucking self, Kolya. Remember why she's here.

I straighten up and release an exhausted exhale. "Pack a bag," I tell her. "If you're late, I'm leaving without you."

25

JUNE

"Here."

That's all Kolya says when he hands me back my phone. There's no ceremony about it. Just the impatient, distracted grunt of a man who has better things to do with his day.

I take it silently and power it back to life. It lights up, revealing that I have several texts from Geneva.

GENEVA [12:33 AM]: We should talk again when I get back from this job in Mexico.

GENEVA: I'm still processing shit. I can't believe you're going to have a baby. And it's not going to be Adrian's!

GENEVA: Fuck, was that an insensitive thing to say. Sorry. I'm just shocked. It's late. I'll text tomorrow.

I scroll down to her messages from this morning.

GENEVA: [8:14 AM] Okay, so I'm on a plane to Mexico. And check it: this dude got me a first class ticket. I am so psyched that I took the job. So fucking worth it. Just for first class. And I haven't even gotten paid yet.

GENEVA: They're serving champagne!

GENEVA: Mom and Dad should see me now. They said my career would never amount to anything. Ha! Joke's on them.

GENEVA: Guess you're used to this life now, huh? With your rich boyfriend and all.

GENEVA: Are you okay? With the pregnancy and everything?

When I look up, there's a shiny black Rolls Royce parked in front of us on the drive. Kolya opens the back door and helps me into the rear seat, then joins me there.

"Did you read my texts?" I ask as the car starts moving.

"Yes." He doesn't bother looking at me, too preoccupied with scrolling and tapping on his own phone.

I sigh. I'm not surprised by the intrusion, and I'm not really disappointed, either. Maybe I'm just disappointed that I'm not more disappointed, if that makes sense.

"I'm going to have to reply to Geneva, you know." He doesn't answer. I sigh again. "Should I tell her that we're going to be in Mexico?"

"Be my guest. Or we can just surprise her at the party. Your call."

"You got us tickets? What? How? Who did you—"

He shrugs and says nothing.

I slump back into my seat and scrutinize him. It's odd: at first glance, you'd never peg him as handsome. Not the way Adrian was, at least, all light and effervescent.

But he does have charisma. It's just the darker kind. The charisma of a canyon you can't see the bottom of, dangerous and tempting.

"You're staring."

I jerk back to reality only to realize that Kolya's piercing blue eyes are fixed on me. A little impatient. A little curious. "Sorry," I mumble. "I was…"

"Yes?"

"Thinking of Adrian," I admit.

He turns his eyes back to his phone as though he's sorry he asked. I let loose the third sigh in as many minutes and start figuring out something to say to Genny.

JUNE: Hey Genny, as it turns out, we can see each other a little sooner than expected. Kolya told me last night after you left that we had invites to the exact same party.

JUNE: So I'll see you there. It was really nice talking with you by the way. That conversation was long overdue.

I read both my texts a few times over. They feel stilted and awkward, but I press Send before I can talk myself out of it. Swiping out to my text message inbox, something catches my eye. I scroll down, getting more and more worked up as I go, until I can't help but turn and glare at Kolya.

"You bastard."

He sighs. "What now?"

"You had someone impersonate me and text everyone I know!"

He doesn't even bother pretending to be apologetic. "I did you a favor. Would you rather have just dropped off the face of the planet without a word to your landlord or the people you work with?"

"Don't pretend you did this for me," I spit at him. "You did this so that no one would sound the alarm and call the cops on your ass."

He seems to find that amusing. "You say that like the police would be able to do a goddamn thing to a man like me."

I can't help but shiver at the audacity in his tone. He really believes that he's untouchable. And who knows? Maybe he is.

"That job meant something to me," I say coldly. "I enjoyed it."

"Did you?"

I pull back. "I—yes. I mean, yeah, of course."

At last, he puts his phone down and turns his full attention on me. It's what I've been after since the moment we got in the car, but now that I have it, I'm not so sure I want it after all. It's overwhelming. The way those eyes suck me in and drown me. The way that sharp chin frightens me. The way those hands, lying carefully in his lap, look so dangerous without having to do anything at all.

"You're one of a handful of barely-paid administrative grunts slaving away for the dance theater you used to perform in," he says. "You stayed because it was the closest you could get to the thing without actually being allowed to have it anymore. Life took dancing from you, and you're *begging* for it back with everything but your words. Pleading. Crying at the doorstep, asking for fifteen more minutes onstage, pretty please with a cherry on top."

Thud. Thud. Thud. Every sentence lands like a slap across my face. I open my mouth and close it a dozen times without so much as a single word coming out. What can you say to a savage, unvarnished truth like that?

Ouch, I guess.

Before I can get myself together, Kolya glances out of the black tinted windows. "We're here." He climbs out without bothering to ask if I'm ready.

I sit there by myself for a few moments. Long enough that my door is opened by the chauffeur. He helps me out by my elbow. I squint into the sun for a minute before the blurriness resolves itself and I realize I'm looking across an ocean of tarmac at a sleek private jet, humming in wait for us.

The chauffeur bows and disappears. When he whisks the car away, he reveals Kolya towering there, eyes ice-cold.

"This way," he says with a thin ripple of sarcasm as he jerks his chin toward the only plane in sight. "That one's ours."

Again, he doesn't wait for me. He just charges off impatiently, like I'm the inconvenience in his life instead of the other way around.

I follow in his footsteps, but when I get to the staircase, I pause. I wring my hands with uncertainty. My leg is mostly healed from my fall the other day, though I still get the odd twinge of pain if I move too fast.

That's not what's slowing me, though. It's my knee—the old knee, the first hurt. It's aching in a way that's almost more than physical. More than bone-deep. Like the next step I'm taking is meaningful in a way that I need to stop and recognize.

It hurt that same way when I knelt at Adrian's gravestone.

"Are you okay?" Kolya asks from the top of the staircase.

"Fine."

I'm hoping he just leaves it there. But then his outstretched hand materializes in front of my face. I stare at the calluses lined along his pink palm, and I wonder how he earned each one.

Without thinking, I slip my hand into his—and just like that, the pain recedes. I mount the first step, leaning on him more than I need to. Another step. Another. He helps me up the rest of the flight of stairs and into the belly of the plane.

He guides me down the aisle, the air surging with the scent of jasmine and leather, then coaxes me into one seat and takes the seat opposite. The window beckons, huge and inviting, but Kolya keeps his eyes fixed on me.

As the stewardess runs through takeoff instructions, he looks at me.

As the pilot chirps our itinerary over the intercom, he looks at me.

As the engines roar to life and the wheels begin to turn and we accelerate down the runway, faster and faster, lifting off into the air, he looks at me.

Until at last, we break out over the sea of sun-dappled clouds. Only then does he look away, but when he does, it's just to glance down at the cupholder of my seat. Confused, I follow his gaze—and there, I see a lemon soda waiting for me, still cool and slick with condensation.

I wish I had a word for how that makes me feel.

26

KOLYA

"I have something for you."

June recoils as though I just told her to strip naked and dance. Her hazel eyes shine with suspicion. "You have… something… for me?"

I reach under the seat and withdraw a sleek back briefcase. Just small enough to be innocuous, at least in my opinion. Looking at June's face suggests a whole other story. I offer it out to her.

She wrinkles her brows. "I don't smell poison. Or rotting body parts."

"What an asset that nose of yours is," I say dryly.

She takes a deep breath, sets the case in her lap, and clicks open the silver clasps. Then she opens it gingerly.

"Oh my God," she blurts, looking up at me slowly. "This is— There's a diamond necklace in here. Why are you giving this to me?"

"It's a gift. If you show up on my arm, you're going to have to look the part. That requires diamonds."

Her gaze falls back to the jewels. "They're beautiful."

"That's why I picked them."

She looks at me with a perplexed expression. "You're a very confusing man, Kolya," she says softly. "You realize that, don't you?"

"I wouldn't read too much into it. In my world, gifts are transactional, not emotional."

I fucking despise having to say them, but my words have their intended effect. Any sign of happiness in her face dissipates instantly. She falls back into her seat. Her eyes veer towards the window and she seems to forget I'm there at all.

It's probably best that way. The two of us alone together for any length of time is dangerous. I'd been naïve about that before, but I'm smart enough to pay heed to the warning signs now that I've collected a fair few.

She closes her eyes somewhere in the middle of the flight, and then she sleeps through the rest of it. I don't know how to feel about that. The only thing more infuriating than talking to her is not talking to her. The only thing harder than being with her is being away from her.

If that's not a warning sign, I don't know what is.

∼

"Whoa…"

I glance at her face. The wide eyes, the stunned expression. I've seen this kind of glitz and luxury so many times before that it's lost the power to leave me awed.

But now, I can see it all through her eyes. It's like being born again.

She marvels at every detail she sees as we make our way through the hotel. Corinthian columns pave the way to the suites. Gilded portraits shimmer on every wall. The carpet underfoot is lush enough to drown in.

Two butlers stand outside our doors. As we approach, they open the room for us in unison.

"You gotta be kidding me," I hear her mutter under her breath. "This is unreal."

She's so impressed that she's forgotten to pretend to be unimpressed. She's also so busy drooling over the balcony that she doesn't even notice when the butlers slip out of the room and leave the two of us alone together.

Although she catches on pretty fast when she turns around with flushed cheeks and finds me standing there, watching her.

She looks around, suddenly aware of how lethally quiet it is. "This is insanity."

I shrug. "It is what it is."

"Do you really travel like this?" she asks. "The private jet, the insanely luxurious hotels? Did... did Adrian?

"He knew what he was giving up when he left."

"Right." Her expression quirks strangely. A sense of defensiveness on his behalf, maybe? "You know, this is all pretty cool. But it's just stuff. Geneva, on the other hand… She'd go bananas over this place."

"The two of you are very different."

She raises her eyebrows. "Yeah, well, I can say the same about you and Adrian."

"Adrian was more like me than he cared to acknowledge," I grit out. "He was just too much of a coward to admit it."

"Adrian was not a coward," June insists, though I'm not sure even she believes that. "He just had a lot of demons. He didn't know how to get rid of them."

"Or he was too weak to try."

She shakes her head. "I don't understand you," she says. "Sometimes, you talk like you loved him. And then there are other times when it seems like you hate him."

"That's the pot calling the kettle black, if I've ever heard it."

She considers that for a moment. "You're not wrong." She plays with the bracelet on her wrist for a quiet second before looking up at me again. "You know, our parents had high standards for Genny and me. A lot of the time, that meant pitting us against each other. We were too young to know any better, so we rose to the bait. We became each other's competition. In our own ways, we both craved our parents' approval. But even when we excelled in school, brought home prizes, won medals, it never lasted. So we tried harder. I did, at least. I threw myself into dancing. And Geneva—I suppose she decided that she'd rather force their attention than win their pride." Her eyes turn glassy for a moment. "She started partying a lot, creating trouble, making the wrong kind of friends."

"Seems like she still has that talent."

June throws me a glare. "She was just a kid who was hurting, and she wanted to be seen. Isn't that what we all are at the end of the day? Isn't that what we all want?"

I glance at her, at all the compassion contained within those shining irises of hers. "Something tells me you're trying to make a point about my brother and me. Be careful what you assume, June."

"I don't have to assume anything," she retorts. "I saw his childhood with my own eyes. Your father was a bully and a beast. A hundred times worse than my parents combined. Adrian had troubles, but he was a good man."

It's amazing—she really does believe that. Despite how he left her. Despite how he treated her.

"How can you cling to that?" I ask in disbelief. "Even after everything you found out since his death?"

She lets out a small, staggering sigh. One that sounds like it's sat in her chest for years. "The last few years of our relationship were tumultuous. But it wasn't his fault. The Accident derailed us. Adrian drank a lot; I just retreated inside myself. But we were both experiencing a loss. We were both mourning our careers. We were mourning the future we thought we'd have. It brought out the worst in us."

She looks up at me, half-defiant and half-pleading. She wants a kind of absolution that I can't give her, though.

"What kind of person would I have been if I'd chosen to judge him based on his darkest moments? I chose instead to focus on his best moments. And before The Accident, there were so many."

I shift in my seat, suddenly cautious of what I'm about to hear. I know things about their relationship that I probably shouldn't. But this is different. June is offering me an intimate look into their lives, and I'm not sure I want or need that view.

Right now, in the light of day, I can still convince myself that she's nothing more than a means to an end. But it's already hard enough to keep up that illusion when the night comes. If she insists on continuing to shove my nose in her soul, there soon won't be anywhere for me to hide from what she does to me.

"You lived in motels a lot as children, right?" she asks abruptly, like she's trying to change the subject.

I nod. "That's true. We did."

"Adrian didn't really give me details, but he told me he hated it there. He said that your father did things he shouldn't have done in them."

"That's true, too."

She frowns. "What kinds of things?"

I grimace and close my eyes. "I think you know, June."

When I look at her again, her cheeks are flushed with color. "There was this story. It was the only story Adrian ever told me about his childhood," she whispers. "It's the reason I fell in love with him in the first place. I suppose I'm just happy to find out that it's true."

"What story did he tell you?"

She hesitates for a moment before she begins. "He told me that he met a young girl in one of those motels. He struck up a friendship with her, and he learned that she had been forced into prostitution when she was thirteen and she'd been passed from man to man for the last three years." She smiles a little, through the velvety haze of emotion shining from her eyes. "He was a teenager himself, but he was outraged for her. He hated the fact that a woman could be used like that, and he knew that he had to get himself out of that life. But first, he needed to help her."

Jesus Christ. My knuckles have gone white now, not that June notices.

"And he did," she says, her tone shining with pride. "He got her out from her pimp's clutches. He tucked her away somewhere safe. He got her a place to stay and a job. He helped her rebuild her life. That story made me see him as he really was. A strong man, a righteous man. A compassionate man. Someone who couldn't just sit by and watch someone else suffer. He hated injustice, and he worked to change it. He saved that girl's life." She takes another breath and looks at me. "That is how I remembered him on all those dark days when he was the worst version of himself. When he drank or yelled or broke things. And that is how I choose to remember him now. Not as the drunk who couldn't bear his grief. But as someone who felt so much for others."

Adrian. Fucking Adrian. He's been dead more than three months, but it feels like he's still here. His lies keep creeping along with lives of their own. Like ghosts. Like spiders in the corner, rats in the woodwork. Skittering just out of sight.

"Kolya," June says softly, "why do you look so mad?"

Her eyes are wide with uncertainty. I could spare her the truth and simply let her believe the glowing ideal of whom she thought Adrian was. But that would be kind.

And I have never been a kind man.

"My brother always did have a talent for taking credit for the actions of others," I snarl.

Her face drops immediately. It's almost like she's been anticipating this very reaction. Like she's half-expecting it. Why else would she believe it so easily? Why else would she look as though she's experiencing his death all over again?

"We did live in motels throughout our adolescence. And there was a young prostitute who needed help. But Adrian was not the one that saved her. I did."

I meet her eyes, just to make sure she can't run from the truth.

"Adrian didn't tell you his story. He stole mine."

27

JUNE

"You're lying."

He looks bored, but the harsh angle of his eyebrows betrays a darker emotion. "I have no reason to lie."

"Except to make Adrian sound like an asshole."

"He *was* an asshole."

"Yeah, well, so are you."

I get to my feet and storm towards the balcony. For a moment, I think about flinging myself off it. Or better yet, maybe I'll fling him off it. Anything to get out of his oppressive presence. Anything to get his voice out of my head.

He's already in your head.

"Shut up!" I say out loud to the ghost I can't seem to get rid of.

"You need to breathe," Kolya says, embodying all the calm I seem incapable of corralling. "Would you still rather cling to a fantasy of him, rather than accept the truth of who he was?"

I turn to face Kolya. He's still in the same position, one leg cocked confidently, his eyes trained on me. "There is more than one truth to a person. Adrian was—"

"Adrian is dead," he growls, his tone sinister. "It's time you accept that."

I shake my head in disbelief. "No wonder he stayed away from the family. Why would he want to have a relationship with someone like you?"

Kolya snorts. "He was more than willing to have a relationship with me when he needed something," he says. "He just never told you when he decided to pull out the begging bowl."

My mouth is already open before I realize I have nothing to say. I snap it shut and turn to the side so that he can see only my profile. Not that I can hide from him. The longer I spend with Kolya Uvarov, the more confident I am that there isn't one single, solitary pocket of shadow on this entire godforsaken planet that he can't see into.

"It's not right," I say quietly, after the silence has seeped into my pores and turned my body cold to the touch. "To attack a dead man, I mean. It's not right. It's not like he can defend himself."

"Why would he need to?" Kolya asks. "With you here to do it for him?"

"I'm his girlfriend!" I cry out, turning to face him again.

"You were. Not anymore. He's not coming back."

I recognize the emotion in his voice—anger meets grief—maybe because I'm trying very hard to suppress my own dose of the stuff.

"I have a right to mourn."

His blue eyes flash with fury, but for the life of me, I can't figure out what he has to be so angry about. Adrian may have stolen his story, but Kolya doesn't seem like the kind of man who'd be so infuriated by something like that.

"Is that really why you fell in love with him?" Kolya asks suddenly. "That story?"

I feel the color rush to my face. I try to hide my blush behind the answer. "Yes," I mumble. "I mean, it wasn't the only reason. But it was a part of it."

Kolya shakes his head. I notice how his jaw tightens, his fingers clench. Like he's trying to hold himself back. It's as if every demon he's spent a lifetime burying in that deep, dark hole he calls a heart is clawing up at the surface now. I can practically see them prodding at the underside of his skin.

And for some reason, that devastates me.

"You're really not lying to me, are you?" I ask softly. "You meant what you said. It's your story, not his."

His eyes splinter, but inwardly this time. Not aimed at me but at himself. "If you doubt me," he growls, voice so low it's barely audible, "then talk to Milana."

That throws me for a loop. "Why would I talk to Milana?"

"Because she was there," he says. "She was the girl in the story."

I feel a strange kind of coldness spread across my body. Or maybe it's not cold at all.

Maybe this is just how betrayal feels.

I don't remember sitting down, but when I look up again, I realize I'm on the sofa right opposite Kolya. "Why did you tell me?" I blurt. "You could have let me believe that Adrian was the savior. That his story was true. Why expose him now?"

He doesn't answer right away. When he does, his voice is drawn tight and haggard. "I figured that you'd been lied to enough for one lifetime. I thought you'd appreciate something different for a change."

I don't know why I struggle with those words. It's a beautiful answer, but I'm scrutinizing it from every angle, looking for —*hoping* for—a crack in the facade.

And then I find it. Whether I truly wanted it or not, I'm still not sure, but I find it.

"You want to show me that you're different from him."

Kolya's eyes boil dark as he gets to his feet. "I couldn't care less what you think of me. You're the one determined to compare us."

Then he turns away from me and stalks into the bedroom.

A smarter, more patient woman might have just stayed put and given him time to cool off. But apparently, I'm not very smart, or very patient, because I follow him to find him angrily ripping the comforter out of its neatly tucked corners.

"What are you doing?"

"I hate made beds."

I'm on the verge of laughing at the ridiculousness of something so petty when I see it again: another crack in the facade. Another ugly truth lurking behind the beautiful lie.

"Because they remind you of the motels."

He whirls around, his eyes are so dark now that the blue seems all but extinguished. "There you go again, assuming I have the same demons in my head that Adrian did."

"Don't you?"

He bristles visibly, and for the first time, I start to realize that maybe those walls of his aren't as impenetrable as I first thought. The more time I spend with him, the easier it is to see the shades of his past. They're taking on color now. Coming to life.

He abandons his assault on the bed, leaving one side tucked in and the other crudely ravished. "You can take the master," he grunts.

"Okay," I whisper.

He must've expected an argument, because he freezes for a second before exhaling and relaxing. Those broad shoulders come down from where they're pinned up by his ears. The muscles smooth out.

I wonder what other cracks there are in his foundation. I want to strip him and inspect him inch by inch in pursuit of them. I've seen him shirtless before, but it was from the window of my bedroom on the second floor. I wasn't nearly close enough to notice birthmarks, tattoos, freckles and scars. The things that tell his story.

And I'm curious.

Are you now?

I actually flinch at the sound of Adrian's voice in my ear. Sometimes, it's so clear that he might as well be standing right next to me.

"What's wrong?" Kolya asks.

"Nothing."

He frowns. "You should get some rest."

"I don't need rest," I say quickly—but only because I don't want to be alone.

He hesitates, then starts to make for the door.

I find myself pivoting in his direction. "Kolya?"

He stops at the threshold, his hand on the knob, and arches his brow.

"Adrian used to do that, too," I whisper. "Pull out the bedsheets so they weren't tucked in so tight. He said seeing a perfectly made bed felt too sterile for him."

Kolya's expression is back to being coldly apathetic. But this time, I can see past the mask of indifference. That's all it is—a mask.

"Is it the same for you?" I ask. I must sound like an idiot. Only an idiot would try to peel back the layers of a man who's made it clear that he's not interested in being exposed.

"Take a nap," he says, but his tone isn't as harsh as it was before. "When you wake up, we'll go out."

He snaps the door shut, leaving me with a curious sensation in my belly. I should ask where we'll go, what we'll do, what the future holds for him and for me and for all of us ensnared in this fucked-up nightmare.

But I don't.

It's enough that wherever we're going, he'll be with me.

Pathetic, Adrian scoffs.

"I know," I say with a sigh. "I know."

28

JUNE

"A hike?" I repeat, incredulous.

"It's when you walk through nature for an extended period of time."

"I know what a hike is, asshole. I'm just surprised that that's what you have planned."

He sighs and folds his arms over his chest. "Dr. Calloway told me that your ankle has healed well enough to be able to incorporate some light exercise into your routine. There's a number of hiking paths just behind the hotel. We explore and provide for your medical needs at the same time. Two birds, one stone."

I glance down at my jeans and thin sweater. "I may not be dressed right."

His eyes sweep over my body, but his gaze doesn't linger. "You're dressed fine. Let's go."

A motorized golf cart with a surly driver in a hotel uniform is waiting for us outside. Kolya helps me onto the back seat and then drops in next to me. As soon as I'm in place, the cart whirrs and whisks us off.

We wind up through the hills. The air grows thinner and sweeter as we get away from the hotel. I close my eyes and breathe it, wondering when I'm going to wake up from this never-ending dream.

I only open my eyes when we slow to a stop. I notice money exchanging hands as I step off. Then Kolya hoists the black backpack he'd brought with him onto his shoulders and gestures for me to start walking up towards where the treeline begins higher up the slope. A trail disappears into the mouth of the woods.

"Was that hush money?" I ask once we're on the trail. It's eerily silent, eerily still.

"To hush who about what?"

"The fact that the driver dropped us off here," I say. "So that when my body goes missing, he won't talk." I turn my attention to his bag. "And what's in the backpack? The weapon you're going to use to bludgeon me to death? I'm telling you right now, I won't go down without a fight."

Kolya chuckles. "I have no doubt about that." He keeps walking, offering me no further explanations.

I pick up the pace and catch up to him. "My sister will notice if I go missing. You realize that, right?"

He stops walking and turns to me impatiently. "Fifty dollars doesn't exactly do the trick when you expect someone to keep their mouth shut about anything. Never mind a murder."

"Oh." My cheeks color with embarrassment as the way more obvious, way less hysterical truth slaps me in the face. "You were tipping him."

"Bingo, Sherlock. But if you'd like to be murdered when we finish our hike, I can organize a larger sum deposited in his pocket later today."

I throw him a glare to hide the fact that I'm still blushing. "You can't blame me for assuming…"

"Yes," he retorts, "I can. I told you I'd protect you. Murdering you would defeat the purpose."

I hesitate, then sigh. "So what's in the backpack?"

"Just walk, will you?"

With no other choice, that's exactly what I do. The trail is steep and unforgiving, as is the dry red soil underfoot. It's an hour of one foot in front of the other. By the time we reach the top of the trail, I'm winded, sweaty, and on the verge of asking whether he would be willing to carry me back down.

Kolya notices before I can even speak. "Pick a spot and sit down," he orders. It's a testament to how weary I am that I don't even bother arguing.

My legs cry with relief when I park my butt down in the grass under a shady tree with feathery leaves that hang low. I lean my back against the cool bark and sigh. "I should have thought to bring water."

That's when Kolya takes off his backpack and pulls out a couple of bottles of water. In rapid succession, he also reveals half a dozen glass containers filled with food.

"You packed a picnic?" I ask, my mouth hanging open in dumbfounded shock.

He opens a container containing the chunkiest sandwiches I've ever seen. "Roast beef," he explains, handing one to me. "With garlic mayo and extra salty pickles."

I give him a searching glance. I've been asking for extra salty pickles in my meals for the last few days. There's no way the maids would be reporting details as insignificant as that to him... right? And even if they were, surely he wouldn't care enough to remember?

"Not interested?"

"No, I am, I am," I say hurriedly, taking the container from his outstretched hand.

I chew idly, but my mind is racing. He brought me up here for a picnic? A picnic for the two of us? That can't be right. There's bound to be a catch that I haven't picked up on yet. Or maybe he's trying to cushion some bad news he's yet to give me.

I feel my appetite take a hit as I start overthinking.

Then Kolya sighs. "What are you worried about now?"

I swallow the bite of food in my mouth. "You gotta admit, this is kinda unusual."

"Eating?" he asks with disdain. "Eating is unusual?"

"In this context, yeah. We're in a meadow straight out of *The Sound of Music*, with a light summer breeze and the smell of lilacs in the air. I half-expect the birds to start doing showtunes."

Kolya rolls his eyes. "We just hiked for an hour, June," he says. "You're pregnant. I brought food. That's all there is to it."

I repeat the words to myself in the same clipped, no-nonsense tone he used. *I'm pregnant. He brought food. That's all there is to it.*

"Thanks anyway," I mumble softly.

He nods dismissively and finishes his sandwich in two more wolfish bites. Then he pulls out a can of soda and starts downing the contents. With his head knocked back and his eyes turned away from me, I take the opportunity to observe him.

His Adam's apple bobs up and down, and I feel a strange sensation of heat spread through my arms and legs. The moment the soda can leaves his lips, I turn away quickly before he can catch me gawking.

He might not notice. But I do.

Shut up, I snarl to Adrian. *No one asked you.*

"Do you ever hear him?" I ask aloud on a whim.

"Excuse me?" Kolya asks, his eyes hauntingly blue.

"Or maybe not hear him, but like… think about him. Adrian, I mean. About what he'd say about… stuff."

"Not unless I have to."

I feel my eyebrows pull together. "When do you have to?"

"When you ask me questions about him, mostly."

He doesn't look particularly annoyed, but there's this vein at the side of his forehead that I'm beginning to notice more and more these days. It thrums like it has a life of its own. "Does it bother you that I talk about him?"

He grunts something that sounds like "no," but I can't be sure. Then he lies back against the grass and his expression is completely lost to me. I want to edge closer, but I can feel a prickly, don't-touch-me energy radiating from him. So I sit there, trying to catch a glimpse of his face, pretending like I'm not doing exactly that.

29

KOLYA

I've honed my skills over the years. I always think ten steps ahead. The result: I never make mistakes twice.

The trick to never repeating a mistake, however, is admitting you made one in the first place. And I've always been good at that.

Like right now, for instance.

This picnic was a bad fucking idea.

I realize that the second she pulls off her thin sweater to reveal the tight tank she's wearing underneath. There's enough perspiration on her body to turn it clingy and slightly see-through.

She gathers up her hair and ties it up into a high, messy bun on top of her head. All that serves to do is bring my attention to her long, slender neck.

It's the first time I notice the scar. It's tiny and sickle-shaped, tucked just beneath her jaw. A curl of dark hair falls from the bun and temporarily hides it from view.

"Where'd you get the scar?" I ask. Before I can stop myself, I sit up, lean in, and run my thumb across the mottled surface of it.

June's fingers float up to stroke it the same way I did. "Oh. That. It's... it's not a big deal."

I arch an eyebrow. "Bar fight? I should see the other guy?"

She smiles. "No. Not quite."

The truth hits me like a bolt of lightning. I grit my teeth and look down in my lap to make sure she can't see the burning anger flit across my eyes. I only look up again when I'm in reasonable control of my face.

"My brother."

She exhales sadly. "It was a long time ago."

"Tell me."

"It was the second time he fell off the wagon," she explains, gazing out into the distance. "It was also the longest time he went without a drink. After we both realized he had a problem, that is. He'd collected his three-month chip." Her voice is drenched with disappointment. "We were supposed to meet at this restaurant downtown after work, only Adrian didn't show up. I called him a bunch of times, but he didn't answer. So I just gave up and went home. And that's where I found him. Face down in the shower with the water running. He stunk of vomit and cheap booze. From the smell of him, I guessed he'd been drinking for hours."

She stops for a moment, like the weight of the memory is too heavy for her to keep going. Then she waves off her pain. "Anyway, long story short, I got him half-conscious and into our bedroom. He started talking on the way to the bed. He was dreaming, or maybe he was just remembering something; I'm not sure. But he wasn't really aware of where he was. I managed to get him on the bed, and I was checking the bruise on his head, when he started screaming at me not to hurt him. I tried to calm him down but it was like he couldn't hear me. That's when he… he… grabbed me."

"He tried to strangle you?" I ask softly.

She frowns. "It wasn't nearly so dramatic. He was seeing things, he was scared, he thought he was protecting himself. And then I screamed and he snapped out of it. He begged me to forgive him. He didn't mean to hurt me."

"Is that what he told you every time he hurt you?"

Her jaw clenches. "You don't understand," she mumbles, dismissing the conversation completely. "And now, it's raining."

I turn my face up to the sky and feel a raindrop land on my cheek. "Make room," I tell her, moving against the trunk of the tree she's resting against.

We're shoulder to shoulder now. Inconvenient. It almost makes me want to brave the rain to reinstate some distance.

Then she meets my eyes, and I meet hers. And our gazes sort of… stick. Her lips part ever so slightly, and I can see her cheeks redden. But she doesn't avert her gaze.

And then, just when I think I'm past the point where people can surprise me… she leans in.

The moment that follows lasts damn near forever. Her lips are parted just enough for me to see that jagged sliver of blackness. To smell the sweetness of her breath, suffused with the oncoming rain. It's floral and wild and in that forever moment, I drown myself in how much I want her. It's wrong—*she's not yours, she's never been yours, she was never meant to be yours*—for me and for her alike, but fuck, I want her so goddamn bad I can't bear it.

Then the moment passes.

Maybe that's for the best.

Because I don't deserve anything anywhere near as pure as her.

∽

June checks her phone the minute we get back to the hotel, but it's more like she wants an excuse not to look at me.

"Any word from Geneva?"

"No," she says, putting the phone down. "She's probably just busy."

"You're very good at making excuses for other people. Did you know that?"

She turns to me with a frown. "Why did you take me on that hike today?" she demands suddenly, her eyebrows knotting together with irritation.

"Dr. Calloway—"

"You already told me what she said," she snaps, cutting me off. "But you could have sent me on that hike alone. Or with one of your goons. You didn't need to come with me."

I keep my tone carefully detached and uncaring. "If you didn't want me there, you could have just said so."

"That's not the point."

"Then get to the point."

"Well—I think… The point is—" I turn my eyes on her and whatever she's trying to say dries up on her tongue. "Forget it. I'm going to my room."

She tries to slam the door behind her, but it doesn't actually shut properly. I settle on the couch with my legs kicked up. The position offers me a direct view into her room, but since the door is currently only ajar by a quarter of an inch, it hardly matters.

My hand drifts to my chest, rubbing the scars there through the fabric of my shirt. I saw June eyeing me earlier. As if she could see what's etched into my skin. The evidence. The proof. The story.

At some point, I fall asleep. But when I sleep, I don't dream—I just remember.

I'm in the throes of old, unwelcome memories when I hear a moan coming from inside June's bedroom.

I awaken and jerk upright, oddly affected by the sound. The door's still slightly ajar. I walk over, careful not to make any noise.

Then I hear it again. Another moan. This one is far more definitive.

I feel excitement shimmy down my spine like a shot of whiskey on a cold day. I push the door open a fraction more, and I'm afforded a direct view of the massive four-poster bed.

Lying right in the middle of it is June. She's wearing something thin and flimsy hiked up around her hips. She's got her hand tucked between her legs and her head tilted back. Her lips are parted and her chest is rising and falling with the musical lift of her moans.

I should step out.

But instead, I find myself stepping right in.

I walk right to the foot of the bed. By the time I reach it, I'm painfully swollen and in danger of doing something really fucking stupid.

I take another step forward, but I'm so lost in the way her fingers are rubbing her clit that I'm not as careful as I should be. The sound of my shoe on the wooden floorboard creates a creak that causes June's eyes to shoot open.

With a gasp, she launches herself upright and pulls the covers over her half-naked body. Her cheeks are flushed with color. A mix of exhilaration and embarrassment. There's shame, but the moment the shock of seeing me wears off, it's replaced with indignation.

"What the hell are you doing here?"

I smile, but it's a hard smile, strangled by desire. "I'm sorry I disturbed you."

"No, you're not."

"Tell me something."

"Oh, sure," she says, all flushed and snarky. "Let's have a nice little conversation right now, shall we."

I ignore it. "Who were you thinking of?"

She's so taken back by the question that she forgets to look furious. Instead, her eyes go wide and her eyebrows reach the peak of her glistening forehead.

"I... I—"

"Come on, June," I encourage. "Give me an honest answer, and maybe I'll leave."

She swallows nervously. Her voice, when it finally emerges, is a delicate, husky rasp. "You know who I was thinking about. That's why you walked in. It was you, Kolya. I was thinking of you."

I walk around and stand at the side of the bed. She sits up, eyeing the foot of distance between us warily.

The crepe silk slip she's wearing floats over her body like a breeze. She might as well be naked. Which is precisely why I rip it off her with one firm tug. One of her hands lands on her bare belly for a moment in wordless shock.

I grip the nape of her neck and I press my thumb against the scar that my fool of a brother left on her. Her expression has that dreamy quality that tells me that her better judgment has taken flight for the moment.

Mine left a long time ago.

But walking away now is not an option. Not when those hazel eyes of hers are begging me to fuck her.

"Kolya…"

That does it. I pull her face to mine and slam my lips down on that supple mouth of hers. She tastes of salty pickles, of lemon soda and sweetness. Of forgiveness. Of redemption.

Of the greatest mistake I'll ever make.

My hands slip down to her ass as she takes two fistfuls of my shirt and starts to pull it off of me.

I push her hands away twice, but she still doesn't seem to get the message. "June…"

My voice comes out ragged and rusty. Her fingers tremble with unease, but she pauses and looks up at me. She still doesn't suspect a goddamn thing. And why would she? This secret is buried far deeper than all the others.

Her face is puckered in a tempting little frown. "Why not? You're the one who walked in here, remember?"

"And I'm not going anywhere. But my shirt stays on."

That seems to snap the dream-like expression right off her face. "I… I don't understand."

"You don't have to understand."

Her fingers pull back tentatively, breaking contact between us. The heat that just a moment ago felt addicting and unbearable at the same time is completely gone now. The room feels cold. Arid. A tundra where neither of us belong.

"What don't you want me to see?" she whispers.

I don't bother answering, mostly because I don't know where the fuck I'd even begin with the story written on my skin. I just turn and leave. I go as far as I can, all the way to the opposite side of the suite. But no amount of distance will be enough.

Not now.

Not that I know how she tastes.

30

JUNE

I'd hoped that a night of sleep would help wash away the residual shame and humiliation after what happened.

Instead, I wake to find a third emotion to add to the mix. Shame, humiliation, and—drumroll, please—guilt. It's the freaking trifecta and I'm smack dab in the middle.

I know. Fun.

I lie in bed for much longer than necessary, trying to figure out how to face Kolya this morning. Do I give him the silent treatment, or do I just pretend nothing happened?

Childishness or denial—you know life is going well when those are your only two options.

I'm momentarily distracted when the sounds of muted chatter filter their way through the bulky wooden door of my room. Is that a woman's voice I'm hearing?

The swing of conversation sounds much too familiar to belong to one of the hotel staff. Is it possibly... Geneva?

I tug on the white robe with the hotel logo embroidered on the breast and rush to the door in a juvenile attempt to eavesdrop. I press my ear to the wood, but all I hear is faint laughter that's entirely too cultured to belong to my sister.

She wouldn't be laughing anyway. Not in Kolya's presence. I'm fairly certain about that. I check my phone and find one lone message from her, riddled with typos.

Geneva: *hye bum busy—c you at teh party.*

Sighing, I head into the bathroom and get ready for whatever is waiting for me outside this room. Once I'm dressed, I pull my hair up into a high bun. It wasn't lost on me that Kolya kept staring at my neck yesterday the whole time my hair was up. I'm reasonably sure it was only partially to do with my scar.

Which, of course, he'd noticed. The man notices everything, especially the things I'd really prefer escaped his attention. It'd be impressive if it wasn't so damn infuriating.

But as much as he gets under my skin, I seem to be able to do the same with him without even trying. I spent a fair amount of time last night trying to figure out why he wouldn't let me take his shirt off. It seemed like an obvious, not to mention expected, ritual insofar as sex usually goes.

Maybe it's for the best, though. It certainly derailed the bad decision we were about to make together.

In the mirror, I stare at the scar at the right-hand side of my neck. It's sickle-shaped, the exact arc and thickness of Adrian's thumbnail. If I close my eyes, I can feel the skin breaking all over again. My scream was the only thing that made him let go.

"I'm sorry, Junepenny," he'd said, tears streaming down his face. *"I—I didn't know what I was doing."*

"You thought someone was trying to hurt you," I'd told him. *"It was like you were seeing someone else."*

"I was."

"Who?"

He only shook his head and hugged me tighter. I'd held him throughout the entire night. I'd held him until he was completely sober and shaking with withdrawal symptoms. He turned his face up to me in the morning.

"I don't deserve you," he whispered.

That was the first time I had the thought. The Thought, as I came to call it. Capitalized, copyrighted, trademarked. A thought that I had always felt deep down, but never had the courage or wherewithal to decipher.

Is it better to be wanted—or to be needed?

In the end, I keep my hair up and head out of the bedroom to find that the woman's voice I'd clocked earlier belongs to Milana. She's sitting at the breakfast table by the balcony, right next to Kolya. The table is groaning under the weight of the biggest breakfast spread I've ever seen. Two dozen kinds of breakfast pastries radiating the scent of so much butter and sugar it should be illegal. Tossed in the mix is coffee, tea, fruit juice, other things I don't even recognize.

"Good morning, June," Milana says brightly.

She looks effortlessly flawless in a dusty gold blouse with a deep neckline and black silk pants. On anyone else, her towering heels would look strange in the light of day, but somehow, they manage to look just right on her.

Her blonde hair is tied up high, much like mine is. All that makes me want to do is undo my bun to avoid being compared to her.

"G'morning," I mumble, daring a glance in Kolya's direction.

He's scrolling through his phone with one hand and nursing a cup of black coffee with the other. He doesn't wish me a good morning or look back at me. In fact, he barely acknowledges my presence.

"Why don't you sit down and join us for breakfast?" Milana suggests, gesturing to the empty chair beside her.

I'm not about to cower in my room just because Kolya decided to be strange last night, so I take the seat and grab a croissant while I'm at it. The smell of freshly baked pastry is too delectable to resist. I don't even butter the croissant and after my first bite, I realize I don't need to. It's like biting into a stick of the stuff already.

"Wow, that's delicious," I say with a contented sigh.

"Right?" Milana nods, adjusting the tiny diamond pendant hanging from her neck.

She has a plate of her own in front of her, but it's empty. Honestly, I'm not surprised. She looks like the kind of woman who could subsist on fresh air and chewing gum.

"Tea? Coffee? Juice?" Milana asks with a smile. "There's fresh mango and fresh pineapple if you'd like me to cut you a slice. But if you prefer something different, we can ring down to room service. Anything you like—say the word and it's yours."

She's so gushingly nice that I cringe, feeling guilty about the snarky thoughts I was thinking just a moment ago. "Mango is fine, thank you."

Still smiling, she serves me a slice while I munch on my croissant and try not to look at Kolya. When he puts his phone down, however, I break my own rule and glance up.

His eyes skid over me—briefly, brusquely—before landing on Milana. "Do you have eyes on the venue?"

"They were dispatched this morning," she replies, reaching for her coffee cup. "Things are still being set up. Ravil wasn't on-site."

"No, he wouldn't be. He likes to show up once all the work is done."

"Seems to be a family trait."

I expect Kolya to glower at her, roll his eyes, snap back with something dry and biting. But instead he… smiles.

And as dumb as it is—really, really dumb, I know—I bristle. I get all his sour. She gets his sweet. It doesn't seem fair.

But given what I now know about the circumstances of their relationship, I guess it's not all that surprising. That's a whole can of worms I'm trying really hard to ignore, though.

"I'm heading out."

"Where?" I blurt out.

Kolya jerks his head to me as though he'd already forgotten I'm here. "Out," he repeats shortly. "I have work to do."

"What work?"

I'm not sure why I insist on asking questions that I know he won't answer. Maybe I just want him to look at me, acknowledge me.

"Nothing that would interest you," he clips. "We leave at eight tonight. I expect you to be ready on time."

Then he finishes the last of his coffee and gets to his feet. I watch him stride out of the suite, resisting the urge to shout something at his back just so that I can get the last word in.

I manage to hold it in, though. I'll be a mother soon. I've got to at least try to be a grownup from time to time.

When I turn my attention back to the table, Milana's eyes are fixed on me with something that looks very much like sympathy.

"Don't let him get to you," she suggests before I can even pretend that I'm not bothered by how Kolya behaves towards me. "He's a hard bastard, but underneath all that armor, there's a little pussy cat."

"A pussy cat?"

"Okay, maybe a lion." She smirks, then softens and reaches over to pat my hand. "Trust me, June: I've known the man a long time. He's not as scary as he seems. Not all the time, at least."

"I'm not scared of him."

"Good effort! With a little more practice, that will be much more convincing."

I frown, and she gives me a sheepish smile. "He's not that hard to decipher," she promises. "He's just a man, after all. At the end of the day, they're all suckers."

"Sure," I say with a heap of sarcasm. "It has nothing to do with the fact that you look like a supermodel."

She doesn't fake-humble and wave away the compliment like some women would. There's no false humility in her smile, either. Instead, she nods. "Oh, that's definitely part of it. And it's enough for most men. But others are more complicated. Looks might be enough to catch their attention. But definitely not enough to keep it."

Those eyes of hers are as sharp as they're beautiful. I fidget for a moment, wondering if I'm going too far, before I just blurt it out. "Kolya told me about how the two of you met."

She blinks, looking mildly surprised. "Did he now? He doesn't usually offer up that story to many people. You don't have to look so nervous; I've never hidden my past. I hated being a prostitute, but I've never been ashamed of where I came from. I was a victim of circumstance."

"And… Kolya helped you get out of those… circumstances?"

My words are clumsy, especially in comparison to Milana's confident eloquence. I feel myself shrinking more and more in her presence, and hating myself for it.

"He did," she says wistfully. "He was the first man I ever truly trusted. In fact, he's still the only man I trust."

Something foreign and unwelcome spreads across my chest. "That must have created quite the bond between the two of you."

"It's very hard not to bond with your savior," she says. "But I didn't expect our relationship to turn into a lifelong friendship. That was unexpected."

"Oh. A f-friendship?" I stammer, like a rat sniffing around for morsels.

Milana raises her eyebrows. "Well, since he rebuffed all my attempts to seduce him over the years, a friendship is what I settled for," she giggles girlishly.

"Oh. Well—I mean…" *Jesus, say something, you dolt.* "His loss."

Milana raises her eyebrows, and I feel my cheeks burn red. Why the hell did I choose this moment to turn into a complete spaz?

"June, babe, I'm kidding."

I almost choke on my mango. "Oh. Duh."

She grins. "Kolya and I have only ever been friends. We met so young, you know? We established the kind of relationship that was so platonic that it never occurred to either one of us to make a move on the other one."

The relief I feel is so freaking obvious that I just choose to ignore it. "So you're saying the two… you've never… you know—"

I'm interrupted by Milana's laughter. She's got quite a raucous giggle. It clashes with her ladylike appearance, but that just makes me like it all the more.

"No," she says, when she finally stops laughing. "We've never. Will never, either. I promise you that much."

I can feel my blush get deeper. "I mean, it's not a big jump to make. The two of you are obviously close. And you're both very attractive… and, um… yeah." I button my lips up before more nonsense spills out.

Milana's gaze is direct and searching. No, not searching—she looks like she's already found what she's searching for. "He's a good man, June," she says quietly. "He'll try to deny it, but take it from someone who knows: he is."

"It doesn't really matter to me."

She raises her eyebrows and smiles at the same time. "Doesn't it?" she asks. I feel like she's catching me out without actually coming right out and catching me. I should be grateful for the subtle difference, but all I want to do is get out from under her gaze. Like Kolya, the woman sees too damn much.

"He may have been your savior," I say. "But he's my abductor."

My words don't really land right. They sound weak, rather than accusatory. Milana shrugs them off and pours herself another cup of coffee. "As far as abductions go, you have to agree—this is one of the better ones."

"A gilded cage is still a cage," I point out.

I wait for her to agree with me, but she doesn't. "You're here for a reason, June."

"I'm here for *his* reasons," I correct. "And they're not noble ones. They're selfish. Self-interested."

"Do you really mind that much?" she asks politely.

"What is that supposed to mean?"

She smiles knowingly. "It's just—the way you look at him."

I flinch back, indignant and defensive, and desperate to correct her insinuation. "I don't have feelings for him, if that's what you're getting at. Well, that's not true. I do have feelings. But they're anger and resentment and frustration and irritation and anger and hate and… and…"

"You said anger twice."

"Well, that's how angry I am!"

She nods with a soft grin, and we lapse into silence. I spend the rest of the morning trying to figure out how I managed to get the last word in, but she still had the last say.

31

JUNE

When I come out of the bathroom that evening, freshly showered and smelling of lily and lavender body scrub, I see a packaged dress laid out on the bed for me.

First, I'm struck with excitement. Second, curiosity. And thirdly—annoyance.

From anyone else, it would be a sweet little gesture. Endearing. From Kolya, it's just more manipulation. *Dance, June, dance.*

"What a complete asshole," I mutter to myself as I approach the dress and unzip the bag it's in. "What a pompous, arrogant, self-righteous—

The insult dies on my tongue when I catch sight of the dress he's picked for me. I pull it out like the stuff it's made of could cure cancer and drape it carefully across the duvet.

Okay, maybe I can deal with being dressed. Just for tonight.

"Wow," I whisper, fondling the tiny intricate little beads of the champagne-colored, floor-length gown. It looks like Vera

Wang meets Monique Lhuillier meets Jesus H. Christ with a sewing machine.

The neckline is scooped and low enough that I already know I'm going to be displaying a fair amount of cleavage. The straps of the dress are thin and the silhouette is lithe. It toes the line of being extravagant without ever stepping across. The whole thing looks light as air, smooth as water. I'm honestly terrified to touch it.

Backing up so I don't breathe on it wrong, I nearly trip over something underfoot. Once I get my balance back, I look down to see what it is.

Shoes. Not just any shoes, either. Three-inch, pointed toe silver heels, with a pearl collar around the ankle. They're practically glowing. I'm not gonna lie—my heart flutters just a little.

It takes me almost ten minutes to get the dress on, mostly because I'm worried about snagging the dress or ripping off some of the beading or just exhaling at an inopportune moment. But once it's on, the side zip slides up easily and it hugs my body like a second skin.

Like it was made for me.

I put on the shoes every bit as carefully and walk to the full-length, hand-carved mirror next to the dressing table.

For the first time in a long time, I don't hate what I see.

I don't linger, though. Lingering would bring back those old familiar self-critiques. The scar Adrian gave me. The hair he said was too flat and brittle, the hips that were too wide. The knee that wouldn't bear my weight anymore. The scars on my chest that told stories I wanted so badly to forget.

I spend the next half an hour at the dressing table, putting on makeup and doing my hair. I construct a more graceful updo than the messy bun that's my usual go-to, and I keep my makeup simple. Smoky eye and nude lipstick.

By the time I'm done, I feel good. I feel as though I could stand next to Milana and not be the slightest bit insecure. Well, maybe just the slightest bit.

Clutching this new feeling to my chest, I check the clock. Seven fifty-five. It's showtime.

Kolya is standing by the balcony when I walk out, looking like something out of a dream. The suit he's wearing is perfectly tailored to his large frame, a dark navy that feels like desire personified. Like looking into space on a starless night.

He doesn't immediately turn to look at me. When he does, though, something about him freezes me in my tracks.

It's not quite a glance. Well, it is at first—but then it becomes so much more. His breath catches in his chest. His eyebrows arch. His fists clench.

But it's his eyes I can't look away from. They darken faster and faster until his suit looks pale in comparison. They darken with danger, they darken with lust, they darken with so much of both that it's impossible to tell where one stops and the other begins.

He takes a few steps forward, close enough to make the heat rise to my neck and flood my face with color. He reaches out unexpectedly and pushes a loose curl back behind my left ear.

"You look stunning, *printsessa.*"

Something about the way he says it makes it feel like so much more than four little words. He says it with his whole body. With his whole soul.

The kind of moment that makes you feel truly seen.

"Thank you," I mumble, cheeks heating. "You look alright."

He smiles and then offers me his arm. "Come on. The limo's waiting outside for us."

"Limo?"

"I'd like to make an entrance tonight."

"Something tells me you would have done that regardless."

He shoots me a sideways smirk. "If I didn't know any better, I'd say you're trying to flatter me, June Cole."

"Yeah, well, good thing you know better."

We go downstairs together, neither one of us saying a word. As he helps me into the limo, I suddenly register an onslaught of nerves that I'd been keeping pinned at the edge of my consciousness, like realizing you haven't been breathing.

"So, um… what's the game plan tonight?" I ask tentatively, more than aware that he might tell me that it doesn't concern me.

Instead, he turns to me. His blue eyes seem so much bluer against his navy suit. "We go, we dance, we observe," he says. "We let the night play out. Have you heard anything from your sister?"

"She sent me a text. She seems busy."

"She didn't mention anything else?"

"No. There was no mention of your cousin or any nefarious dealings."

"Isn't she a useful asset?" he mutters with an eye roll.

"Hey," I protest, "she isn't aware of anything that's happening here. As far as my sister is concerned, she's just landed a great job."

"So she's just ignorant. Much better."

I open my mouth to defend Geneva, but I hesitate a little too hard. Sighing, I throw him a defeated glare. "Fine."

He chuckles as the limo rolls up to a glittering building with the tallest columns I've ever seen. There's a whole bunch of staff standing outside the steps. Valets and pursers, greeters in white tailcoats and fake smiles. A red carpet winds up to the entrance.

"Ravil isn't big on subtlety, is he?" I remark, peering out the window until my door is opened by one of the valets.

I get out of the car and step out onto the red carpet. "I've got it from here," Kolya says, appearing at my side and offering the valet a tip in exchange for my arm.

We make our way up the steps. I keep my eyes riveted on my own feet because I'm one unexpected sneeze away from tripping and breaking my tailbone in front of what feels like a million onlookers.

"There she is," Kolya says as soon as we enter the ballroom. That's when I finally look up.

Through the crowd, Geneva appears. She's in a tight black dress with a slit that ends alarmingly close to her lady bits and a neckline that dips down to her navel. Her hair is loose and sleek and there's about three pounds of makeup caked onto her face.

She takes one look at me and her eyes go wide with awe. "Damn, Juju!"

I give her a self-conscious smile and smooth out my dress. "I'd like to take the credit, but it's all the dress."

"Nonsense," Kolya purrs. "You're a vision."

I look at him in surprise, taken aback by the compliment. He's smiling down at me with an affection he's never revealed before. Why would he show it now, in front of all these—

Oh. Right.

He's just putting on a show, like we discussed. I'm such an idiot sometimes.

"I gotta say, the two of you make quite the couple," Geneva says begrudgingly, looking between the two of us as though we're got crowns on our heads.

Kolya wraps an arm around my waist. "Geneva."

Her eyes narrow ever so slightly. "Kolya. Been treating my sister right?"

"As well as Ravil has been treating you, I'm sure."

Geneva's face melts into a pouty frown. "How did you—? Never mind." An influx of people surges through the entrance behind us. When it clears, Geneva's frown is the same, but with a veneer of impatience plastered over it. "Excuse me. I've got to get back to work."

Just like that, she disappears into the swarms once again.

"What?" I snap, feeling Kolya's eyes on the side of my face.

"She's quite something, your sister."

"She grows on you."

"Like a fungus?"

I try to turn my laugh into a cough, albeit with mixed results. Kolya takes my arm again and we wander around the perimeter of the room. I'm not sure exactly how much of this is Geneva's doing, but it's jaw-dropping nonetheless. The whole ceiling glows with fairy lights strung from chandelier to chandelier. It's blinding and soothing at the same time, somehow. I feel like we're floating in a cloud.

"This is quite the crowd."

"The rich, the powerful, the social climbers," Kolya says. "They're all here. Ravil certainly knows how to fill out a ballroom."

"Is that a bad thing?"

"Not for us."

"Because you want it out there that… I'm your—"

"Woman."

I wrinkle my nose up in distaste. "Do you have to say it like that? Like I'm your possession, not your partner."

He is unfazed. "That's how it works in this world."

"Well, maybe your world needs to change a little bit."

He looks at me as though I've just grown an extra limb. "This is the Bratva, June. It doesn't change for anyone."

"Not even you?"

"Not even me," he says in a hard voice. "Come on."

"Where are we going?"

"To the dance floor."

"The—wait, the what?"

In answer, he sashays me onto the dance floor and pulls me flush against his body. I feel winded already and we haven't even started dancing.

I watch the other couples move, and for a moment, I forget that I'm a dancer by trade and that this really shouldn't be such a big deal.

"June."

I look up at those exhilarating blue eyes. "Mhmm?"

"Breathe. This is one area where you can outdo me."

It's all the reminder I need. His grip tightens around my waist as we start moving to the beat of the music. I find myself loosening up with every passing second, relaxing into the melody.

Once I've swallowed the ball of unease in my throat, I realize that Kolya is holding his own. I may be able to outdance him, even with my injuries, but he's no slouch on the dance floor.

"You can dance," I say in surprise.

He smirks. "I don't embarrass myself."

"I must say, you're a surprising man, Kolya. I mean, first the piano. Then the dancing. Next, you're gonna tell me that you can sing."

"Like a drowning cat," he promises me.

I laugh loudly enough that a few of the couples around us turn to look. Is this what it's like to have fun? It's been so long that I've forgotten the feeling.

And I'm starting to associate this feeling with the scent of vanilla. With the musk of rich oak and pine that makes up the foundation notes of whatever aftershave Kolya is wearing.

"If your ankle is—"

"It's not," I say firmly. "In any case, I've danced with a sprained ankle before." Of course, that was before The Accident, but I choose not to mention that.

"Masochist."

"It was a great night," I tell him with a longing sigh. "I had the main solo. Standing ovation when I finished. You've never seen people so excited for ballet before."

He nods solemnly. "You deserve no less."

For a change, his voice is devoid of sarcasm. If I didn't know any better, I'd say he actually means it.

I open my mouth to say something else, but before I can, I see his eyes sharpen imperceptibly. His movements are still confident and graceful, but his attention is fixed on a point above my head.

"Something wrong?"

"We've got eyes on us," he says in a low growl.

I resist the urge to look back over my shoulder. "Ravil?"

"No. But almost as bad."

I feel Kolya's grip tighten around my body. He swings us smoothly off the dance floor, but he keeps his hand on the small of my back.

"Here we go, June," Kolya warns me softly. "Put your game face on."

32

JUNE

The man walking towards us is as tall as Kolya.

He's wearing a white dinner jacket with black pants, a bejeweled watch, and enough confidence to carry off the mismatched look. His dark hair is pulled back into a tight, greasy ponytail and large diamond studs gleam like spotlights on both his ears.

Not Ravil. But someone important. Someone who thinks he's important, at least.

Kolya pulls me closer against his body as the man approaches. I wonder if he realizes he's doing it or if it's just pure, primal, protective instinct.

"Kolya," the man greets coolly, stopping a foot away from us. Much too close for comfort, in my opinion.

It's Kolya who takes a step back, though I'm fairly certain it's all for my benefit. The man smirks as though the gesture is an admission of fear, of weakness. I sense a nonverbal conversation flowing back and forth between the two of them that I can barely understand, like two people jabbering furiously in a language I don't speak. A language of angles and intimidation. Implied threat. Sins and scars from the past flashed at the other like fangs.

"Didn't expect to see you here, Iakov," Kolya replies.

The man—Iakov—grins so wide that I can't help but notice his canines. They're unusually sharp, as if he's filed them into points. He also smells strange. A mixture of ash and incense that makes me want to retch. You know how some smells scream *Run for the hills?* Shit, blood, that kind of thing? This does the same. I want away from this man ASAP.

But Kolya's hand on my hip will keep me safe. I don't know much, but I know that.

"Now, that can't be true," Iakov tuts. "Surely you knew who was throwing this party."

"Must have slipped my attention," Kolya says with a shrug. "I don't usually keep track of the hosts. I just show up."

"How charitable of you."

The man's eyes slide curiously to me, and I shrink into Kolya's side. His irises are an unsettling blue. Not bright and bold like Kolya's. More like… translucent. Alien, almost.

"And who do we have here?" he purrs.

The condescension with which he asks the question rubs me the wrong way. I immediately regret cuddling up against Kolya like some wallflower. Men like him only respond to strength.

I pull myself up to full height and step out from under Kolya's shadow. "I'm June," I say, looking him right in the eye. "And who exactly are you?"

His smile is amused, and much more interested than he was a moment ago. "I'm Iakov. I—"

"I wouldn't trouble yourself, June," Kolya interrupts. "You're not going to be seeing him again after this."

The man arches one thick eyebrow. "Is that right? You're going to keep her locked away, are you? Protective of your little prize, Kolya."

"I'm no prize," I cut in viciously. "Not his, and sure as hell not yours."

The man's other eyebrow rises to meet the first. It's subtle, but enough that I can see the burgeoning respect in his eyes. Then that's gone, smoothed over with placid, malicious amusement once again.

He turns to Kolya. "Your kitten has claws."

Kolya thrums with a dark, wary energy. I know enough about him to be frightened of it. I can't say the same for this greasy ponytail in front of us.

"I assume you walked over here for a formal introduction," he says calmly. "So I'll give you one. This is June Cole, my girlfriend and the future mother of my child."

He delivers the words so smoothly, so naturally, that it takes me a minute to realize just how jarring they really are. When it finally lands, I whirl around to gawk at him. He doesn't look back, though, and in profile, his face gives nothing away.

Iakov doesn't look surprised. "I see" is all he says. His gaze roams over me once again. "Then I suppose congratulations are in order. For more than just the baby." Iakov's tongue flicks out over his dry lips and then retreats again like a worm, leaving slimy spit in its wake. "Though a woman with a mouth like that ought to be taught how to properly use it."

It's like a cold breeze only I can feel passes through me. Wherever it touches, it burns the way frost does. I've never been a violent person in my life, but images flash through my head of attacking this man like a feral wildcat. Baring my teeth, my claws, ripping that ponytail right off his smug fucking scalp.

"You have rounds to do," Kolya grits out. His voice is as icy as that invisible breeze. "I suggest you go do them."

Iakov's eyes twinkle. "But it's *you* I came to talk to, Don Uvarov."

"We've talked. Have a nice evening, Iakov."

Then Kolya pivots, taking me with him toward a bar tucked into the corner of the ballroom. He gets the bartender's attention with only a tap of his finger.

"Whiskey for me. Lemon soda for her."

The man leaps to do as he's told. When he holds out my drink, I take it from him with trembling hands.

It's only a little bit of fear that's fueling the shakes. Fear for my sister, for Kolya, for my baby, for myself.

Mostly, though, it's anger.

I've survived so much, just to be talked about like I'm not even there. To be wielded like a shiny little bauble that men can bat around to their amusement.

I'm getting really fucking sick of it.

"Stay here. I'll be back," Kolya blurts unexpectedly.

I set my drink back on the bar counter. "You're going to… leave me here?"

"I've got eyes on you," he assures me. "You'll be safe. I just need to check in with my men. See if they have any leads on Ravil's location."

That's when I follow his gaze over my shoulder and a stony-faced soldier standing by one of the Corinthian columns.

"Okay," I gulp. "I'll be here."

He nods and heads off in the direction of Mr. Stone Face. I turn to my lemon soda and down it like a shot. I miss alcohol, which is odd—it's the first time I've felt that way in a long time.

The more Adrian drank, the less tolerance I had for it. By the time his third sobriety journey came around, the mere thought made me sick.

Which in hindsight, feels nauseatingly condescending. I deserved the barbs he used to throw at me. *"Oh good for you, June. What a fucking pillar of discipline. You want a damn trophy or something?"*

Not much has changed, croons his voice in my head. *I'm six feet under and you still think you're above me. Though I guess it's literally true now, isn't it?*

"That's not funny, Adrian," I mutter under my breath.

"All alone?"

I gasp, taken unawares by the giant silhouette hanging over me. It's him, the man with the ponytail and diamond studs and the flat, lifeless eyes that make me think of the horror films I used to avoid as a kid.

"I… I'm not alone. Kolya will be back soon." My voice shakes no matter how hard I try to keep it still.

Iakov smiles wolfishly and then licks his lips again. Christ, I wish he would stop doing that. "Did I tell you how ravishing you look in that dress?" he murmurs. "Pregnancy certainly does suit some women."

His eyes slide down to my cleavage. It makes me wish I had a shawl to wrap around my chest. Either that or a suit of armor.

I push myself off the bar stool. "I'd better go look for Kolya. Excuse me," I tell him coldly.

I'm hoping he just lets me go, but it's a shallow hope, dead on arrival. Iakov tails me like a shadow. "Oh my, what a pleasure it is to walk behind you. Why don't you let me keep you company until your man deigns to show up again? A prize like you can't be left wandering around by herself. So many sharks in this room who might try to steal a taste."

I figure I can lose him on the dance floor, but that turns out to be a phenomenally bad plan, because he takes the opportunity to grab my hand and twist me around.

Before I can catch my breath, he pulls me against him and suddenly, we're locked in a dance I never agreed to be a part of in the first place.

"What are you doing?" I snap, looking around desperately, hoping to catch a glimpse of Kolya. Or one of his men, at the very least.

"I'm dancing," Iakov says, giving me a smile that's more of a sneer. "Heard that you were pretty good at it."

I feel a shiver run up my spine. It's an offhand comment, innocuous on the face of it, but I know now that there's no such thing in Kolya's world. How much does this creep know about me? The whole truth, or just part of it? The entire point of tonight is to push the lie. If no one ends up believing it, then where do I stand? What use am I?

"I'd rather not dance right now."

He just holds me tighter. "I would enjoy this while you can. I certainly am. Kolya Uvarov is not the kind of man who likes to share."

Okay, so maybe he does believe our little fantasy. At least that will give me some measure of protection.

I hope.

"That just makes this move really stupid on your part."

Iakov scoffs. "He's not going to do anything. Making a move against me would be akin to calling for war. And that's a big risk for your man."

"Kolya can take you," I say confidently. "And anyone else that comes his way."

He just laughs at me. "He may have the pride, he may have his father's ego, but he has half the strength and less than that in support. Oh, he needs me, little rabbit. He can't afford to act without me."

I stop struggling so hard against his hold and just stare at him, disassociating. This is not my world. I'm in over my head here. But Kolya isn't around to hold my hip and keep me safe. I'm in the deep end all alone and the shark is circling. Do I let him take a bite?

Or do I bite first?

"Why would he need you?" I venture.

"Because I have inside information for him. Not to mention a very generous offer to present."

"Which is what?"

"I'll speak to him about that when the time is right. I just need you to take the proposition to him."

"You want me to play messenger?"

"Precisely." He reaches up and runs the calloused tip of one finger down my cheek. "And what a pretty little carrier pigeon you are."

I resist the urge to bite his finger clean off. Instead, I jerk away from his touch. "I'm not about to take anything to him without knowing what it is. So you can tell me now, or you can fuck right off."

His eyes glow with annoyance. "You've got a bratty little mouth for a woman who—"

"A woman who has Kolya Uvarov's ear," I finish over him with a glower. "If you want his attention, then you need mine first."

It has to be the dress giving me all this confidence, because I certainly don't know where else it might be coming from. As we swing around the dance floor, I notice Geneva on the left side of the ballroom. She's got her eyes on me, her expression partially curious, but mostly just irritated.

Concentrate on the asshole, June.

"You drive a hard bargain," he says, scowling at me. "It's not the only thing you're making hard right now."

He shoves his groin against me, and I gasp with disgust. But I refuse to walk away now, not when I can be of help to Kolya. So I stand my ground and stare at the asshole, refusing to be intimidated.

"Tell me what you need to right this second, or I'm walking away."

I'm talking bolder than I feel. I figure that if he uses force, I can scream, cause a scene. I'm not just gonna offer him the upper hand on a silver platter.

His upper lip curls in distaste. "So be it. Some of Ravil's men aren't happy under his leadership. Many still see Kolya as the rightful don of the Uvarov Bratva. He's made poor choices—one in particular—but if he's willing to reverse that decision now, then he's looking at swelling his ranks until he outnumbers Ravil ten to one."

I feel my breath hitch. "Which decision is that?"

"You don't know?" he asks searchingly.

I keep my expression apathetic. "You're humoring me, remember?"

Iakov gnashes his teeth. "The red trade. Get your man to lift his ban on trafficking prostitutes, and it's a done deal."

I take him by surprise by slamming my foot down on his fancy Italian loafers. He releases me with a sharp intake of breath and I lunge backward, glaring at him with disgust.

"Kolya will never agree to that. Nor would I want him to."

The asshole's eyes narrow. "Then you'd both be making a huge mistake."

"The only mistake I made tonight was letting you touch me. I'll have to shower twice when I get home. Don't you ever speak to me again."

I've already got my back to him and I'm storming away when he grabs me again and twists me back around. "Don't you dare walk away from me, you little fucking slut."

Fears starts edging out my anger. "You… you can't… if Kolya sees the way you're—"

"He won't do a fucking thing about it," he spits in my face. "As I said, hurting me will be the same as calling for war. I'm the key to everything; you're just some whore Kolya knocked up by accident. I'm—"

I cut him off by spitting in his face. The gob of saliva hits him right in the eye, temporarily blinding him. I turn and start to run, but with my bad knee and injured ankle, I stumble the first few steps.

It's all the time he needs to recover and snare me by the bun on my head.

"You fucking bitch!" he screams, causing several of the people around us to gasp and clear the area. "Do you know who I am?! I will teach you a lesson in respect."

He pushes me down so hard that my legs cave and my knees hit the ground. The beads of the dress dig into my flesh like a million tiny needles. He's still got me by the hair, but with his free hand, he starts to undo the buckle of his belt.

Oh God… Oh God… Oh God…

Tears erupt in the corners of my eyes. I can feel everyone in the ballroom watching this play out, but no one steps in. No one speaks up.

I cringe back at the sound of Iakov's buckle coming loose. His face hangs over me, a living nightmare. And then…

I smell vanilla.

I watch as the asshole's expression goes from fury to shock. The knife glints at his throat for half a second before I watch it slice from left to right. Blood sprays out crudely and I feel the heat, the wetness splash on my face.

The next thing I know, I'm being lifted into the air. The air around me ripples with screams. Maybe they're mine, maybe they're not—I can't be sure.

"Grab the sister," I hear a familiar voice command. "Quickly."

"I've got her. Let's go." Another familiar voice. This one female. It has to be Milana.

I want to ask questions, but my mind is too heavy, drenched with fear. The only thing I can manage is resting my head against the broad chest I'm being held against.

As long as I'm here, everything will be okay.

33

KOLYA

"Jesus, can you make her stop that noise?" I growl, shooting a dagger-edged stare at Milana as though she's personally responsible for Geneva's wailing.

"Short of knocking her unconscious, I'm out of options," she hisses back.

"Don't tempt me."

The only reason I keep myself from making good on the suggestion is the fact that June is here, too. Slumped in the seat right next to me, as quiet as her sister is loud.

She hasn't said a word since I slit Iakov's throat. A front row seat to a violent death will do that to you, if you're not used to it. Even now, her face is splattered with drops of his blood.

What I did will have ramifications. Serious ones. I crossed a line, spilled protected blood. But despite all that, my main concern is for her.

Even the sound of her sister's incessant screaming isn't snapping her out of the catatonic fog engulfing her.

I glance back over my shoulder at the back seat, where Milana is trying to get through to Geneva. She'd been restrained with makeshift cuffs after clawing at two of my men. But her mouth is still painfully unfettered.

"Will you calm down?" Milana snaps, a little unruffled by her normal unflappable standards. "We just saved your life."

"My life?" Geneva screeches back in disbelief. "You're all in on this shit together! H-he's a murderer." She turns to me. "MURDERER!"

The woman certainly has a flair for the dramatic. I pull up the partition that separates the front seats from the back. It cuts the sound by half, but I can still hear her banshee screams.

We arrive on the tarmac ten minutes later. I'm the first one out of the car. Milana is the second. "My head is pounding," she complains. "She's got a set of lungs on her. Why wasn't I allowed to gag the witch?"

"Because of June," I growl. "Keep her in there for the moment. I need to make sure June is okay."

Milana nods, and I walk around to the other side of the car and open June's door. She doesn't even glance at me. Her eyes are glassy, unfocused. When I take her hand and pull her from the car, she comes with me without putting up a fight. I walk her onto the private jet waiting for us, engines already purring eagerly.

Forcing her into one of the leather seats, I take the opposite one. Her gaze teeters brokenly toward the night beyond the window. Darkness obliterates everything past the wingtip.

"June."

Her eyes flicker back to me, but they don't focus. I gesture for the stewardess, who brings me a tray stacked high with wet towelettes.

I take one and press it against June's blood-splattered face. She flinches against the cold, but she lets me wipe her face clean. By the time I'm done, she looks like she's checked back into reality. Just barely.

"You never finished telling me about your solo," I say quietly. That gets her attention. Her eyes drift to mine.

"W-what?"

I keep my voice soft and distractingly calm. "Your solo. The night you danced on a sprained ankle. You said you got a standing ovation. Tell me about it."

She nods dumbly. I hate seeing her like this. Like the life has been sucked out of her. "I… I landed wrong. A grand jeté, but the floor was wet with sweat, so I slipped a little when I hit." Her voice is dreamy. Haunted. "I felt the pain shoot up my leg, but I had worked so hard to get there that I didn't want it to be for nothing. So I kept dancing through the pain." At long last, the corners of her lips twitch up in the faintest, vaguest ghost of a smile. "But then they all stood and clapped for me when it was done. My ankle was on fire, but it was the best night of my life."

I smile back at her. What's the warmth I'm sensing in my chest? It feels like pride, but that makes no fucking sense. I barely know this woman now. I definitely didn't know her then. Her past is nothing to me but words—but goddammit, the feeling says it means far, far more than I've been willing to admit.

"Was Adrian there?"

I'm not sure why I ask. I'm not sure I even want to know, and yet I'm curious. Curious to see how many important moments of her life she shared with him. Curious also why the thought of that makes me sneeringly jealous.

"Yeah, he was," she says. "It was during one of the good times."

She stops there. I decide not to pry. Her eyes slide to the dirty towelette in my hands. The red blood stains feel jarring all of a sudden.

"I'm okay," she breathes, but it sounds like she's trying to convince herself more than me.

"I know you are," I say. "The same principle applies here as it did there, June."

She frowns. "What principle is that?"

"Just dance through the pain."

I can see her processing that. Her shoulders seem to gain strength as we sit there in the silence.

"Where's Geneva?" she asks after a few minutes have passed.

"Still in the car. Milana is trying to calm her down."

She takes a deep breath. "I… I thought I could do it. It was stupid."

"Do what?"

"Hold my own. He… Iakov, he had a message for you," she says, trying to remember through the fog of shock. "He had a deal."

"I know."

She raises her eyebrows. "You do?"

"I knew that one of Ravil's lieutenants was unhappy, but until tonight, I wasn't sure which. When I saw Iakov, it all clicked."

I don't let her know what a huge blow tonight has been. I intended to have a conversation with Iakov at the end of the night. After making him run in a few circles first. Instead, he had chosen to approach June. He had chosen to intimidate her, scare her.

And the sight of that fucker forcing my—forcing *June*—to her knees in front of all those people... It was the first time in a long time I've taken such leave of my senses. It was the first time I hadn't bothered pretending to talk myself out of something I knew I shouldn't do.

It was a short-sighted move, and I'm going to pay a steep price for it. But looking at June now, I can't find it in me to regret what I did.

The fucker deserved to die for his sins. I'd cut his throat a thousand times over to keep her safe.

"I-I know this has created problems for you," June says in a timid voice. "But I can't deny that I'm happy you did what you did. I'm happy that asshole is dead. I—" The rest of her words are drowned out by a heaving sob. A tear slips down her cheek and she looks at me through her eyelashes. "Thank you, Kolya. Thank you for what you did for me tonight."

That breathtaking hazel pierces through me for a moment. It makes me forget that I have a massive problem on my hands, and very little in the way of solutions. When she looks at me with that *thing* in her eyes—that trust, there's no other name for it, that's all it can be—nothing else matters.

"You should get some rest," I say gruffly, breaking eye contact.

"Can I ask you a question?" she asks instead. "Why can't you just kill Ravil?"

It's an unexpected question from her. "Because he's my cousin. We're family. *'Krov*. Killing one family member cost me more than half my Bratva. Killing a second would spell the end."

She swallows noticeably. "Did you really kill your father?"

"I did."

More silence follows. It's thick enough to choke on because there are so many things we aren't saying. So many things I haven't told her that she needs to know. But we've come so far that telling her now would ruin everything.

So I keep them in the darkness. That's where they belong.

"Kolya." June is looking extremely pale all of a sudden. "I—I don't know how to ask this… She takes a breath, her eyes turning wary. Nervous. "Adrian's d-death… you had nothing to do with it, did you?"

I should probably have expected this question at some point, but it takes me off guard. "No, *medoviy*. I had nothing to do with Adrian's death."

It's a lie. But now is not the time for confessions.

June needs sleep. She needs peace of mind. She needs to be able to trust me. I see that happen the moment relief floods onto her face and she relaxes back into her seat. She mutters something under her breath that sounds a lot like "thank God," and her eyes flutter closed.

Milana appears at the plane door. She gestures for me, and I get to my feet. "I'm going to go see how things are going. Stay here. I'll be back in a moment."

I follow Milana off the jet. "We should have been in the air by now," she murmurs as we make our way down the steps towards the tarmac. "But the woman won't get out of the fucking car. She goes into hysterics every time I get near her. If this was anyone else, I'd have punched her in the face and been done with it."

"There will be no punching," I say firmly.

Milana throws me some sharp side-eye. "No one ever gets special treatment with you."

I don't bother explaining myself.

We reach the car and I rip open the door. As soon as I do, Geneva is there, filling up the space with wild eyes and froth at her lips. "No! No! Are you going to kill me? What have you done with my sister? Did you kill her? You won't get away with this! I'll—"

"Jesus Christ," I hiss. "You were only restrained because you were stalling our getaway. Shut up for two seconds and you'll be free of the cuffs."

She stops talking, her eyes moving from Milana to me. "Where's my sister?"

"She's on the jet, waiting for you. If you get a hold of yourself, then I can take you up and you can sit with her."

She narrows her eyes suspiciously. "You haven't hurt her?"

"Are you really so blind that you missed everything that happened at the party?"

"I saw plenty," she spits in disgust. "You murdered a man in cold blood."

"I saved your sister from being raped, is what happened."

Geneva sucks in her breath. Whether or not to believe it is the question she's struggling with. She wavers back and forth, but in the end, she settles on defiance.

Guess it runs in the family.

"I don't believe you."

"Then ask June yourself," I say dismissively. "Are you ready to come aboard, or will you need to be bound and carried?"

She sidles to the edge of the seat and props her legs on the tarmac. I move forward to help, but she jerks away from me violently. I reveal the small penknife in my hand. "Just to cut your restraints," I explain.

She goes still, but she allows me to step closer. She doesn't breathe the whole time I'm sawing off the zip ties. I hear her breath release only when the plastic hits the ground.

"Come on," I say, offering my hand. "We'll be in the air in five."

34

JUNE

I wonder if I look as bad as Geneva does right now.

Her dress has ripped at the hemline, so now she has two slits instead of one. Her hair is one giant knot, and the sweat has caused her makeup to run so badly that it looks like her face is melting off.

I appreciate the fact that Kolya and Milana sit at the back of the jet, giving Geneva and me some privacy. My first instinct is to clean her up. I can credit that to years of practice dabbing blood and spit off a drunken Adrian, I guess.

I grab a wet towelette and lean in to try cleaning up Geneva's face the same way that Kolya had cleaned mine. But the moment I move in her direction, she flinches away from me like she's not sure who I am anymore.

"Genny…?"

Her eyes focus on me, uncertain and anxious. Then they flicker to the side, loose and wild in their sockets once again.

She doesn't look back at Kolya or Milana, but it's clear that she's all too aware of their presence.

"I know this is a lot," I tell her calmly. "But we're safe now."

Geneva's eyes bulge. "Safe?" she hisses in a hoarse whisper. "How can you possibly say that? What part of everything that just happened screamed 'safe' to you?"

"Geneva, let me explain—"

"No. We're not talking here. Not while they can hear us."

I dart a glance at Kolya and Milana. They're sitting side by side, murmuring back and forth, faces placid and calm. If it weren't for the urgency in their voices and the blood on Kolya's hands, I might've thought they were whispering sweet nothings to each other.

I wrench my attention back to my sister. "Geneva, please."

She throws me a glare that reminds me of our childhood, of every fight we'd ever had. I know that look. It means that it doesn't matter how well I state my case—she's not going to listen to me until she's ready to.

With a deep sigh, I lean back in my seat and close my eyes. I feel a slight twinge in my stomach, grating and insistent. Resting my hand over my belly, I try to breathe deeply. In all the chaos of the night, I'd forgotten I was pregnant.

My breathing lulls me down. Lost somewhere between my thoughts and my impossibly confused emotions, I fall into a dream that's born out of a memory.

And then even that fades, and all that's left is darkness.

∼

Back at the mansion, Milana points out the room next to mine. "This is yours," she says to Geneva. "For as long as you want it."

"You make it sound like I have the freedom to leave whenever I want to." Geneva scowls. The vein in her forehead is throbbing like it always does when she's worked up.

Milana fixes her with a dead smile. "You do—just as soon as we can make sure it's safe for you."

Geneva turns to me. "They feed you this crap, too?"

"Genny," I say softly, putting my hand on her arm, "I know this is a lot, but it's for your own protection."

"Got it. So you've already drunk the Kool-Aid."

Milana drops the smile like a hot potato. She holds out her hand, palm up. "Phone, please."

Geneva recoils in shock. "Are you serious?"

"You can give it to me, or I can take it from you. Your choice." Milana's voice, as always, is pure, icy efficiency.

"I work out, you know," Genny retorts. "I do Pilates."

If the situation weren't so serious, I might have laughed. As it stands, no one does. "I have black belts in Jiu Jitsu and Tae Kwon Do, I'm trained in every weapon known to man, and I have sixteen confirmed kills from over eight hundred yards away," Milana shoots back without batting an eyelid. "But I'm sure your Pilates instructor is very good."

Geneva's jaw clenches. Too many seconds tick by and I'm worried someone's blood is about to get spilled. Then, much to my relief, Geneva pulls out her phone and hands it to Milana.

"I don't like you," she hisses.

Milana rolls her eyes. "I assure you, the feeling is mutual." She turns to me. "June, are you okay? Do you need anything?"

I shake my head. "I'm fine."

"I know you're tired, but it wouldn't hurt to have a quick check-in with Sara. Make sure everything's okay with the baby. That was a lot of stress to deal with in one night."

I glance at my sister. I want a check-up myself, for peace of mind if nothing else. But I don't want to leave Geneva alone, either. Not just yet anyway. She's fragile. We all are.

"Can I have an hour? I just want to… put my feet up for a bit."

Milana gives me a small, knowing smile. "Of course. I'll let Sara know to expect you."

"Is this the part where you lock us up in our rooms and throw away the key?" Geneva demands, ruining the first pleasant exchange I've had in hours. "Why can't we share a room? Afraid we'll put our heads together and try to escape?"

Milana heaves a tired sigh in Geneva's direction. "If you want to share a room with June, that's your prerogative. I'm only sorry for June."

I grab Geneva's hand and throw Milana an apologetic nod. "She'll be in my room for the time being. Goodnight, Milana."

I pull my sister into my room and shut the door. Geneva stands in the middle of the space, her hands crossed hard over her chest. When she turns to me, she's got her fighting face on.

"It's, like, three in the morning. How're you going to see a doctor in an hour?" she asks.

"She's... on call, sort of."

"And you just jump up to the front of the line whenever you please? What about her other patients?"

I swallow the tang of guilt. "She doesn't have any."

Geneva's scowl deepens as she leans against the bedpost. Her foot starts tapping, sounding like a countdown until she implodes. "Make it make sense, June. I'm sick of playing Twenty Questions with everyone under this godforsaken roof."

Sighing, I sink onto the bed. "I'm her only patient. Kolya hired out her services exclusively for the duration of my pregnancy."

Geneva's eyebrows hit the ceiling. She looks mildly impressed for a millisecond before she wipes her expression clean and goes back to looking indignant.

"Is this how he got to you?" she demands. "The jewels, the clothes, the lavish lifestyle? He bought you."

I bristle at that. "Do you really think I'm that shallow?"

"Sorry," she mutters. "Low blow."

An apology was not something I could have expected as a child, so this strikes me as progress. I try to remind myself that Geneva went through something traumatic tonight, too. I need to be more patient with her.

"Why don't we change out of these clothes?" I suggest. "We can clean up and then… talk?"

Geneva plonks herself down on the window seat, her shoulders hunching with fatigue. "Let's talk now."

I nod. "Okay," I say, shuffling over to take the spot opposite her.

There are only one or two garden lights on, so there's not much of a view at the moment. But Geneva still continues to stare out the window as though she can see in the dark.

"I'm sorry," I say, breaking the heavy silence. "About tonight. You're probably not going to get paid."

Her eyes snap to mine and I brace for a tirade. But then the angry energy surging through her seems to dissipate all at once. "You still have nightmares about The Accident, don't you?" she asks suddenly.

My breath catches in my throat. "H-how do you know?"

"You had one on the flight when you drifted off," she explains in a monotone. "You were tossing and turning, mumbling things. At one point, I heard you say, *'My baby.'* You even grabbed your stomach."

Heat floods my face, but there's no point denying it. Every part is true. "This was the first one in a while."

She nods, and for a moment, it looks like she's biting her tongue. Which is weird, because Geneva is not one for holding back when she has something to say.

She takes a deep breath. "You never really talk about The Accident. The few details I know, I heard from Adrian."

I flinch involuntarily. I wish my reactions weren't such a dead giveaway, but they're entirely out of my control. "I just don't like talking about it."

"That's not exactly healthy."

"Yeah, well, I've made it this far."

Geneva looks at me with pursed lips and a pinched expression. I don't know why, but I get the feeling that she's not telling me something.

"Genny," I say softly. "What is it?"

She meets my eyes for a moment, and I can see the uncertainty there. Simmering like boiling water. "I-I should have been around more during that time," she says. Her voice gets so quiet I can barely hear her. "I should have been there for you."

I shake my head. I wouldn't be ready for this conversation on my best day, and today is most certainly not that. "You had a life to live."

"But you were my sister. And not only did you lose your career, you lost your baby, too."

I freeze, feeling goosebumps pimple my skin, flushing my body with reminders that I don't want. Everything feels a little too close to home, especially now, with the new life growing inside of me. It's like the first green thing poking its head above ground after a wildfire. Like fragile hope.

"Genny..."

"Adrian told me that you refused to talk about the miscarriage after it happened."

I frown. "I didn't realize you were talking to him so much."

She shrugs. "It wasn't 'so much.' Just a couple of calls every month or so after the crash. Mostly because you refused to come to the phone, remember?"

"Yeah," I whisper quietly. "I remember."

The clock ticks in the corner. Every passing second feels like a little needle pricking against my cheek.

"Adrian told me you wanted to press charges."

"I did," I say softly. "At the time, I thought it was the closure I needed to move on. But the thing about a hit-and-run is that there is no closure."

When I first started having nightmares about The Accident, I heard the screeching tires of the vehicle as it hit us. Then those same screeching tires as it drove away. I'd wake up with sweat on my brow and the stench of burnt rubber in my nose.

And I'd curse the invisible person who changed everything.

I only stopped with the curses when I realized they were hurting me far more than they were hurting the person I was cursing. It takes a whole lot of energy to be angry.

So one day, I just decided to stop. Life is tiring enough without clinging to anger.

It took a while to really believe that, though.

Geneva places her hand over mine. "I haven't been a very good sister to you, have I?"

I sigh deeply. "We haven't always been good sisters to each other," I correct. "But we can change that now."

Geneva smiles. "Yes, we can. And this time, I'm not going to leave you, June. I'm not going to abandon you when you need me the most. I'm here. I'm not going anywhere. But…"

I frown. "Genny—"

But she steamrolls over me. "It's no coincidence that you've started having these nightmares now, June," Geneva insists. "This is your conscience trying to warn you. Kolya is trouble. He's dangerous. He's going to end up hurting you."

I can't blame her for thinking that, but I'm hoping I can make her understand. "He's—"

"We watched him murder a man today!" she insists. "In front of a room full of people." She cups her ear and leans toward the windowpane, as melodramatic as ever. "But I don't hear any police sirens coming this way, do you?"

"I know it looks bad, Genny—"

She rears back in disbelief. "You can't possibly be taking up arms for this guy, June."

I pinch the bridge of my nose. My head is suddenly pounding, as if someone is whaling on the inside of my skull with a jackhammer. "You don't know everything that's going on. I mean, I don't, either, but you don't know—There's… there's this guy. Another guy. Like Kolya, but he's—"

Fuck, I'm screwing this up so badly. It's absolutely essential that I make Geneva understand, for both our sakes, but the pieces just won't lie in their places for me to show her how it all looks from a distance.

I take a deep breath and try again. "The man who was hosting this party, who hired you to host—his name is Ravil Uvarov. He might be going by a different name, I'm not sure.

But that's not the point. The point is, he's Kolya's cousin. They were both a part of the same Bratva, before Ravil decided to break off and start his own."

Geneva looks eerily calm as I explain all this to her. Not even the part about the Bratva seems to elicit much of a reaction.

"The fact that I'm pregnant complicates things. Ravil doesn't want Kolya to have a direct heir to the Bratva crown. The man that Kolya killed tonight, he was trying to hurt me. He would have, if Kolya hadn't… done what he did."

Geneva doesn't say a word for several seconds after I finish talking. "Genny?"

She blinks once and her eyes focus on me. Sharper and less puzzled than I ever would've expected. And when her voice comes out, it sounds like Milana's.

Icy. Cold. Detached.

"That's not the story Ravil told me."

35

JUNE

"I'm sorry—what?"

Geneva adjusts her position and takes a breath. "Ravil met with me when I landed in Mexico," she says. "He wanted to tell me the real story."

"But I just told you the real story."

"Honey, you've been brainwashed," she says in a tone that's sickly sweet and condescending. "The big brute out there has gotten into your head. Made you think he's the knight in shining armor and you're the damsel in distress. Ravil told me the truth. The *real* truth."

"I haven't been—"

"Kolya killed his own father, did you know that?"

I swallow my words. I'm chewing on the inside of my cheek hard enough to draw blood. Even before I say anything, I know how it's going to go. There's no way to say *Yes, I knew that* without confirming her belief that I've been taken in by a handsome face and a few smooth lies. "Listen, Geneva, you don't know the circumstances."

It strikes me the second I say it that I don't know the circumstances, either. I just assumed, as with every other decision he's made in the last few days, that Kolya had a good reason for doing what he did.

Not that it started out that way. When I first arrived in this house, I'd been dead-set on escaping. Somewhere along the way, though, I'd just accepted my fate. Got comfortable. Hell, I literally slept with the man who abducted me.

I feel a disengaging coldness spread through my body. Like real life is peeling off of me, leaving me behind. Is it possible that Geneva is right and I have been brainwashed? Am I a sucker?

My heartbeat starts to feel a little uneven.

"Hey," Geneva says, grabbing my hand. "I can help you, June."

I try to breathe through the panic. *Think, June, think.* Why did I start feeling safe with Kolya in the first place? There were definitely reasons. There were. There had to be. So why can't I think of any of them right now?

"June. Look at me."

I focus on Geneva. She looks completely in command of herself. A far cry from the hysterical woman that Kolya and Milana forced into the back of his car in Mexico.

"Ravil was worried about you. That's why he sought me out. He wanted to make sure he could trust me before he told me any further details. That's why he hired me."

"Geneva, I've met Ravil. I've spoken to Ravil. And so I really, really need you to believe me when I say this: he can't be trusted. He was trying to win you over. To get inside your head so that you could get inside mine."

She sighs heavily, like she was expecting exactly that response. "You may be carrying Kolya's baby, but don't let that be your life sentence."

I'm on the verge of telling her that the baby's not actually Kolya's, but I stop myself at the last moment. This all just feels so *wrong*. Those aren't my sister's words coming out of her mouth. They're the words of a yellow-toothed smirker who laid his hand on me in Kolya's blue room in a way I'm still feeling all this time later.

I brush my hair behind my ears and try to compose myself, though it feels mostly like a failing effort. "It means a lot that you're here, Genny. It means a lot that you want to be there for me. But I trust Kolya. Ravil is not who you think he is."

"Maybe not. But neither is Kolya."

I look at her and she looks at me, and for a moment, it feels like we are what we've always been: two people who will never agree. Eye-to-eye in person, yeah, but never eye-to-eye on anything that matters.

Then, to my surprise, Geneva sighs. She reaches out to pat my hand where it's lying lifelessly in my lap.

"Are you okay, Juju?" she asks. I look down at her fingers stroking my knuckles. A few beads from my dress are missing. Lost in the rush out of Mexico, I assume. It makes me unreasonably sad. Things this pretty shouldn't be ruined by events this ugly.

I nod. "I think so. Tonight was… a lot."

"The baby…?"

"Is fine, I think," I say, placing my palm over my belly. "I don't feel like anything's wrong."

"Good," Geneva says with relief. She squeezes my hand again. "This baby's going to be fine, hon. You're not going to lose this one."

I give her a shaky smile. "I'm still scared. But I'll be fine once I see Sara. Once she confirms that—"

"Can you trust this doctor?" Geneva asks abruptly. That snaky gleam is back in her eyes. "I mean, Kolya is the one who hired her, right?"

I breathe through my panic. I'm not sure how the instinct to defend Kolya got so strong, but it feels like a betrayal to sit here and listen to Geneva accuse him of things that I don't believe he's guilty of.

You're a little naive on that front, though, aren't ya, sweetheart?

I cringe at Adrian's voice. *You're a little biased.*

And you're a little fickle. I haven't even been dead that long. Barely cold and you're already moving on.

I jerk upright and pace away from Geneva. My head is pounding with unease. I'm too confused to think straight.

"Honey, you should lie down," she suggests.

"I don't want to," I say, trying to breathe through the weight in my chest. "I-I need to get out of this dress."

I unzip myself on the way to the bathroom and shut the door before Geneva can follow me in here. I turn the shower on, but after I strip off the dress, I stand in front of the sink and stare at my reflection in the mirror.

It's subtle, but there's a new curve in my belly that wasn't there before. Like the beads on my dress, that makes me sad, too.

Because I've been down this road before. I carried my last baby for almost five months. We knew what we were going to have—a baby boy. He had fingers and toes and hair and a smile. I felt him quickening inside of me. *Life.* Vibrant and hopeful.

I close my eyes and the tears spill free.

Adrian was holding my hand tightly as the doctor told us the sex. When he walked out to give us a moment of privacy, Adrian had kissed my forehead and tap-danced his hand over my exposed belly, still slick with the petroleum jelly from the scan.

"You're going to be a great mother, June Cole."

"How do you know?" I asked, more fearful than I expected to be.

He shrugged as though it were the most obvious answer in the world. "You take care of me."

I open my eyes and focus on my reflection in the mirror once more. My eyes are drawn and gray with weariness. There's no other indication of what I've been through in the last day, the last month, the last year. Kolya wiped away all traces of blood.

Maybe that's another reason I decided to trust him.

He's the first person who's ever shown any interest in taking care of me.

36

KOLYA

"I don't trust the sister," Milana says, blowing out a plume of smoke.

I grimace. "I don't, either. But we couldn't just leave her there."

"Why not?" Milana demands. "Now, she's our problem, not Ravil's."

"She's still June's sister."

Milana raises her eyebrows and puts down her spent cigar. "Hm."

I roll my eyes. "I hate when you do that."

"Do what?" she asks innocently.

"When you 'Hm' at me instead of just saying what you're thinking."

"Ooh, testy tonight, are we?"

"With good reason. I shouldn't have killed that motherfucker. He deserved it, but I should have held back," I growl, reaching for the half-empty glass of whiskey in front of me.

I don't even want a drink. I just want something that burns going down.

"You should have," she agrees. "But you were hopped up on testosterone. *Tarzan protects Jane, ooh-ooh ah-ah.* That kind of thing."

I drop the whiskey glass down on the table in disgust, ignoring how it sloshes over the rim and onto my hand. "She's not my woman."

Milana eyes me with a knowing smile, then shrugs. "Coulda fooled me."

"This is about the child. The pregnancy. That's all."

Milana shifts in her seat, cocking her legs in the opposite direction. She doesn't say anything, but I can practically feel her thoughts like a hailstorm, peppering me one after the next.

"You really think this baby is the answer?" she asks at last. The room feels stuffy and silent.

"Since I'm not planning on having children and my brother is dead—yes, I think this baby is the answer."

She eyes me warily. Then her hand flickers towards her stomach like she's cradling something. I follow the movement before bringing my gaze up to meet her own.

"I never thought I'd want children of my own," she admits. "When that bastard had me sterilized, I was honestly relieved. Because it meant I would never bear a child that was a product of all that fear and hatred and ugliness. My children would never suffer because they'd simply never be born. A blessing in disguise."

Her fingers twitch slightly, as though she's trying to reach for something that's no longer here. In the end, she just brushes a hand over her face, like she's trying to brush the sadness from it.

It took her years to drop her mask with me. The mask she wears around men.

"But then again, what did I know?" she asks, meeting my eyes. I've never truly seen Milana cry. The closest I've come to seeing her that vulnerable is in moments like these, when her eyes get glossy. There's the promise of tears, but I know I'll never see them. She'd die before she let them fall.

"I was fourteen years old when he did it to me," she whispers. "Fourteen years old. It wasn't until recently that I started feeling a… a stirring."

She gives me a self-conscious little laugh. I'm not sure which of us it's meant to fool.

"Sometimes," she says with a forced smirk, straightening herself up, "I forget I'm still a woman."

I decide to let her get away with the faked nonchalance. "No one could ever forget that you're a woman, Milana."

She smiles tenderly. "You realize that the only time you ever flirt with me is when you're trying to make me feel better?"

I run my fingertip around the damp edge of my whiskey glass. A high keening sound wails out into the room, ethereal and unsettling. After a while, I stop and fix her with my gaze again. "If you've had enough of this life… I wouldn't hold it against you, Milana. You know that, right?"

She nods. "I know. But this is the only life I know."

"Then we'll figure something out. Everything can be fixed one way or another."

"You don't have to keep compensating for what happened to me, Kolya," she tells me softly. "It wasn't your decision. Or your legacy."

"I carry the shadow of that legacy with me still," I tell her. "I am the don of the Uvarov Bratva, whether some men are willing to accept that or not."

"You don't need those men."

I scoff. "I don't have the numbers, Milana. Ravil—"

"Fuck Ravil," she hisses. "The man is like Adrian, only with power. The two of them are cut from the same cloth. Manipulative cowards who rode on the coattails of their betters."

The impulse to defend my brother is muted, almost nonexistent. I'm not in the mood to be generous to his memory tonight. Which is not a feeling I'm accustomed to experiencing.

Maybe that has something to do with the woman he left behind.

I've always stood up for the little shit, even when he didn't deserve it. That was my responsibility as his older brother. That was his right as the younger sibling. We would always be bonded by our shared childhood, by the demons we faced together and the nightmares we tried and failed to outrun.

He used to slip into my bed at night when he was a boy. Until our father found out and placed our bedrooms in separate wings of the house, with a guard outside our doors to keep us apart.

"You are not helping him by protecting him, Kolya," my father had snarled at me after a night in the cellar with the rats to make me more amenable to his lessons. "You are ensuring his failure."

Was my father right? Is that why Adrian hadn't been able to resist the allure of the bottle? Is that why he'd become a selfish, short-sighted flight risk, the kind of man who left scars on his woman's throat and tears in her eyes? Had I turned him into a coward by standing in between him and everything he was frightened of?

Is all of this my fault?

"It's not, you know," Milana says softly, breaking into my thoughts. "You didn't do this. You're not to blame for Adrian's mistakes. He was a grown man."

He may have been, but I take my promises seriously. And I'd made him one a long time ago. When he was still climbing into my bed at night, trembling head to toe from terrors only he could see.

"I'm scared," he used to tell me. I was the only one he ever admitted that to.

"Sometimes," I'd whisper back under cover of darkness, *"I'm scared, too."*

"Really?" he asked with wild, shocked eyes.

I nodded. *"Everyone feels scared sometimes."*

"Not Otets. He's not human."

It certainly felt that way when we were growing up. The first time I saw him bleed was a revelatory moment. I had no idea our father could bleed at all.

"He is human," I assured Adrian. *"And one day, you're going to be bigger than him."*

He had laughed at that and curled his hand around my arm. *"Will I be stronger than him, too?"*

"Ten times stronger."

"Maybe then he'll stop hurting me," Adrian ventured.

"I will stop him from hurting you," I said firmly. I was nine years old. I had no right to make that kind of promise, but I was young enough to believe that one day I would be taller and stronger than our father. And that I would be brave enough to enforce my view of how the world should be.

It wasn't that I was wrong to believe it; I just underestimated how much strength it would take.

I underestimated how much it would cost me.

"You promise?"

"I promise, sobrat. *I swear it."*

I raise my eyes and find Milana observing me curiously. "Where did you go?"

"Back to the past."

"Any part of your past in particular?"

I know where she's going, and I don't want to hear it. Which is exactly why I get up and walk to the bar, even though I still haven't finished my whiskey.

"Kolya."

I ignore her and cross the room to the dark mahogany bar with the carved wooden paneling on top to store wine glasses and the like.

I changed a lot about this house once it passed over to my control. I'd actively removed all signs of my father's taste. He'd preferred his bars sleek and modern. Marble counters rather than wood. Bottles hidden away rather than displayed for everyone to see.

I ripped them all out and crushed each one to rubble.

"You need to tell her, Kolya," Milana says abruptly.

"I don't need to tell her anything," I snap, keeping my back to her as I rest my forehead against the cool wooden wall.

"You're going to need her cooperation going forward," Milana warns, ever the pragmatist. "If she finds out later—"

"She'll just have to deal with it."

"The Accident—"

"Enough."

I never raise my voice, but the change of tone is all I need to get my point across. She falls silent, but I hear the click-clack of her heels as she walks over to me.

"Kolya," she says when she's close, "why did you pick me as your right hand?"

I turn to her slowly. "You fishing for compliments?"

She smiles. "Just answer the question."

"Because you didn't shut up even when I told you to."

She grins sadly at me. "Exactly. I've never been a yes woman. You can count on me for the truth even when you don't want to hear it. But I'm not talking to you now as your right-hand woman. I'm talking to you now as a woman, period. If June finds out the truth later, it will hurt her, and it will undermine all the progress you've made. You can't expect her trust if you don't give her yours."

"My trust was never on the table."

Milana rolls her eyes. "Don't give me that. You may not want to admit it, but you like her."

"She's my brother's woman."

"She was," Milana agrees. "But as far as Ravil and his men are concerned, she's your woman now. That's all that matters. And that is precisely what's going to force him to show his hand."

I narrow my eyes at her. "You have a plan?"

"I do," she says with a half-hearted smirk. "But, fair warning—you're not going to like it."

37

JUNE

I stop short when I walk into the medical room a few days after we get back from Mexico.

Milana is in there already. She's leaning forward, resting her face in both her hands. I can tell from her lack of reaction that she hasn't even noticed that I've just walked in.

Which in and of itself strikes me as weird. Milana notices everything.

I can smell the faint pervasiveness of surgical disinfectant—and beneath it, the thin veneer of desperation. Or maybe it's sadness.

Or maybe I might be reading a little too much into things.

Milana's shoes are thrown to the side of the chair and her legs dangle in the air, like a bored six-year-old. The dress she's wearing is loose-fitting today, and it doesn't quite suit her.

"Milana?"

She snaps upright, her expression fraught and complicated before she wipes it clean. "June, hello. I didn't realize you had an appointment with Sara today."

"Oh, I didn't," I say, realizing that I've walked in at the worst possible time. "I just wanted to refill my vitamins. I figured I'd come here and do it myself."

Her usual aura of composure is fragile at best. She looks tired. As I move closer, I realize she's wearing only a little lipstick and not much else. Again, very much out of character.

"I'm sorry, I'll leave," I say. "Just... are you okay?"

She meets my eyes and pushes herself off the chair. "Do I look okay?"

The question isn't as antagonistic as it seems on the face of it. It's more like she's genuinely curious. "Well, you don't look like you normally do."

Milana laughs suddenly, and the sound makes me jump. "No, I suppose not. I don't feel like I normally do, either."

"Should I get Sara?"

"She'll be out soon. She's probably trying to figure out how to break it to me," Milana says.

I frown in confusion. "B-break it to you? Break what?"

"That there's no hope for me. I can't have my own children. I will never have my own children. That he took that away from me."

There's a wildness in her eyes that terrifies me. But in the next instant, they fall flat and lose their spark.

In its own way, that's just as scary.

"I'm sorry," she says. "I didn't mean to freak you out."

"No, no, you didn't. Of course you didn't."

She shakes her head and wraps her arms around her body like she's cold, though the room is comfortably warm. "It was stupid of me to hold out hope. He was not the kind of man who did anything halfway."

"Who are you talking about?"

"The fucker who bought me from my mother at twelve," she whispers in a hard, haunted voice. "The bastard who gave me a hysterectomy at fourteen. The fucking pimp who sold me from one man to another to another."

I'm dumbstruck. Some words just aren't meant to go together. Some things are too horrible to be real.

But the look in her eyes says it's real. It's all very, very real.

Before I can come up with an appropriate response, Sara walks out of a room in the back. She stops short when she sees me standing there. "June?"

"Sorry," I fumble. "I came to refill my vitamins."

Sara glances towards Milana and then back to me. "Would you mind waiting outside for—"

"No," Milana cuts in. "It doesn't matter if she hears. It doesn't matter who hears. Just tell me what I already know."

Sara's eyebrows flatten, and I feel my heart drop for Milana. "I'm sorry, Milana. He did a thorough job."

Despite the fact that she already suspected the answer she'd get, I watch as her face crumbles. Her body follows suit.

I move forward at the same time Sara does. We attach ourselves to her sides and hold her upright. Her neck drops and I hear one heart-rending, guttural sob escape her lips.

It feels like it's being pulled out rather than let out.

"It's okay, Milana," I tell her, stroking her hair, because I remember how soothing it was when the nurse did that to me right after The Accident that cost me my first baby. "It's okay. Let it out. Just cry."

She shakes her head for several seconds before she speaks. "No," she gasps, and it sounds like every word she utters is taking a toll on her body. "If I let myself cry... I'll never stop."

38

JUNE

When I walk back into my bedroom, I find Kolya sitting by the window waiting for me. This is the second time in an hour that I've walked into a room expecting to see one person and getting another.

I just hope that whatever is coming isn't going to be as draining as what just passed.

"Where's Geneva?" I ask.

He doesn't look at me when he answers. "I banished her to her room for the next few hours."

I raise my eyebrows. "And she went, just like that? Didn't realize you have actual magical powers."

I expect a smile, but his face never cracks. He just gestures for me to come forward and sit down, which instantly puts me on high alert.

"What's going on?" I ask tentatively as I inch towards the window seat.

He still won't look in my direction. "Sit down."

"I don't want to sit."

He sighs and finally drags his eyes over. "I'm not in the mood to argue, June."

I shiver under his gaze, but I stand my ground. "You're the one sitting here in my room," I remind him. "I've had a really tough afternoon and I'm not in the mood for games, Kolya."

He glares at me for a moment. "I need to send a message to my cousin."

I try very hard to keep my expression from giving anything away. I've decided not to tell Kolya about Ravil's conversation with Geneva. It's immaterial, since Geneva isn't working for him anymore. If she ever even was to begin with.

"Which involves me how…?"

"It involves you because… we're going to have to have a wedding."

I stare at him, waiting for him to deliver the punchline. There has to be a punchline, right? Because I'm pretty sure he mentioned a wedding. In no sane world does that not function as the beginning to a joke.

"Um… I'm sorry, I don't—"

"As far as my cousin and his men are concerned," he interrupts emotionlessly, "you are pregnant with my child. At the moment, you're just a woman I knocked up. But getting married—it lends legitimacy to our relationship. And to the child you're carrying."

He's speaking way too fast. His tone is throwing me, too. It's cold, apathetic. Almost robotic.

"Is this your idea of a romantic proposal?" I say with a nervous laugh.

He blinks placidly. "This isn't a joke, June."

My mouth snaps shut. Along with my sense of humor. "It has to be a joke, Kolya. Because it sounds like you're saying that you want me to marry you."

"The wedding would be fake."

"Oh, okay. Then that makes all the difference," I retort sarcastically. "This is insane!"

"No more so than the last several weeks," he points out.

"As true as that is, I'm still not marrying you."

"I wasn't really asking."

He stands up and heads for the door as though that's the end of the conversation. "Kolya!" He doesn't stop walking until he's at the threshold. Even then, he throws me a glance like it's an afterthought. "What does a fake wedding entail exactly? What's the point? What's it going to do?"

He sighs wearily. "It's going to force my cousin to make his move."

"What does that mean? What move?"

"Your guess is as good as mine."

39

JUNE

I pace back and forth until the news has sunk in. Then I head over to my sister's room. I recognize the guard standing outside her door.

"I want to speak to my sister. Let me in."

To my surprise, he shrugs and steps aside. "Genny?" I call out the moment the door shuts behind me.

She bursts out from the bathroom almost instantly. "June! What did the beast want?"

"Well…"

Her face falls. "Oh no. It's bad, isn't it?"

"It's… um… not bad, per se."

Geneva crosses her arms over her chest. "Spill, Junepenny."

I shoot her a disgruntled glare. Sometimes, it feels like she's purposefully trying to remind me of Adrian. It's not like I need the reminder. I'm carrying around the reminder inside of me.

"He thinks we… that we should get married."

"What?!" she screeches.

"Will you shush?" I hiss, glancing back towards the door. I grab her arm and pull her deeper into the room.

"H-he proposed to you?"

The way she says it snaps me out of the fog I'm in. Of course she thinks Kolya proposed to me. She believes that I'm carrying his baby. She believes that I'm with him.

Because that's what I told her.

I lied to my sister. And right now, I can't really remember why. Is it as simple and as pathetic as "Kolya told me to"?

I feel my heart shudder as I wonder where to go from here. Come clean or keep the charade alive? Geneva's eyes are zinging with fire, and it's making me nervous.

"Yes," I say, because making a decision right now is just too hard. "He did."

She grabs my hand and stares down at my empty left fingers. "Without a ring?"

I bite my bottom lip. "He had a ring; it just didn't fit. He's going to get it resized."

"That's a metaphor if I've ever heard one." She lets go of my hand, but only to lock onto my upper arm and drag me even closer. "This is exactly why we need Ravil, June! He can save us from this. You don't want to go down this road. I know you don't."

She's wrong about so many things. She's wrong that we need Ravil. She's wrong that Ravil could ever stop Kolya from doing exactly what he wants.

But most of all, she's wrong about the very last thing she said.

I *do* want to go down this road with Kolya. I want everything he's sworn he'll never be able to give me for real.

That's the scariest part of all.

40
———

JUNE

I pinch my nose to keep the sneeze from blowing through the entire room. But everywhere I turn, there's another huge arrangement of flowers.

I manage to avoid sneezing on the roses and carnations, only to spray a display of purple orchids that just happened to be my favorite.

"Oh my God, I'm so sorry!"

The florist just shoots me a polite smile. "Not to worry, dear." I'm fairly certain her tolerance is a direct result of the fat check Kolya is cutting her and her colleagues for this pre-wedding presentation.

Of course, I'm just guessing here. I haven't seen Kolya in almost three days. Not since he dropped the bomb on me and then casually strolled out of my room.

A gentleman would have given me some time to process the information and let it sink in. But Kolya proceeded to inundate me with wedding decisions that needed to be made post haste... because the wedding would be taking place in three weeks.

Three. Weeks. Three freaking weeks!

In that time, I have to decide between a dozen different venues and half a dozen different prix fixe menus. I have to pick between a harpist and a string quartet, I have to choose place settings, themes, lighting.

And of course, flowers.

Which brings us back to the sneezing.

This might be a fake wedding, but it sure as hell feels real.

"June? Have you made a decision yet?"

I turn to Anette, our wedding planner. For as much as I've seen her versus Kolya in the last three days, you'd think she was the one I'm marrying.

"The orchids," I say, eyeing the purple bouquet with regret. "They might have to be sanitized, though."

She nods briskly and marks her clipboard. I don't think I've ever seen her without it in hand. I'm genuinely concerned her skin is fusing to it.

"Perfect," she says. "Great choice."

Not that I can take her word as gospel. She's given me seventeen "good choices" so far. I stopped believing her somewhere around number six.

"We should really get going," she says. "Cake tasting in an hour, and crosstown traffic can be such a nightmare."

"That's today?" I'm desperate to get off my feet, although the idea of cake makes my stomach growl with hunger. I haven't eaten since this morning, and even then, I only managed two pieces of dry toast. My appetite hasn't been what it was, ever since Kolya's visit.

"Yes," replies Anette. "There's a car waiting out front for you. Text me your decision once the tasting is over, and I'll organize everything with the baker."

"Wait—you're not coming with me?"

"Not this time," she says, marching towards the door. "I'll see you tomorrow, darling."

I sigh and slump forward. I'm exhausted in a way I didn't know it was possible to be. I feel like a conceited bitch for being worn out by discussions of tulle versus silk, but there's no mistaking the bone-deep weariness that's dragging me down to the earth.

But when I feel eyes burning a hole in the side of my head, I jump and yelp with a sudden shot of adrenaline.

"Dammit, Milana!"

I should've known it was her. Neither Geneva nor Anette could ever be so eerily silent.

The smile she gives me is tentative at first, but it grows more sincere as she walks over. "Wedding planning has been keeping you busy, huh?"

I take a deep breath. "I still can't believe this is happening. Have you seen my sister, by any chance?"

"She's already in the car."

"For the cake tasting I forgot was happening today," I say bitterly.

"I know it's a lot."

She looks like her old self again. She's wearing black pants, a gorgeous cashmere blouse, and four-inch heels. Her makeup is impeccable and her composure is bulletproof.

"Yeah," I grumble. Then I pull myself together. "But I'm not gonna complain about it. How are you?"

"Fine," she says breezily, as though she doesn't know why I'd even bother asking. "You should get going. I think they're waiting for you."

"They?"

She gives me a wink. "We'll catch up later," she says, in an offhand way that makes me realize she has no intention of talking about what happened in the medical wing the other day.

I understand where she's coming from. I've been guilty of the same thing, as Geneva pointed out to me not so long ago. I give Milana a wave goodbye and head outside.

But instead of the single car I'm expecting, there are two. One is a conservative sedan, as inconspicuous as possible. The second, parked right in front, is a massive black Mercedes. Not inconspicuous in the least.

The door to the Mercedes opens from the inside, and a tide of vanilla rushes over me.

"Kolya."

"Come on," he says from within the darkness of the car. "We don't have all day."

I cross my hands over my chest and stay put. "You're coming with me for the cake tasting?"

"So it would seem."

I roll my eyes. "Of course you'd choose to come for the errand that involves dessert. Where were you when I was picking out place settings?"

He chuckles. "Your sister's going to get impatient if we don't get going soon."

I lean in and take a quick look around the Mercedes's spacious insides. "Where is my sister?"

"In the car behind us."

I frown. "Why?"

"Because I didn't feel like driving with her."

"Kolya!"

His smirk just gets deeper. "I'm letting her come. But my magnanimity only extends so far."

I should be pissed at him. I should make this harder for him. I should slam the door in his face and walk over to the sedan so I can ride to the bakery with my sister.

Instead, I find myself getting into the Mercedes.

"Lemon soda?" he asks, offering me a cold bottle from the mini fridge underneath his seat as the driver pulls away from the curb.

"No," I tell him sharply, even though I really could use a lemon soda right about now. "Where the hell have you been?"

"Planning. Strategizing. Organizing."

"You told me this was a fake wedding."

"And so it is."

"Then why does it feel so real?"

"Because that's the only way I'm going to be able to convince Ravil that it *is* real," Kolya says. He pulls out a little black box from his pocket and hands it to me unceremoniously. "Speaking of making things look real, here."

My eyes glide from the box in his hand to his face. It's completely expressionless.

"Aren't you supposed to be on one knee for this part?" I ask, mostly teasing, but slightly distracted by the way my heart seems to be thumping a little harder and a little faster in my chest.

He rolls his eyes and opens the box himself to reveal a marquise diamond ring sitting on a plush pink cushion. I practically have to shield my eyes so as not to be blinded.

"That's no fake ring…"

He surprises me by putting the box down and taking my hand. Then he slides the ring onto my finger without permission. He looks down at it for a moment.

"It's a perfect fit," he declares, his gaze rising to meet mine.

Then he drops my hand without warning. It lands on my lap with an unflattering thwack

"Do you like it?"

I glance at him, cheeks burning. "Does it matter?"

"If we have to do this, I'd rather you have things that you genuinely like," he says in a matter of fact tone. "So if you don't like the ring, I can—"

"I like it," I mumble.

He nods. "Good."

It's hard not to look at the damn thing. No matter how hard I try, my eyes go straight to it. I'd always expected to wear a ring one day; I'd just never expected Adrian's brother to be the man to give it to me.

"What's wrong?" Kolya asks.

I shake my head. "It's just... weird. I'm not much of a jewelry person."

"You don't have to wear it all the time. Just when you're out in public."

I spin the band around my finger. It really is a perfect fit. "Adrian was the ring person in our relationship," I blurt out. "Never took the stupid thing off."

Unconsciously, I lift my hand up and touch my cheek. He left a mark with that cursed thing the night he died.

Kolya doesn't offer up an opinion. He just sits there, gazing out the window. "I never asked what the insignia meant," I realize aloud. "Two swords clashing against one another. I just thought it was pretty."

It was a heavy ring. Heavy enough to cut. Heavy enough to scar. Heavy enough to last.

"We're here," Kolya says abruptly, as the Mercedes comes to a stop in front of a gorgeous little cake shop with wooden framed bifold glass doors and potted greenery as far as the eye can see.

Kolya strides past the wicker chairs, beneath the yellow pinstriped awning, and breezes indoors. I wait by the Mercedes until the sedan's door opens and Geneva flies out looking positively murderous.

"That bastard locked the car so I couldn't get out or even roll down the windows!" she snaps. "You couldn't even see me waving at you because of the damn tint."

I just barely manage to suppress the snort in my throat. "I'm sorry. But if you were a little less antagonistic towards him—"

"It takes two to tango!"

"I'll talk to him."

"It's cute that you think you have any clout with a stubborn ass like that."

That stings a little more than it should, but I pretend as though I don't care. I hook my hand through Geneva's arm and pull her into the cakery.

"Whoa…"

"What?" I ask, looking at Geneva with concern. "What's wrong?"

But she's not looking around us. She's looking at *me*. "Is that a diamond?" she gasps, gawking down at my finger. "Or a boulder?"

I give her a self-conscious smile. "It's a little big."

Geneva clicks her tongue against her teeth. "He's got taste, I'll give him that. And it's no less than you deserve."

"I must be having a stroke, because I'm pretty sure that was a genuine compliment." I grin and blush at the same time. "But really, thank you, Gen. Now, come on—I smell chocolate."

The entire front-facing wall is counter space that displays a smorgasbord of cakes, pastries, and sweet treats. My nose is drowning in caramel, butter, cocoa, and every other sweet note known to man.

"Cake, Genny," I say, gesturing towards the display case. "How can you be anything but happy when there's cake around?"

"Because I don't share your insane sweet tooth," she says with a roll of her eyes. "Now, if you'll excuse me, I need to use the restroom. Or do I need your fiancé's permission for that?"

I roll my eyes back at her and wave her away. "Happy peeing."

I notice Kolya in conversation with someone I can't see behind the open doors of a separate room of the café. The doors are painted with a pattern of daisies and peonies. Beyond them are three narrow tables, each of them groaning under the weight of half a dozen different cake samples.

The woman speaking to Kolya turns to me with bright eyes and an enthusiastic expression. "And this must be the future Mrs. Uvarov!" she greets, extending her hand for me to shake. "I'm Elinor Martin. It's a pleasure."

"The pleasure's all mine. This is an amazing place you've got here."

"It's a family business," she says proudly. "I'm the third generation to take over. Please, Mrs. Uvarov, take a seat."

Have I morphed into Mrs. Uvarov already? It feels strange, but I don't correct her. Instead, I take the seat she's offering me beside Kolya.

"We've got a wide selection of savory pastries for you to whet your appetite," Elinor tells me. "You'll need some palette cleansers to break up all the sweetness. Can I offer you tea or coffee?"

"Tea would be wonderful, please."

She bows her way out of the room, leaving Kolya and me alone, surrounded by cake, flowery wallpaper, and more of the flourishing green house plants. "This is... crazy," I say, looking around the room in awe.

"If it's not to your taste—"

"It's perfectly to my taste."

He nods, satisfied with my answer. I watch him carefully, refusing to drop my gaze, even when he matches it. "Something the matter?" he asks in his careless, aloof way.

"I was just thinking that for someone who claims not to care about me, you sure do seem to care about whether or not I like things."

"I never said I didn't care about you," he says gruffly, almost defensively.

I raise my eyebrows. It might be the nicest thing he's ever told me. I glance towards the open swing doors that lead to the main café, but there's no sign of Geneva, and I have to admit, I'm relieved.

It's not a generous thought, but I can't help wishing that she had stayed back for this outing.

I can't help but wish that, for just this evening, for just this moment... it could be just Kolya and me.

41

KOLYA

I've been avoiding her for the last three days for this very reason.

She could come to do this alone, or with Anette and her annoying older sister. But I had to give her the ring, right? That's all I came for. Beginning and end of it.

It has nothing to do with the fact that I wanted to see her, wanted to spend some time with her. It has nothing to do with the fact that I missed her.

Those things, to the extent that they're even true, are irrelevant. We should be keeping our distance.

It just becomes hard to remember that when you're trying to figure out which diamond will flatter her eyes the most.

She starts to say, "Kolya, you—"

"Here they are!"

June's jaw drops as she takes in the older couple standing behind Geneva. She gasps, "What are you guys doing here?"

I wince and close my eyes.

June's parents.

Fucking fantastic.

I have no doubt I can thank the sister for this little surprise. Sure enough, the little she-devil makes eye contact with me and waggles her eyebrows. "Hope you don't mind," she says cheerfully. "I thought I'd make this a party."

"Y-you invited Mom and Dad," June observes. She's trying hard to keep her bearings as she rises to her feet to give both her parents a stiff hug.

"Surely you're not disappointed to see us," June's mother remarks, though her eyes are locked on me.

"Of course not," June replies. Her voice is a little too high-pitched to be convincing.

I get to my feet. "Mr. and Mrs. Cole, it's a pleasure to meet you."

Both of them look me up and down with scrutiny. "I must say, our pleasure at meeting you is somewhat sullied by our shock," the old man says with a weird, brittle kind of formality. At my side, June has shrunk back into her seat like she wants to wink out of existence.

I notice the glare she throws her sister, but Geneva is too busy watching the show like it's a matinee.

The man sniffles. "We didn't realize that June was even dating again."

"I must say, June," Mrs. Cole says, flinging her ice-cold stare in June's direction, "it was somewhat of a shock to hear that you were engaged to another man so soon after Adrian's death."

June flinches when she mentions Adrian, but Mrs. Cole either doesn't notice or doesn't care. She starts fumbling through an answer—"I—It was…"

"I helped June through Adrian's death," I say, stepping in smoothly. "And in the process, we fell in love."

I can feel the tension wafting off June, even from here. But I focus my attention on the Coles. If Geneva thought she could throw me with this surprise visit, she's got another thing coming.

"Your daughter is a wonderful and accomplished woman, and I knew I couldn't just let her walk out of my life. So I pursued her. In the end, I wore her down."

The Coles exchange a glance. "But to be *engaged*," Mrs. Cole protests in a murmur. "And so soon!"

I rest my hand on June's shoulder. "When you know, you know."

Mr. Cole's eyes land on my Rolex. "Then congratulations are in order," he says gruffly, pulling out a chair and sitting down. "Bridget, sit."

Geneva's eyes keep bouncing between us, but I never let the silence simmer for too long. Within a few minutes, I have more pastries and tea brought out for the couple, and I'm telling them all about my businesses, both foreign and domestic.

They seem like a discerning couple, but apparently, I pass muster because within the first half an hour, they're smiling and talking more freely.

Geneva's face stays locked in a permanent scowl. When I meet her gaze, I arch one eyebrow pointedly and she rolls her eyes in disgust.

"All these cakes are simply divine," Mrs. Cole says after an hour's worth of small talk and sampling. "You certainly have excellent taste, Kolya."

I incline my head and offer her another piece of cake. "That's a wonderful necklace you're wearing, Bridget."

"Why thank you. They're not real pearls, unfortunately."

"Well, we have to remedy that," I tell her. "My jeweler has an eye for fine pieces. I'd love to send you a little gift."

Her eyes go wide, and she's not the only one. The entire table looks gobsmacked. "Oh, goodness no! I couldn't let you—it's far too generous."

"Nonsense. Nothing is too good for my future mother-in-law," I tell her with my most charming smile. Then I turn it on Mr. Cole. "Pearls do go quite nicely with a new Rolex. The two of you will look smashing."

The old man hems and haws, but even as he does, he goes red with delight at the prospect. "It is quite refreshing to meet such a driven young man. So unlike all the other ruffians these two brought home."

"I never brought anyone home," Geneva snaps, sulking now that her plan has backfired. "But maybe I should have. Guess it was easier than I realized to impress the two of you. A few fancy gifts and you're pissing yourself with pride at your future son-in-law." Her words are pure rat poison.

Mr. Cole's smile drops instantly and Mrs. Cole turns to me in horror, before glaring at her daughter. "Geneva! Stop acting like a petulant child. Kolya, I am so sorry for my daughter's behavior."

"Geneva."

Everyone turns to June. This is the first time she's spoken in at least twenty minutes. Her eyes are fixed on her sister. The hazel in them burns dark like firewood.

Geneva exhales sharply. "Excuse me. I'm going to get some air."

She leaves the table. June glances at me regretfully, but before she can apologize, her mother beats her to it. "Kolya, I can't apologize enough. My daughters have never been very disciplined."

"I'm a dancer," June interrupts. "Discipline is built into the job."

"Are you still, though? I didn't realize you were dancing again," Mrs. Cole says in a tight voice.

"You know I can't."

"Oh, darling, dancing was always a pipe dream. It was never very realistic, now, was it?"

"How would you know?" June demands. "It's not like you or Dad ever came to one of my performances."

"June," Mrs. Cole says with a nervous glance in my direction, "there's no need to get worked up."

"Exactly," Mr. Cole jumps in. "In any case, we're very happy for you. You seem to have finally turned your life around."

"Oh yeah?" June fires back. "Tell me, how exactly have I 'turned my life around'?"

"Well, you've made a great choice in agreeing to marry this fine young man here," Mr. Cole says, shooting me a smile. I'm pretty sure I can see giant Rolex watches swimming in his eyes when he looks at me. "This will be the best contribution you can make to society."

June opens her mouth to answer, but nothing comes out. She's too flustered to defend herself right now.

So I decide to do it for her.

"Neither one of you preening fools knows your own daughter very well if you think that marrying me is the best contribution she can make to society," I snarl. "She's bright and beautiful. More importantly, she's kind and caring. She has a lot more to offer the world than to simply take on the mantel of wife and mother. I'm sure she'll excel at both roles, but that is most certainly not all she is or can be."

Mr. Cole is staring a hole in the floor between his feet.

Geneva, back and leaning in the door, applauds sarcastically. "Wow, what a speech."

But it's Mrs. Cole who catches my attention first. She doesn't look as put-off by my rebuke as I might've expected. Her eyebrows are furrowed in concentration.

Then she looks up at me. "D-did you say *'mother'*?" Mrs. Cole asks abruptly. "June… are you pregnant?"

Fuck me.

Geneva cackles behind me. "Oopsie! Looks like you've let the cat out of the bag now."

"Are you?" Mrs. Cole asks June, ignoring her eldest daughter.

June hesitates for only a moment. Then she inflates her chest as pridefully as she can. "Yes, I am."

"And when were you going to tell us?"

"I guess I hadn't really thought about it." June sighs. "This is not the way I wanted you guys to find out, and I'm sorry about that. But I am getting married, and I am having a baby. You guys have never been very enthusiastic about my life decisions. I didn't think this time would be any different."

"Well, that… that's—"

"Accurate," she says, sticking to her guns. "I just didn't want the judgment. Not this time. Not with this."

Mr. Cole lurches to his feet suddenly. "That's no way to talk to your parents," he scolds, though his face is burning with embarrassment. "I won't sit here and be criticized for your poor choices. Call us when you decide to behave like a proper daughter. Bridget, let's go."

Then the two of them storm off.

The silence doesn't last long, though. "I cannot believe you called Mom and Dad down here," June hisses, turning to Geneva.

She shrugs. "I thought it was important that they knew."

"That wasn't your call to make!"

Geneva shrugs again, but this one is a little more self-conscious. "I honestly didn't think you'd be this upset about it."

"No, you thought you'd pull them down here and create a whole awkward thing out of it. You were hoping to trip Kolya up, right? You didn't think about me at all!"

"I—that's not what—"

"Save it," June snaps. "Let's just go home."

She leaves Geneva standing there, frazzled. I follow her out, feeling strangely proud. The girl can look like a Bambi-eyed fawn sometimes, but she's got claws when she needs to.

We get into the Mercedes, and I immediately pull up the partition to separate us from the driver. "June, I'm sorry about what happened there. It was a mistake to mention the baby."

She looks straight ahead for a moment. Her shoulders are tense, almost as tense as they were when her parents were with us.

Then she takes a deep breath.

"I'm not mad about that. I mean, yeah, I was thrown. But I'm not mad." She squirms uncomfortably in place. "I wanted to tell you that the way you defended me, what you said back there in the café about me… It meant a lot. I know you were probably just playing your part. I'm sure you didn't mean any of the things you said, but—"

"I meant it," I tell her firmly. "I meant every fucking word."

Her eyes darken instantly. The next thing I know, she leans in and kisses me. Her lips press against mine, earnestly and enthusiastically, for the length of one shuddering breath before the self-consciousness creeps back in.

She pulls back, her face flushing with color. "I—I'm sorry. I shouldn't have done that."

I place my hand under her chin and force her eyes up to mine. "And I shouldn't do this."

Then I kiss the ever-loving fuck out of my bride-to-be.

42

JUNE

I straddle him and wind my fingers through his hair. It's thick and soft and smells faintly of sandalwood.

His hands start on the small of my back and then slowly slip down to my ass. The friction between us builds as his erection rubs against my inner thigh.

I break the feverish kiss we're locked in and stare down at Kolya. His eyes are dark and filled with unadulterated desire. It's almost enough to make me forget my self-consciousness.

"Kolya…"

He starts unbuttoning the front of my dress. My half-cup bra leaves my breasts spilling out a little, and he kisses them tenderly.

"Kolya, I—"

"Stop thinking, June."

"We're in a car—Driving—There's a—"

He chuckles. "The partition is soundproof. But if it makes you feel better…" He grips me tightly as he leans forward, taking me with him. I can't see what he's doing, but a second later, music floats through the air. Classical and lyric-less, but it's loud enough to make me feel comfortable.

"I want you now," he growls as he straightens back up. "And I'm not waiting anymore."

That's all it takes to convince me. That and the hungry look in his splintering blue eyes. I raise my hips and he pulls down my panties, then discards them like they offended him by ever daring to cover any part of me.

He undoes the remaining buttons on my dress, gets rid of my bra the same way he got rid of my underwear, then drags a finger down my bare torso all the way to my naked pussy.

This isn't the first time I've found myself completely naked before him. The first time we had sex was the same. Me—completely naked and completely vulnerable. Him—more or less completely clothed.

This time is no different. He doesn't seem in any hurry to take off any of his clothes. The only thing he allows me to do is unbuckle his pants and unzip him free.

I hold his cock in my hand and rub it slowly, all the while keeping my eyes on him. I have to admit—despite my reservations about having sex in a moving vehicle, it's also strangely exciting. My heart is thumping fast, drowning out all the voices in my head that wonder if this is such a good idea after all.

I expect to hear Adrian's voice loudest among them, admonishing me for moving on so fast, just like my mother said. But there's nothing from him. Radio silence.

I've heard him less and less over the last few days. It's as if he's disappearing altogether.

I ought to be sad about that probably. But maybe that silence is why I feel so much less guilty about what's happening right now.

When I pull back, raw-lipped and breathless, Kolya runs two fingertips along my bottom lip. Then he forces both fingers into my mouth.

"Suck," he orders.

I do as he says.

He watches me the entire time, and with every new suck, I feel myself getting wetter and wetter. Once I release his fingers, he slips them inside me.

I gasp, my grip loosening around his cock for just a moment as my body short-circuits. I bury my face in his shoulder and drink in that rich scent of sandalwood and vanilla.

I wonder if he tastes the way he smells, so I run my tongue along his neck to find out.

He doesn't.

He tastes even better.

"Fuck," I moan as his fingers slip deeper inside me.

He squeezes my ass, encouraging me to raise my hips. The moment I do, he pulls me back down on his lap, sinking into me in the same breath.

I cry out as he fills me up with one savage thrust. Maybe the running water from our encounter in the shower had distracted me from just how big he is, because this time, I really feel it. Every inch of it.

For half a minute or more, I just sit there on his cock, getting used to his girth. Then, when I can finally breathe again, I start moving, raising my hips and then lowering them back down again and again.

I go slow until I get a good rhythm going. Once I do, it's impossible to take it slow anymore. I ride him hard, slamming myself down on his length. Each thrust sends more adrenaline skittering through my veins. He burns beneath me. A furnace of brutal, all-consuming heat.

I brace myself against the onslaught of tremors that race down my spine until they finally break loose and overwhelm me. Then I'm coming and gasping his name in spluttered half-syllables.

But the whole time I'm coming, he never stops thrusting upwards. He fucks me right through the orgasm, and he doesn't stop, even when I go limp like putty on top of him.

He just starts moving a tiny bit slower. When I'm finally calm, he pulls my right nipple into his mouth and starts sucking gently.

And just like that, I feel the needles of desire ravage my body all over again.

I pull at his hair while he brings me to my second orgasm, a little slower and softer and fuzzier than the first. Only then does he give way to his own pleasure. I keep my eyes on him as the muscles of his face contract. His eyes narrow in concentration and the vein at the side of his forehead stands out starkly.

His jaw tightens and he lets out a small, barely audible grunt as I feel him erupt into me.

A wild thought runs through my head as he unleashes: *I'm glad to have a part of him inside of me.*

It's gone as soon as it came, leaving me wondering where that came from, why I thought it, what it might mean.

My forehead comes to rest against his. For a moment, I can't quite tell our breaths apart. I can't tell where he ends and I begin. He doesn't push me off him, and my legs are locked so tightly around his hips that I'm not sure I can move by myself.

He doesn't say anything, and neither do I. But there's a lot I want to say. How on earth can we have a fake wedding after we shared that together? Fake weddings are for fake connections, aren't they? And this feels so damn real.

More real than anything I'd shared with Adrian.

The moment that thought hits me, I feel horrible. All the guilt I'd managed to stave off up until now comes rushing back.

I have no right to compare the two of them like that.

I marshal what's left of my strength and slowly peel myself off Kolya's lap. He doesn't fight me. He just watches as I put my clothes back on. Then I fall into the seat beside him, spent and conflicted.

"The car's not moving anymore," I observe after a few seconds.

"We're home."

Home. It sounds right, but it shouldn't. This isn't my home. It was never supposed to be. I've gone along with too much already without asking questions.

"Kolya—"

Knock-knock-knock.

I jerk upright in a panic. Kolya sits up calmly. He buttons up the top two buttons I'd managed to work loose and swings the passenger side door open.

Milana is standing outside with a grim expression. "I'm sorry to interrupt," she says. "But I need you inside urgently."

She barely even glances at me before she turns and strides into the house. Kolya looks at me, one raised eyebrow saying everything he would never say out loud.

Then he follows her inside.

43

JUNE

I end up following Kolya to one of the larger sitting rooms on the first floor. Fire burns in the hearth and the arched windows draw in a soft breeze from outside.

A young woman waits by the fireplace. She's wearing a humble blue dress with a torn sleeve, and her dark brown hair spills down her back in large, elegant curls that make her look like something out of a fairytale.

Then she turns her face towards Kolya and me, and I realize that the expression on her face is the stuff of nightmares, not fairytales.

I stop at the threshold, transfixed and afraid, but Kolya follows Milana right into the room.

He kneels down next to the girl and says something to her, too low for me to catch. She nods once and then her neck drops. Her body shudders with devastating sobs, but no words that I can make out. Just pure anguish.

Weirdly enough, it reminds of Milana's anguish when she told me what her past had done to her, what her pimp had taken from her. It's the kind of anguish that has to be kept caged so it doesn't destroy everything in its path.

Milana looks up and spies me standing by the door, watching the scene unfold. She walks over, the sound of her heels muted by the thick carpet underneath her footsteps.

"Why don't you head upstairs, June?" she suggests. Her tone is polite, but there's no denying that it's a dismissal. "You look tired."

"What's going on?" I ask, looking past her.

Kolya gets to his feet. "Milana."

Milana gives me a bracing nod and the two of them trade places. I expect him to give me an explanation, but all he says is, "You should go upstairs now."

I bristle at the harshness in his tone. What hurts the most is the fact that I feel like it's deliberate. A way of discouraging me from asking questions. *Stay in your little corner, Junepenny. Don't even pretend you belong in rooms like this.*

"Who is she?" I ask anyway.

"I need you to go upstairs, June. Now."

I swallow my pride and go.

44

JUNE

I manage about three hours of fragmented sleep after that, and then I find myself wide awake, staring at the ceiling and wondering how I'm going to get through the night.

I abandon any hope of sleep and pull on my green silk robe, then leave my bedroom and walk downstairs in search of a glass of water and leftovers from the fridge.

The house feels different at this time of the night. Quiet, calm, teeming with secrets I've yet to uncover and stories I've yet to hear.

On the first floor, I'm about to veer towards the kitchen when I notice the golden glow of the fireplace emitting from the open door of the sitting room. I change course and go toward it.

She's still here—the girl from before. She's in different clothes now, though. Dark sweats and a long-sleeved pajama top, both of which look a little too big for her.

She catches my shadow from the corner of her eye and jerks to the side, her eyes going wide with fear.

I hold up my hands and freeze. "I'm sorry. I didn't mean to scare you."

The girl's eyes relax just a little, but her body stays curled in the same defensive position. "Who are you?" Her voice is soaked in fear and suspicion.

"My name's June. Who are you?"

"I'm Star." Then her eyebrows pinch together as if something in what she said pained her. "That's not my real name. I don't know why I said that. I'm Angela, actually."

"It's nice to meet you, Angela. Do you mind if I join you?"

She shakes her head, so I sit down in front of the fireplace, keeping a good three feet of space between us for her benefit.

She has a lovely face, heart-shaped and delicate. Her eyes are a deep, warm brown that matches the color of her hair perfectly. But things are swimming in there that I'm not sure I was meant to see. Harsh fears, bad dreams. Memories she'd rather forget.

I turn my gaze to the fireplace, only because I don't want her to catch me staring at all the scars on her body. There are two fresh wounds on her face, and several old ones scampering down her arms.

"Are you like me?" she asks abruptly.

"What do you mean?"

"I mean, did you come to Don Uvarov for help, like me?" she asks. "I… I didn't know for sure if the rumors were true, but I knew I had to try. I thought, if there was a chance it was true, and Don Uvarov was helping girls like me... then I had to try."

Despite the heat coming off the fireplace, I feel suddenly cold inside. "I'm sorry," I say softly. "For everything you've been through." It's just a guess, but it feels like the right thing to say.

She frowns. "But were you... like me? Did Ravil...?" Her voice fades away like she can't bear to finish the question.

I shiver. "Not quite, I don't think. I'm here for... different reasons. It's a long story."

She nods and turns her forlorn gaze back to the fireplace. "So's mine."

"I'm sorry if this is a stupid question, but... are you okay?"

She doesn't take her eyes from the fire. The flames dance in her eyes. "I don't know yet," she admits. "I think today's the first day I've felt like maybe I will be okay. One day."

Her scars glare at me, each one more alarming than the last. They look so out of place against the peaceful quality of her features. She can't be more than nineteen or twenty. Too young to carry so much permanent damage around with her.

"Do you want something to eat?" I ask.

She looks at me as though she's surprised by the question. "Now?"

I smile. "There's nothing like a midnight snack to make everything feel a little bit better. Trust me on that." I go to fetch a tray from the kitchen, load it up with food, and return, setting it down on the hearth between us. Angela hasn't budged from her perch.

"Help yourself."

She bites into a slice of pizza tentatively. Her face seems to quiver with relief. "I haven't eaten pizza in, like… six years, maybe."

"Six years wasted then," I say with an awkward laugh.

Angela smiles shyly. "Yeah. Maybe."

I swallow hard. Maybe it's pre-maternal instinct, or just plain stupidity, but my fingers are itching to reach out and smooth her wounds away. The fresh ones on her cheek especially. I let my hand float halfway across the space between us before I stop myself and sheathe my hand back in my lap.

"Can I ask you another really rude, way-too-personal question, Angela?"

She nods with a mouthful of pizza.

"Who hurt you?"

She glances down at her arms as though she's forgotten she has scars at all. They gleam in the firelight like they're absorbing the glow. Swallowing it up in a way that strikes me as unsettling.

"I gave myself these two," she admits, pointing at her fresh cuts. "Trying to get out of the building they had me in. There was a wire fence I had to slip under." Then she points to the largest scar on her arm, still scabbed over and nasty-looking. "I needed stitches for this one. My second pimp did this. The stupid thing was that I actually liked him at first. Isn't that crazy? He seemed nice. I was young enough that I thought maybe he cared about me."

I reach out and put my hand on hers. She flinches, but she doesn't shake me off.

"But I realized that it was just an act. He didn't care about me at all."

"I'm sorry, Angela." The words fall flat. Nothing I can think to say sounds big enough for what she's been through. I don't even know half of what she's suffered.

She touches her cheek and winces at the sting of pain. "This was him, too. He had this big ring that he never took off. He got mad and *bam,* there it goes. I hated that stupid ring."

I feel the tang of vomit rushing up my throat. I bite down to hold it back, and a second later, I taste salty blood instead.

"June... are you okay?" Angela asks, realizing that I'm not looking so calm anymore.

Before I can think of how to answer, I hear a sound behind us. Angela and I turn at the same time to see Kolya standing by the door. The moment he sees my face, his expression darkens.

"Angela. You should be in your room, sleeping."

She stands up nervously. "I'm sorry, Don Uvarov. I couldn't sleep."

He moves forward, making sure not to touch her. "There'll be plenty of time to talk later. For right now, get some sleep. You can take the snacks up if you want."

She throws me a glance, and I manage a smile, even though my blood is pounding like a full-swell symphony in my ears. "Go on, Angela. Sleep well."

"Thank you," she says tenderly.

She grabs a handful of snacks and heads out of the room. Kolya watches her go. Then he turns his eyes on me. For once, I think I can read what's in them.

And it reads something like the truth.

45

KOLYA

"You heard the tail end of that conversation, didn't you?"

"You should sit down, June."

She ignores me. "Your brother wore a ring. I think I mentioned that to you," she says, her eyes burning darker than the fire next to us. "I think I mentioned it to you today, actually. Two swords clashing. The exact same as what Angela just described to me."

"And you think her pimp and Adrian are the same person?"

I don't know why I'm taking this stance. Chalk it up to habit. Even after all this time, I still feel the need to keep my promise and protect him. Despite the fact that he stopped deserving it a long time ago.

"Do *you?*" she asks, throwing the question back at me.

I take a deep sigh. And then I just concede the truth. "I've been trying to figure that out myself."

Her eyes go wide. "Wait. So you don't know for sure?" she asks suspiciously. "But—you know everything."

I almost smile. If this whole fucking situation wasn't so cursed and convoluted, maybe I would have. "I'm glad you agree. But my brother's life was a mystery to me. Part of that was my fault. I chose to keep him at arms' length when I realized he had a problem."

"A problem?"

"The drinking, June," I remind her softly. "It started early."

She looks confused for a moment. "No—no, that's not true. When we met, he was fine. I mean, he drank, but it was never, like… excessive." I can see her mind whirring with effort as she tries to determine if her memories are accurate or just fantasies dreamed up to paper over the hideous face of her reality.

But that fails, of course. When it does, she shivers despite the oppressive heat in the room. "The drinking only got bad after The Accident."

The Accident.

She's just given me the opening I need to give her the rest of what she doesn't know. But for some reason, I can't bring myself to cross that line. Not now. Not when yet another part of her past is crumbling right before her eyes.

And since I can't give her that truth, I choose another one. "The drinking started when he was a teenager," I tell her. "When he was about seventeen. He went through a hard time with our father and alcohol was the only thing that seemed to help him."

"That was years before he met me."

I nod. "He had many masks, June. And he wore them well. He was charming and smart enough to pull them all off, make them convincing. He knew what to say and he knew when to say it. The only person he couldn't bullshit was me. Which was probably why he started to resent me in the end."

The silence is strained and painful. It's funny how both of us have handfuls of memories of Adrian's pain—both the pain he suffered and the pain he caused. Memories that only *we* have. She has hers. I have mine. They differ in content, but it all hurts the same.

"How common can a ring like that be?" she whispers. "A gold ring with two clashing swords? It has to be Adrian. We should talk to Angela some more. Ask her to describe —Maybe—"

"Angela has been through enough," I say firmly. "I don't want to inundate her with questions before she's ready to answer them."

"She was talking to me."

"Do you really want to make her feel like she's only important as a source of information? Do you want to minimize her suffering?"

I'm not a fan of manipulating June the way I'm doing. But I'm doing it to protect her as much as Angela. Angela can only tell her what I already suspect—that my brother had fallen even further into the abyss than I had initially suspected.

But I still have no idea about the extent of his dealings. And until I do, I want to make sure that June is shielded from the worst of his mistakes.

"No," June says, looking down at her feet. "No, of course not."

"I'm sure she'll be open to sharing her whole story with us when the time is right," I continue. "But right now, she came here for refuge. Our job now is to make sure she's protected. Ravil's men will no doubt be searching for her."

"Will they know where to look?" she asks tentatively.

"He knows I'm opposed to the prostitution trade, and he knows I don't participate in it, but he has no reason to believe I would actively move against him this way. Still, he'll probably have eyes on me regardless."

"Because of me," June infers softly.

"Yes. Because of you."

She shakes her head and her shoulders hunch forward as she tries desperately to hold herself together.

I take her hand and coax her onto the sofa. Then I sit down beside her. I can't scoop the nightmares out of her skull with my bare hands, though I would do it in a heartbeat if I could. She doesn't deserve to be tortured by them. *Give them to me*, I want to tell her. *I'll take the torture on your behalf. I'm the one who deserves it.*

"Kolya," she says, looking up at me abruptly. "I need you to be honest with me, okay?"

I nod, bracing myself for her next question.

"What do you think?" she asks, her voice straddling the line between calm and hysteria. "Do you think he was... that Adrian was... involved in this? Do you think he was hurting innocent women?"

I have some evidence to support that theory, but even still, it's hard for me to wrap my head around. My own brother, working against me, in the one industry I swore never to be a part of.

The worst of it was that he'd been there when I made the decision. He saw what led me to it. He'd looked Milana right in the eye and I was so certain that he noticed what I did—how deep some wounds really go.

Things happened after that, of course. Life happened, in all its ugliness and glory. Considering everything that we went through, I can understand his resentment—to a certain extent, at least. I can see where his respect for me had turned to bitterness, even hate.

But this?

This seems so far beyond that.

"I don't know, June."

She narrows her eyes. "You know something," she insists. "You know something, and you're not telling me."

"I knew that he regretted leaving the Bratva," I tell her. I'm giving her scraps when I should be serving her the whole damn meal. "He was angry with me for that."

"Why would he be angry with you for that?" she asks. "If it was his choice?"

"It was his choice to leave," I admit. "But he was young. Too young to realize everything else he would be giving up."

"Like what?"

"Like... this," I say, gesturing to everything around me. "The wealth, the luxury, the influence. He thought he wanted to be free of the life, but he just wanted out from underneath our father's shadow. By the time he figured out that getting one would cost him the other, it was too late."

"Too late for what?"

"You can't just walk out on the Bratva and then walk back in again," I explain. "He wasn't just anyone, some rank-and-file nobody; he was the son of the don. He cut ties with our world, changed his name, and disappeared. It isn't the kind of decision that can be unmade."

Tears are beginning to form at the corners of June's eyes. "He did always seem like he was… searching for something. Something he lost."

"Life in the real world was a cruel awakening, once the novelty of his freedom had worn off."

"Are you saying you wouldn't let him rejoin the Bratva if he asked?"

I shake my head. "Like I said, it's not as simple as walking back in when you've walked out. He had lost face with my men. They saw him as a coward. Many weren't afraid to say so to his face."

"What did you do?"

I raise my eyebrows. "I can't stop men from talking, June. My brother thought I could. But if I went around cutting every tongue that said something I didn't like, I'd have an army of mutes and a mountain of tongues and neither one would do me a damn bit of good. Not that it stopped him from pleading with me anyway."

She nods, shaken but understanding. "W-when was this? How long ago?"

"The first time he formally approached me about returning was five years ago."

She sucks in her breath. "That was... around the time we met."

Before or after—that's the question swimming around in her eyes. But she doesn't allow herself to ask me. Instead, she wraps her arms around her body like that's the last thing keeping her intact.

"Angela, she... she said certain things. About her pimp." She sniffles, then catches herself and stiffens her chin proudly. "That he was charming. And she thought he cared about her. At the beginning, at least." She stops for a moment to settle her shaking voice. "It reminded me of Adrian. That, and... and the ring she described."

"June," I say, placing a hand on her shoulder, "you need to breathe."

She looks up at me as though maybe I have the lifeline she needs. "I made excuses for him for so long," she says through the half-formed sobs. "Whenever he said something cruel, or got a little aggressive with me, I explained it away. Sometimes, *I* even comforted *him* after the fact. He was always sorry in the mornings. He was always sorry when he was sober." She shakes her head in self-disgust. "I never thought of myself as a fool."

"You're not a fool, June."

She laughs humorlessly. "Of course I am. I look back at every sincere moment I thought we had, and now, it just feels like... it feels like he used me."

I want to reach out. I want to touch her. But it feels wrong to do that now, when she's trying to unravel her past with him.

All this shit is melting together. There are no more boundaries to keep the world in order. It's just a blood-soaked fucking mess from start to finish.

"He was real to me," she murmurs. "But was I real to him? Was I anything to him?"

"I know he cared about you," I tell her, because as much as I want her to hate Adrian, I don't want her to feel like he never loved her. "He tried to get sober for you, June. He didn't succeed, but he tried, again and again. It wasn't for anyone else that he made the attempt."

I can see her trying to cling to those words, but they might have come too late.

"His sobriety attempts never lasted though," she says. "I suppose that says it all, doesn't it? I wasn't enough."

"Don't do that to yourself. Don't blame yourself for his weaknesses."

"I can't really trust myself anymore," she whispers softly, as if she's talking to herself. "I thought what we had was real. I thought he really loved me."

"Not everyone's version of love looks the same."

She locks her eyes on me, desperation mingling with sadness. It's like she's experiencing his death all over again. My heart—what's left of it—breaks right along with hers. "You know what's insane?"

"Tell me."

"I feel like I'm making the same mistakes all over again. Because," she says, and then stops short, as if that's the only thing she wanted to say. She swallows hard and takes a breath that leaves her shoulders shaking. "Because lately, I've realized that... that I have feelings for you."

I'm not expecting that. I'm not sure what she's expecting, either. But to my surprise, when she meets my eyes, it's not even expectation I see there. Just... resignation. Disappointment, perhaps. Masochism, almost certainly.

"And you wanna know what the *really* crazy part is?" she says, glancing away from me self-consciously. "I actually thought for a moment there that you might have feelings for me, too."

Jesus Christ. My entire body feels like a fucking live wire, and for the first time in my life, I have no idea what to do about it.

"But like I said, I can't trust my own judgment anymore," she says. "I'm only saying this because I'm so, so tired of pretending. Why even bother? The truth is pretty damn obvious. I stopped fighting you because I started to care about you. I resigned myself to living here because I wanted to be close to you. And when you mentioned the wedding..." She looks down at the ring on her finger. It glints back at both of us like it's alive, like it knows what's happening between us. "I was actually excited. Because even though you told me it was fake, somehow, I managed to convince myself that maybe a small part of it was real."

What the fuck is this feeling I'm having? Nerves? Is this what nerves feel like? Is this how it is to be human, to be vulnerable, to be alive?

If so, I despise it.

"I was willing to go along with everything, the pretense, the fake wedding, all of it, because I'd convinced myself that you cared about me. But—if that's not true, if I'm just a pawn in your game… please tell me," she begs. "Please let me go."

It takes me a dozen painful, thudding heartbeats to realize she's waiting for an answer. She's waiting for me to confirm or deny.

Do I have feelings for her, or don't I?

"June…" My voice breaks on the rocks, hoarse and useless. I'm being strangled by years of training. Years of repression working like a muzzle, rendering me silent.

What would I even say if I could? *Feelings for her?* If they exist, I'm barely even aware of it. I keep them frozen and locked away. Saying them out loud—to *her*, no less—is un-fucking-fathomable.

No. I can't. I am my father's son. I am my brother's keeper. I am Kolya Uvarov, don of the Uvarov Bratva…

And I am too far gone to be redeemed by her love.

"The wedding has to go on as planned," I hear myself say, cold and determined. "Feelings have nothing to do with it."

Her face crumbles. Before I can figure out how to salvage whatever we might've had, she's on her feet and moving towards the door.

I should stop her. I *want* to stop her.

But I can't.

It's a bridge too far for a heartless fuck like me.

46

JUNE

"... June?"

I look up and squint against the fluorescent lights overhead as Sara removes the blood pressure collar from my arm. "I'm sorry, did you say something?"

She smiles pleasantly. "I was just asking if you were okay. You seem a little distracted today."

"Oh. Yeah. Sorry. I didn't get much sleep last night."

"Any particular reason?"

I think about Angela. About the man whose baby I'm carrying. About two swords crossing in an emblem made of gold and stained with blood. It feels like there's so much information swirling around in my head that I can hardly keep track of everything I'm feeling.

"So many reasons I can't count them," I admit in a tired mumble.

Sara's eyebrows furrow down. "Stress isn't good for the baby, June," she advises. "Your vitals are good for now, but if there's something that's weighing on you—

"I don't belong here, Sara."

She stops short. The concern in her eyes deepens. "I was under the impression that you were happy here," she says diplomatically. "You seemed to be. For the last few weeks, at least."

I place my hand over my stomach, disappointed in myself. "I suppose I was. But only because I was in denial about a lot of things."

"Okay," Sara says, "now, I'm officially concerned. Talk to me. What's going on?"

I shove myself off the examination table and start pacing slowly. I have a decision to make and my window to make it is getting smaller and smaller.

Last night was revelatory about more than just my past with Adrian.

It was revelatory about my future, too.

"What's going on with me is that I don't want to be a pawn in men's games anymore," I say. I repeat what my sister had told me from the beginning.

I'd alienated her in the last few days. Despite the fact that she is here because of me. Despite the fact that she is only trying to help me.

More than that, actually—I hadn't just alienated her; I straight-up lied to her. She doesn't even know that Adrian and Kolya were brothers yet.

"Kolya is trying to protect you, June," Sara suggests. She puts her hand on my arm, forcing me to stop my pacing. Her eyes are intense and alert and intelligent. Friendly, too, but can I trust her friendliness? Or is that just another classic naïve June mistake?

"That's what he told me, too," I say with a fierce nod. "But maybe that was just what he knew I needed to hear. Let's face it—he's not interested in protecting me. He wants my baby."

"Two things can be true at the same time."

I frown and pull away from her. "I shouldn't be talking to you," I say coldly. "You're in his pocket. He's bought you like he buys everyone else."

Yeah, maybe I'm looking for a fight today. The more I think about things, the more worked up I get.

Unfortunately for the petty voices in my head, though, Sara doesn't rise to the bait. She takes a deep breath and just keeps looking at me with unadulterated concern. "I can see why you might think that. But I had money before Kolya Uvarov and I'll have money after. I didn't take this job for the pay out."

"Then why did you take it?"

"Because I like Kolya," she says simply. "And I trust him."

"That's easier to do when you're not a prisoner in his home."

"You won't be a prisoner for long, June. This is just a safety precaution. An extreme one, I'll give you that. But—"

"There are no buts, Sara!" I explode. "I shouldn't be here! Neither should my sister."

"Listen to me," Sara says, grabbing my hand again. Except this time, there's nothing remotely calm about the strength of her grasp. "I'm not sure how much you know about Ravil and his—"

"I know enough."

"Good. Then you should know that leaving yourself vulnerable to him would be catastrophic," she says urgently. "I've treated several of the women who've lived under his thumb. The stories I've heard… They're gruesome, let's just leave it at that. And that's coming from a doctor who's seen her fair share of corpses splayed open on examining tables."

She lets her fingers go slack. "No Bratva don can ever be called a hero, June. But Kolya sure comes close. I don't agree with everything he does, but in this one thing at least, he has my complete and total support. That's why I like him. That's why I trust him. That's why I'm here." She takes a deep breath and adds, "And that's why you're here, too: because it's the safest place for you to be right now."

I have to admit, she's convincing. There's a part of my soul that wants so badly to believe he's a good man. That he'll keep me and my baby safe out of the goodness of his heart and nothing else.

Stay here, it's begging. *Trust him.*

But I can't see a way for me to stay.

Not when staying means falling even harder for Kolya. Not when staying means giving away more years of my life to yet another man who doesn't love me.

I have a child to think of now.

I avoid her eyes, trying to hide my inner thoughts from her scrutiny. "I have to go," I tell her. "I just want to be alone right now."

Sara sighs. "I understand. If you ever need to talk…"

"Yeah. Thanks."

She gives me a bracing smile that I can barely return. Then I leave the medical wing and whisk back to my bedroom. I don't quite have a solid plan, but it's taking shape bit by bit.

I have to leave—that much is obvious. I have to leave precisely because I want to stay so badly. There's no way I can go through with a fake wedding to a man I have real feelings for, knowing he doesn't care about me in the same way.

It would be the emotional equivalent of self-flagellation. And I'm done doing that.

It's no longer enough that I love the man I'm with.

I want him to love me, too.

First comes first, though: I need to talk to my sister. I need to explain things to Geneva. Maybe not everything, and maybe not right away. But she needs to know enough to explain why we need an escape plan out of this monster's labyrinth.

I get to the landing that leads to our adjoining rooms—when I notice a shadow to my side. I stop short, my eyebrows pulling together.

"June."

"Kolya," I whisper, my heartbeat thudding unevenly against my chest.

Seeing him today, after the declaration I made last night, feels even more painful. It crosses my mind that I might be running from heartbreak, rather than running towards a more independent future.

After all, if he had given me anything other than a rejection last night, I wouldn't have been contemplating escape. I'd be contemplating a white picket fence, a shaggy golden retriever, and two point three beautiful children with splintering blue eyes. I'd be contemplating his ring on my finger and his taste on my lips.

I'd be contemplating a beautiful lie.

"I'd like to speak to you for a moment," he rumbles. It's not quite a question—Kolya never really asks those—but it's as close as he'll ever get to asking my permission for something.

It makes me very nervous.

"I was just on my way to see my sister."

"You can see her later," he says, his voice downshifting into something darker and sharper. "Come with me."

He turns and leaves. He doesn't even glance behind him to make sure I'm following. As my heartbeat rises heavily, I force my feet forward in his wake.

He leads me down to the second-floor office. The darkness swaddles us as we step inside. The blinds are drawn tight and a thin wreath of cigar smoke floats through the air, still fresh.

That makes me nervous, too.

"What's going on?" I ask, right before I hear the click of the lock. I twist around to face him. His blue eyes are the only twin points of light in the darkness. "What is this? Why am I here?"

"Trying to run would be foolish, June," he says bluntly. "You've tried it before and it hasn't worked. This time won't be any different."

My eyes go wide as I realize the obvious explanation. "I just left her office. She must have ratted me out the moment I stepped out the door. That fucking bitch."

"Sara was concerned about you. That is all."

I laugh darkly. "Of course. I'm such a fool. Obviously, she'd go running to you the moment my back is turned. She's just another one of your minions."

Maybe I will get the fight I'm after today. And this match-up seems so much more appropriate. If a little uneven.

"Sara cares about you."

"Bullshit!" I yell. "If she cares about me, she cares about me the way that Adrian did. Which is to say, not at all."

Kolya fixes me with his composed, apathetic gaze, completely unmoved by my outburst. I wish I could shake some emotion out of him. Something that would betray what he's really thinking. I wish I could crack him open with a hammer and see what, if anything, is inside.

"This is all your fault," I spit at him.

"Is it? Go on. Tell me why."

It's like he's the professor and I'm the student who can't seem to wrap her head around the topic at hand. "You should have done whatever it took to keep Adrian from the bottle. You should have let him back in the Bratva, if that's what he wanted. Who cares if he wanted to join your little fucking boys' club again? But no. You had to be all high and mighty about it. So yeah, it's your fault. No wonder I could never help him. He didn't need my help; he needed *yours*."

He just stands there, taking it.

"You should have done more," I continue. "You should… you should… have given him a purpose. Given him direction. If you'd been there for him, then maybe, maybe—

"He wouldn't be dead right now?" Kolya supplies quietly.

Is that what I'm mad about? The fact that Adrian is dead? My hand unconsciously twitches in the direction of my stomach. I may be carrying his baby, but in many ways, his absence in my life has been a relief.

Kolya takes a step towards me. I freeze.

"If I had been a better brother, Adrian wouldn't be dead right now and you would be free to be as mad at him as you want to be. You would be free to question him, challenge him, hold him accountable for his sins."

As Kolya speaks, his words slip slowly into my head and lodge themselves there. I have been spoiling for a fight today, but the person I'm really mad at is not here to take the brunt of it.

I lock eyes with Kolya, wondering how, in a matter of mere months, this stranger knows me better than anyone else ever has.

It started with lemon soda and the scent of vanilla. And now, here we are.

Who the hell knows where we'll end up next?

"Adrian's demons were not ones I could conquer on his behalf, June," he tells me gently. "I tried. Believe me, I fucking tried."

His tone isn't quite as apathetic as his expression suggests. I find myself taking a step closer, leaning toward his warmth like a flower seeking sun.

"What happened?" I whisper, before I truly know if anything happened at all.

"You don't even know his real name, do you?"

I suck in my breath. Of course he had a different name. *Adrian* —it's so wholesome, so All-American, so obviously fake. Somehow, in all this time, I've never thought to question it.

"Bogdan," Kolya fills in. "My brother's name was Bogdan Uvarov."

"Bogdan," I whisper, trying to associate the name with the man I knew. It doesn't fit. Not at all.

"By the time we hit our late teens, our father decided that I had been protecting Bogdan for long enough. He wasn't satisfied with the progression of Bogdan's training. So he decided to take matters into his own hands."

The phrase alone has me shivering. I know what it means now when a man like Kolya "takes things into his own hands." And if I've learned anything about his father, it's that he was capable of far uglier things than Kolya would ever do.

"We were called into the cellar late one night. There was a woman gagged and bound to a chair. I was told to stand in the corner and not to interfere, no matter what. My father ordered Bogdan to kill her."

"Why?" I whisper, even though I know it's a pointless one. Stories like this only end one way.

Kolya shrugs. "To this day, I don't know what her crime was. It could have been as big as betraying my father to our enemies, or as small as being insufficiently polite. He didn't see the world in shades of gray, or even black and white. It was one color only: red like blood."

My body goes cold. I want to tell Kolya to stop, but my mouth has gone numb.

"The first thing Bogdan did was look at me. Our father pulled out his gun and pressed it to Bogdan's temple. He told him that if he looked at me again, he'd be dead. I had to stand there and watch."

"H-he did it?" I ask, even though I already know the answer.

"With his bare hands. She screamed and clawed at his face, but he did what he was told to do."

My stomach twists with horror. Had I really spent years with the man in this story? Had I kissed his brow at night and told him everything would be okay in the morning? If only I'd known. I'd never have said such things. How could anything be okay after that?

"No. No. No," I say again and again, as though my sheer willpower can turn back time and stop this from happening.

"My father had Bogdan bury the woman's body himself. He was never the same after that. He had always been a little lost, but after that, he was utterly broken. He followed our father's orders like a trained dog. He became as ruthless, as cold as he was told to be. So you're right about one thing, June: it is my fault. If I had done what I did sooner, I would have spared so many so much pain."

I feel my legs buckle, so I limp over to the couch and sit down gingerly. My entire body ripples like jelly. And at the same time, it feels like there are a thousand different needles pricking at my skin. Pins and needles, but painful. Excruciating.

"He walked away from the life he knew, thinking that was what he wanted. But it was too late. Neither one of us realized that until later. Changing his name and identity couldn't change what he'd done. His demons followed him into the outside world, and he unleashed those demons on the people he found there."

He doesn't have to say the last piece: *people like you.*

I haven't heard Adrian's voice in my head for a long time. Probably around the time I started developing serious feelings for Kolya. I felt guilty for that for a while.

But not anymore. Now, I'm glad I don't have his voice haunting my thoughts.

I don't want to know what he would say.

"Your suffering is a byproduct of my inaction," Kolya says, pulling my back from the abyss I'm close to falling into. "I was the one who sent Adrian out there."

"Kolya…"

But my voice trails off. I don't know what I want to say.

"You've been a pawn for long enough, June," he continues quietly. "Telling you about my past has forced me to realize something: I refuse to turn into my father. And I don't want to be like my brother, either. I've kept you in this house because I thought I could protect you. I thought I knew better. But that was my mistake—believing I had the right to make the choice for you."

My eyes go wide.

"So if it's really what you want, I will cancel the wedding," he finishes. "I will let you go. Say the word, and you'll never see me again."

47

KOLYA

I'm not in my body. I'm floating out of it, above it, watching this scene play out from afar.

Did I really just release her? Did I really give her permission to walk away from me?

It goes against every instinct I have to let her go. Not just because she's in danger if she does, but because—

Because...

Fuck.

"Kolya."

I pull my eyes up to meet hers. Those perfect, deep hazel eyes that seem to contain the world's warmth in their center. She takes a tentative step towards me. "Y-you're really going to let me leave?"

There's no going back now. "If that's what you choose."

She stares at me as though she's searching for something. Then she takes another uncertain step forward.

"Why?"

"Why?"

She nods. "Tell me why."

"I just did," I snap impatiently.

She doesn't so much as flinch. In fact, she looks as though she's lost the ability to feel fear in my presence. "I will leave," she says, and something inside me cracks open. It can't be my heart, because I'm pretty sure I lost that a long fucking time ago. "But first, I need to know. I need to know if the real reason you're letting me go now is because… you do have feelings for me. Feelings like mine."

Silence. My heartbeat is so loud I'm sure she can hear it. *Ba-boom. Ba-boom.*

"You should be halfway out the door by now," I growl at her.

She refuses to take her eyes off mine or let me take the easy way out. "Not until you give me an honest answer."

"June—"

"Kolya," she fires back, taking the final step that puts her right in front of me. Her chest is practically shoved up against mine. She looks up at me like a little lioness, ready to go in for the kill.

All fierce determination. All unfettered pride.

"There were two boys in that story you told me. The boy who was forced to do horrific things and the boy who was forced to watch helplessly. I don't doubt that you have your own traumas, your own pain. It must be easier to shut your heart away so that you can't feel any of it anymore."

She raises her hand and places it on my chest, right over my beating heart. It's as if she's trying to remind me that I have one.

"Denying your feelings doesn't mean you don't have any," she says. "So for once, stop denying—and give me an honest answer."

Her voice hitches up. Tears pool in the corners of her eyes. They turn her hazel irises into a bed of embers.

Fuck, she's beautiful.

"Do you have feelings for me, Kolya?" she asks, simple and forthright.

I've spent most of my life lying. I've always had a good reason to. But right now, staring down at that unflinching gaze, I realize I've run out of reasons.

I've run out of road—the path my father laid at my feet has come to a sudden and abrupt end. There's an abyss waiting for me, and I can't see the bottom from where I'm standing.

If I take one step forward, I'll fall in.

If I say one word, I'll fall in.

Every cell in my body is screaming at me to shut my eyes and back away before I do something I cannot undo. So I take one deep breath and do the bravest thing I can.

I jump.

"Yes," I whisper. "Yes, June. I've loved you from the first lemon soda."

At first, I get no reaction at all. And then, her face splits open in a smile that's laced with tears.

Her fingers twist into the front of my shirt, pulling me to her like she's scared I might bolt. A part of me is tempted to do exactly that. There are so many feelings coming at me so fast that my instinct is to fight back.

But those eyes have a hold on me that is far stronger than my sense of self-preservation.

I cup the side of her face with my palm and stare down at her. I never let my gaze linger too long before, just in case she suspected what I already knew but refused to admit to myself.

That she means fucking everything to me.

She smiles up at me, the corners of her eyes going all soft and hopeful. I kiss her tenderly, breathing new life into our complicated dynamic. It might still be complicated afterwards, but for right now, it feels natural.

It feels right.

It feels inevitable.

She doesn't even try to take my shirt off this time. But she strips down quickly, as though she's desperate to be rid of her clothes.

She's never been this bold before, or this free. There's not a shred of self-consciousness left in her. Her eyes are alight with desire as she bares herself to me.

I unbuckle my pants and she pulls them down. The moment my cock springs free, I grab her by the hips and hoist her up around my waist. Then I walk us backward until her back hits the wall. She gasps as my cock hits her slit. She's soaking wet. So wet that I slip inside her without any effort at all.

Like I was always meant to be there.

And from that point, there's no way I can hold any part of me back. I fuck her hard as she clings to my shoulders, her eyes rolling back in her head. I keep my gaze on her face, her gorgeous lips, the perfect curve of her neck.

I want to memorize this moment. I want to burn in this heat.

I manage to stave off my orgasm long enough to give her one. But the moment I can feel her cumming around my cock, I let go. I pump into her a few more times, draining myself empty, and then I drop my forehead onto her shoulder.

Her arms loop around me, gripping me tightly, holding me as much as I'm holding her.

It's all over so fast. I carry her back to the couch, muscles sore and protesting. I place her on it and settle down on top of her, angling my body to the side a little so that my entire weight is not crushing her.

She stares at me unabashedly, toying with my hair like she's never felt anything quite like it before.

We lie there in the silence for God knows how long, drinking in the luxury of being with each other. Of *choosing* to be with each other. Without the pretense or the power plays.

I've fucked a lot of women—but it's never felt like this.

This is the first time it's felt real.

"Kolya… what's going to happen with Angela?"

I clear my throat. "There's a community of women who have something of a rehabilitation center out west. For people who have suffered like Angela has. Milana will place her there for the time being. Once she's back on her feet, we'll help her get a job, an apartment, and an alias if she wants one."

June smiles sadly. "You've done this before."

"More often than I'd like."

She runs her finger down the bridge of my nose. "You're a good man, Kolya Uvarov."

"Bite your tongue."

She laughs, and the sound sends this strange, giddy thrill straight through my metal heart. "I don't feel guilty anymore," she says, her voice crackling in the silence. "Do you?"

"I never did."

"I never felt safe with Adrian," she admits quietly, her smile fading as she speaks. "I was with him for years and I never felt like he was truly mine. And after The Accident… losing the baby… my life with him just felt off-kilter. I guess, in a way, I was waiting for us to break."

She's so lost in her thoughts that she probably doesn't notice how stiff I've become in her arms.

The Accident.

The one secret I've yet to tell her. The one she most deserves to know.

"I don't feel that way with you, Kolya," she murmurs. "I feel safe. Whole."

I have to fucking tell her. She's going to see my scars eventually. And when she does, she's going to ask questions. Questions with answers that can only break her heart.

"I love you, Kolya," she whispers to me. "In a way I've never loved any other man."

Fucking tell her. Tell her, you coward. Tell her, tell her, tell her.

"June…"

"And I want the wedding to be real."

I pull myself up on my elbow to look down at her. "Excuse me?"

She nods, tears glistening like sapphires in the corners of her eyes. "I don't want a fake wedding, Kolya. You and me… This isn't fake. So why should our wedding be?"

And just like that, I decide that our future is more important than my past. Telling her now would only break her heart, and now that she's given her heart to me, I have to protect it.

No matter what it costs.

48

JUNE

"It's not too late, you know. I can cause a distraction and you can get the hell out of here."

I turn to my sister with my eyebrows knitted together. "Another runaway bride joke. How original."

Geneva crosses her arms. "What makes you think I'm joking?"

I sigh and walk over to the bagged gown laid out on the bed of my hotel suite. "Shouldn't you be changing into your bridesmaid's dress?" I ask as I unzip it to reveal the shimmering opal fabric.

"Fine," she snaps irritably. "I'll go change now."

She heads into the bathroom, and I revel in the silence. The suite has been bustling since the moment we arrived three or four hours ago. There was the makeup team, the hair team, plus Anette and her many clipboard-bearing minions.

They all had questions on top of questions. Flowers and seating and timing and songs and ushers and this and that and that and this.

It was all so overwhelming. Geneva had to remind me of my answers seconds after I'd given them.

But the end result is beautiful. Four hours as the focal point of an army of hair and makeup artists left me glistening like something ethereal.

Van and Marilyn had created an intricate vine of French braids that wove and threaded through one another. My makeup was mostly natural, with a little extra oomph around the eyes and deeper color on my lips. It's fairytale bride with an edge, and I approve wholeheartedly.

Now, the last piece of the puzzle is the dress.

It took half a dozen fittings to get the gown to lie just right without revealing my small but growing baby bump. The work was worth it. The crepe and chiffon float like they've never heard of gravity, and the off-white color with pale blush detailing glows like the deepest part of a pearl.

Not strictly speaking traditional, but I kind of like that about it. This wedding isn't strictly speaking traditional, either.

The last week has been a flurry of final stage planning.

It's also felt like the beginning of the rest of my life.

Being with Kolya—really, truly *being* with him—felt like the relationship I'd always hoped that Adrian and I would one day mature into. A week of waking up in his arms, of making soft, slow love in the dawn… I didn't know it was possible to love and be loved like that.

Of course, the one shadow hanging over me is my sister's sour face. She pretends to be supportive, but in odd moments, I've caught her dark looks, her worried glances.

I just don't know what she'll do about them.

The door opens and the silence is punctured by the snip-snap of high heels and a whole lot of confidence. Milana walks in looking like a Grecian goddess in a Vera Wang gown that includes a full-on cape. The dress is a dark, rich purple and the cape is a shadowy black that matches her dusky makeup perfectly.

"You look amazing," I tell her, breathing in the subtle cloud of Chanel number five that billows around her.

She tosses her head to the side playfully. "You should be dressed by now."

"Sorry, I was about to. Then I got lost in the silence."

"There'll be silence enough after the wedding." When I frown, she laughs. "That was in no way a dig at marriage. I just meant you won't have to deal with all this wedding hoopla."

I smile. "No offense taken."

"Let me help you into the dress."

I shrug off my lavender robe and get to my feet. I stand there in a nude lace bra and matching panties that don't cover much of anything.

Milana gives me an approving nod before floating the dress in front of me so that I can step into it. It takes her only a few moments to zip me up and twist me around to face the full-length mirror.

"There," she says, pushing my hair over my bare shoulders. "Now, that's a fucking bride."

I laugh. "Do you think he'll like it?"

"He'll like anything you're in," she assures me, brushing out my skirts just a little before she moves to stand in front. "You should know your parents are out there."

I frown. "Are they seated?"

"They were hovering a little down the hall, so I assumed they wanted to see you. I pointed them in the direction of the ceremony hall. They can wait their turn."

I give her a grateful smile. "Bless you."

"Do you need a little liquid courage before your solo walk down the aisle?" she asks, pulling out a tiny little silver flask from a fold in her dress.

"I'm pregnant, Milana," I remind her.

She rolls her eyes. "I know. It's not from me; it's from your future husband."

I take the flask and have a modest sip, knowing what it'll be before it even hits my tongue. I have to control my laughter so as not to spit out the mouthful of lemon soda.

I swallow and shake my head. "He knows me well."

"Then you're one of the lucky ones," Milana says, gliding a hand over my belly without the faintest bit of jealousy.

I haven't brought up the day in the medical wing again. Milana made it clear that she didn't want to discuss it, and I intend to respect that. Even if she deserves the chance to fall apart in the arms of someone who cares about her. She hasn't said so, but I know she appreciates my willingness to pretend like I didn't see her at her most vulnerable moment.

I bite my lip. "Milana… I might need to pee."

She laughs. "Well, you are pregnant. I suppose it's to be expected."

"Urgh," I groan. "I just put the dress on. Wait—hold on. False alarm, I think."

"Are you sure?"

I nod. "I think so. How long do I have 'til show time?"

"I'll go check. But not more than twenty minutes or so." She heads for the door, her cape swishing in the soft breeze floating in from the partially open French doors of my balcony.

I'm starting to get nervous. But it's more excited nerves than anything else. "Milana?" I say quickly, before she can shut the door behind her.

"Yes?"

"How is he?"

She smiles. "Handsome and confident as always. You can't crack that composure with Thor's hammer." I giggle, but she continues. "I think he's a little nervous, but only because this is so important."

I exhale slowly. "Thank you."

She gives me a wink and closes the door with a sharp click. Right on cue, the bathroom door opens and Geneva walks out of the bathroom in her pale lavender chiffon dress and a scrunched-up expression on her face. "She gone?"

"Were you waiting for her to leave?"

"Duh. That woman freaks me out."

I frown. "Why?"

"Because she works for *him*. Something's off about that relationship."

"Nothing's off about that relationship," I snap defensively. "You're not giving either one of them a fair shake."

"Considering the first impressions they made, I don't think I need to." Then she seems to notice for the first time that I'm in my wedding dress. "Wow, Juju. You look amazing."

I ignore the compliment. "Sit down, Genny. We need to talk."

"Whoa, sounds serious. You gonna break up with me or something?" she asks. "Because I don't think you have that option with siblings."

"Just sit," I say impatiently, conscious of the time. Sighing, she sits down on the edge of the bed and I join her there. "I know you don't like Kolya, but he is going to be my husband."

"I know," Geneva sighs. "And you're having his baby and—"

"That's just the thing," I say, placing my hand on her arm. "I'm not."

Geneva freezes for a moment, her eyes flitting to my stomach before moving back up to my face. "I'm not sure I'm following. You are pregnant, aren't you?"

I take a deep breath and a leap of faith at the same time. "The baby is Adrian's, Genny," I tell her.

Silence.

Silence.

Then...

"WHAT?!"

I stare at her calmly so that she understands that I'm not kidding.

"How... how is that—wait! Does Kolya know that?"

"Of course."

Geneva frowns. "I don't understand."

"That's because you don't know the whole story. Maybe I should have told you sooner, but I'm telling you now. And I need you to just sit there and listen, okay?"

For once, she nods wordlessly.

"Adrian had this whole past life I didn't know about. The night he died was the same night I found out that I was pregnant. And right after that, I met Kolya at his funeral."

"You met him at Adrian's funeral?"

"They're brothers, Gen."

She just blinks at me. "Adrian was born Bogdan Uvarov, Kolya's younger brother. He left the Bratva when he was younger and took a different name to get away from the world he knew. Except... he couldn't really give it up the way he thought he could." I take a staggering breath. "There was so much he kept from me. So much he lied about. And being the naive idiot that I was, I never asked too many questions."

"Y-you're going to marry Adrian's... brother?" Geneva asks slowly.

"It was only ever meant to be a fake wedding," I tell her. "A way to throw Ravil off."

"Ravil?" she asks. "How does he fit into this?"

I nod. "Ravil is Kolya and Adrian's cousin. He formed a competing Bratva with a breakaway faction of Kolya's. And now, he feels threatened by the fact that Kolya will soon have an heir."

Geneva frowns. "So it's not Kolya's baby you're carrying…"

"But Ravil doesn't know that."

Slowly, she starts to get it. Her eyes go wide. "You were trying to trick him into believing that you were carrying Kolya's baby so that he would have the upper hand."

I nod. "Exactly."

"But… I still don't get it. What's in it for you? Why are you going along with this?"

I take her hand and hold it tight. "I'm going along with it now because I love him, Genny," I say, looking her in the eye because I want her to know how much I mean it. "I love him and he loves me."

"And how do you know he's not manipulating you like Adrian did?"

It's a fair question, but it hurts regardless. I had been prepared to walk away from Kolya and the whole wedding. The only reason I hadn't is because he convinced me that his feelings for me are real.

What if it had all been an act?

I consider that for all of five seconds before I fall back on the last week with Kolya and everything we've shared in that time. It isn't just about what he said, it's about what he did.

Pressing a fresh lemon soda into my hand every time I finished the last.

Massaging my knee every night before bed to ward off the phantom pain.

Pulling me close into his arms when I dreamed of crashing glass and screaming metal.

It wasn't all an act. It couldn't be. No one is that good an actor. And I'm not the naïve girl I used to be. He is a Bratva don and I know he has to do awful things sometimes. But the way I see it, he does far more good than bad.

And that, for me, is enough.

"I know it," I say with conviction.

But Geneva barely hears me. "Listen," she says urgently, "this actually might work out. I can still try to contact Ravil. He'll help. Especially now that I know you're not carrying Kolya's baby. Ravil has no reason to hurt you."

I grip her hands tightly. "I need you to hear me, Genny," I tell her. "I'm staying because I want to. Not because I'm being tricked or used. This is right. I didn't expect it. I doubt he did, either. But somehow, impossibly, we fell in love. I want to be his wife. And he's willing to raise my baby as his own. He'll protect us both."

"Honey…"

"Genny, please," I beg. "Trust me."

She takes a deep breath and exhales slowly.. "Okay," she says. "Okay then…"

"So you're going to give Kolya a chance?"

A shadow passes over her face. "Y-yes."

"Good," I say, breathing deeply as I get back on my feet. "And just so you know, he and I have talked about our... situation. He's keeping you in the mansion because he wants to protect you, too. But if you want to get back to your apartment, that can be arranged. You'll just have a little security to be on the safe side. Just in case Ravil tries to contact you again."

She looks at me a little glassy-eyed, clearly still in the middle of processing everything. "Okay."

I give her a quick peck on the cheek. "It's all gonna work out, Gen. I can feel it. Now, if you'll excuse me, I really need to pee now. Get me out of this dress fast."

Smiling distractedly, she unzips me and I jump out of the dress and run into the bathroom. I pee, check my makeup and hair in the mirror, and then head back out to the room to Geneva.

Except that she's not here. The room feels eerily quiet.

"Genny?"

I check the balcony, but she's not there, either. I circle the suite twice before I'm forced to conclude the obvious: she's gone.

My heart thuds uncomfortably. What mistake did I just make?

I just wanted to tell her the truth. I owed her that much.

Knock-knock-knock.

I grab my discarded robe and pull it on, with a strange ringing in my ears. I cinch it tight at the waist and step to the door.

But when I open it, no one seems to be standing on the other side.

Frowning, I walk out into the hallway. That's when I spot him: the bodyguard who'd been assigned to stand sentinel outside my door. He's lying on the dark carpet, bleeding from the head.

I back up, a scream lodged in my throat.

But instead of hitting the wall behind me, I back right into the arms of someone whose face I can't see. I open my mouth to let that scream loose. Before I can, I feel something sharp and painful slide into my neck.

The scream withers on my lips.

And the world goes black.

49

KOLYA

"How're you feeling?" Milana asks as she steps up to my side at the altar.

The hall that June and I picked for the ceremony is the largest ballroom at the Grand Ritz. In just a few minutes, it will be the place where we're joined forever as husband and wife. And it won't be fake. It will be real.

To her. To me. To everyone seated here to witness it.

What a fucking miracle.

"It feels…"

"Surreal?" Milana offers with a knowing smile. "I agree. Can't say I ever thought I'd see the day."

"That makes two of us."

"But you know what?" Milana says. "You and June—it makes sense. And that's saying a lot, considering how the two of you came together. I just hope…" She trails off. "I'm sorry. I told myself I wouldn't bring this up today."

I don't have to ask what she's talking about. "I've decided not to tell her."

"Kolya!" She pulls to the side, and her dark cape swishes dramatically with the movement. "How are you going to keep it from her? It amazes me that you've managed to hide your scars from her this long. But after you're married…?"

"I guess I'll have to lie," I drawl. "In the big picture, it's the least of my sins."

"Sounds like a healthy marriage."

"You're in no position to lecture me about what's healthy and what's not," I snarl before I can stop myself.

Her face floods with hurt. I know the only reason I can see it is because she's letting me see it. Then she plasters her mask back on and turns towards the waiting crowd.

"She should be here by now. Maybe I should go and check on her. Where is Anette? She was supposed to give June the cue."

"Milana—"

She turns to me with a tight smile. "Hey, don't worry about it. This is your wedding day. We shouldn't be fighting."

"We never fight," I remind her.

"Only because I let you think you're right most of the time." She scans the ballroom. "But seriously, where the hell is Anette?"

I feel a weird little spike of tension in my spine as I survey the guests. Most are long-time allies; the rest are my most trusted Vors, along with their various plus-ones. Vetted and double vetted, every last one of them.

So why do I feel like something is off?

"I'm gonna go check on things," Milana announces. She's clearly experiencing the same sense of unease.

I stay rooted in place for half a beat before I abandon my post. "I'll come with you."

"You're the groom."

"I'm also the don."

Some of my Vors stand up as I walk past, their faces alert and ready for anything. "Boss?"

"Be ready," I let them know. Just in case.

The moment we clear the ballroom, I know something's definitely not right. The atmosphere is rife with tension and panic. Hotel staff is rushing from corridor to corridor like a bunch of headless chickens.

That's when I spot one of my men. I'd assigned Knox to the security detail at the elevator. He rushes forward, face taut with tension.

"The wedding planner is down," he says. "I rode up to the bridal suite, and she was lying on the floor just in front of the elevator."

"Where's the security detail?" I demand furiously. "They're supposed to be guarding the bride!"

"All three were tranqued," Knox tells me. "Looks like an inside job."

"Goddammit," Milana growls, dashing over to my side. "The fucking sister."

"Where is she?" I hiss, turning to Knox.

He clearly doesn't know who I'm referring to. "I checked the bridal suite. The sister wasn't there and neither was the bride. But—"

"But what?"

"Her dress was," Knox whispers. "The gown was sitting there on the floor…"

I turn to Milana, who looks flushed and fierce. We both spit the same word in unison.

"Ravil."

50

JUNE

I wake up.

Well, sort of. More like I'm caught halfway between a dream and utter blackout. Things have shapes and colors, but nothing is set in stone, everything is fluid, the world won't obey its normal rules.

I'm aware of a ringing in my ear that sounds vaguely like Bach's Fugue in G Minor. My feet tingle automatically, as though encouraging me to dance.

And for a moment, my heart lifts at the prospect. Then I get a whiff of something salty and metallic, and the smell yanks me right back to reality.

A reality where I'm a dancer who can no longer dance.

A reality where I'm a bride without a groom, a woman without a future, a mother without a hope.

My eyes snap open and I sit up with a gasp that suggests that something weighted was lying on my chest all this time.

Except there isn't. My arms and legs are free, too. There's nothing holding me down, nothing restraining me.

I check my watch. I should be walking down the aisle now. And yet, I'm lying on a massive four-poster bed in a room I don't recognize. The thick, velvety curtains are drawn, leaving me to pick through the near darkness for clues.

What the hell is that smell? Cloves and something else… Pepper? Why does that scent ring a warning bell?

"Hello, June."

I scream.

"You," I gasp as I finally spot the silhouette slouched in the far corner of the room.

As I watch, the silhouette pushes off the wall and draws the curtains a few inches to the right. Light creeps into the room in a narrow beam…

And Ravil Uvarov steps right into it.

"Welcome to my humble abode," he croons. "It was so sweet of you to have your wedding this close to my home. That was convenient. Although, I am a little hurt that I wasn't invited."

As far as I can tell, it's just the two of us in here. Which is one person too many, in my opinion. I get off the bed, my robe billowing treacherously around my bare legs.

"That's a beautiful garment," he remarks.

I make sure to keep the bed between us. "You know if you're going to kidnap a girl, you could at least wait until she's fully dressed."

He smirks at me, his eyes flaring brightly. "Is that what my beloved cousin did?"

"What did you do to Kolya?"

He looks surprised by the question. "I've done nothing to Kolya," he says. "We're family. I would never hurt him."

"Where is he?"

"If I were to take a wild guess, I'd say he is standing at the altar waiting for you to float down the aisle towards him," Ravil says with a self-satisfied little chuckle. "If you look to the left, you can see the Grand Ritz from here. Maybe you'll even spot him through the window."

I don't look. If Ravil expects me to take my eyes off him for even one second, he's delusional.

"What's the matter, darling?" he asks, turning his gaze back on me. "You don't look very comfortable. Perhaps a wardrobe change is in order."

He gestures towards a huge armoire standing tall in the corner. I deliberate for a moment before I decide it's best to play along. But I keep him in my peripheral vision the whole time as I pad over and tug the doors open.

Ravil doesn't make any attempt to help me, but I'm thankful for that. I want him to keep his filthy fucking distance.

There's a bunch of clothes hanging on the inside. All women's, and all dresses that remind me a little of the outfit I saw Angela in the first time I met her. Floaty materials, soft silhouettes, and pale pastel colors. The kind of clothes you dress dolls in. Feminine and dainty and somehow nauseating.

And so many of them. Why would any one woman need…?

Oh.

My stomach twists when the truth hits me. They're not for any "one" woman. They're for dozens. Hundreds. As many women as Ravil and Adrian and the men who work for them can get their hands on.

I snatch the dress closest to me and turn to Ravil in disgust. "You're a fucking monster!"

He seems amused by my fury. "Why is that? Because I have good taste?"

"The curtains behind you would beg to differ."

His smile stays in place, but it becomes tighter, more forced. "I see my cousin didn't take my advice. A woman who talks back quickly loses her appeal." He points at a folding dressing screen over my shoulder, a bamboo frame with canvas stretched taut across it.

The canvas is marked with art—row after row of dancing little swans. It makes me sick. "If you'd prefer to change in privacy," he says.

I retreat behind it, making sure I keep his blurred silhouette in my sights. When he can't see me, I exhale and my whole body sags forward, preemptively defeated. Through a nearby window, I can see the high arches of the Grand Ritz.

Nothing has ever looked so far away.

Don't you dare quit, says a new voice in my head that sounds the way vanilla would sound if it could speak. *Don't you give him the goddamn satisfaction.*

Kolya's voice is right. I grind my teeth, strip quickly, and pull on the puff-sleeved white dress I grabbed from the wardrobe. It's not the white dress I was expecting to wear today, but that's okay.

Soon enough, it'll be red with Ravil's blood.

I step out and eye him warily. He's sprawled on the bed now, hands tucked behind his head like he's ready for a nap.

"How did you get past Kolya's guards?" I ask quietly.

He grins. "I had to kill quite a few. The sad part is that they never saw me coming. And of course, I had a mole on the inside, which expedited matters significantly."

I freeze. He's giving me a smile that makes my spine feel like jelly. "M-mole?" I repeat. Though I know the answer before it even leaves his lips.

"I think you know her. In fact, I believe you're related."

"Geneva." I breathe out her name like it's a curse.

He chuckles darkly and nods. "I must say, she's not nearly as pretty as you are, but she's a lot more interesting. A lot more cunning, too. She managed to conceal her burner phone from you and my cousin quite expertly."

I think back to the night of the ball. To all the moments that followed. Geneva had never been a fan of Kolya, but she'd been so vehemently opposed to him right from the beginning that I should have suspected something.

I *did* suspect something, actually. I just chose to believe she would side with me. I chose to believe she would trust me. I chose to believe in my family.

Apparently, I chose wrong.

"Where is she?"

"Safe," he promises. "She made me promise not to hurt you. It seems you told her some pretty horrendous things about me."

"None of them were lies."

"How do you know?" he asks, sitting upright. "You're only repeating what my cousin has told you. What makes you think you can trust him?"

"Because I know him."

He raises one eyebrow. I hate how it looks so similar to when Kolya does it, and yet so wrong at the same time. It's a familiar gesture in an unfamiliar face, and the effect is physically repulsive.

"Do you now?" he asks rhetorically. "It's funny—I convinced your sister that you were hoodwinked by Kolya's charms. I convinced her that you were brainwashed. How ironic to find that I wasn't lying?"

I shake my head. "It's just like an arrogant man like you to assume that a woman doesn't have opinions on her own. I can make up my own mind about people, Ravil. You're just pissed off I didn't settle in your favor."

"So you went along with the whole fake baby plan because… why, exactly?" he asks. "Because you loved him?"

My hand lands protectively across my belly. "It's not a fake baby."

"It might as well be. Adrian's child is of no value to me."

I shudder a little at the implication. The way an unborn baby's life can be reduced to just an asset or a liability. He notices my disgust and his smile becomes wolfish. Then his eyes flatten with anger, and I realize that I'd prefer an actual wolf.

"You have made me a fool," he growls. "You and Kolya both. I believed the bullshit fable you peddled and now, my men do, too. If I were to reveal the truth, they would believe it was a self-serving lie."

"They would also think less of you for being fooled in the first place," I point out before I can think better of it.

He pulls back his lips to reveal his sharp teeth. "That, too. Which leaves me with only one option."

My hair stands on end and my breath hitches in my throat. I could've kept my mouth shut, but what would that have done? Only delayed the inevitable for a few seconds more.

"You're going to kill me," I guess.

Ravil recoils like I spat in his face. "Kill you? Of course not! Killing *'krov* is a grave sin in the Bratva."

I roll my eyes. "Right, because it's so hunky-fucking-dory in the real world."

He shakes his head sadly. "Kolya learned that to his detriment. And since I don't plan on repeating his mistakes, I'm not going to kill you." He pauses before he breathes, smirks, and says, "You're going to kill yourself."

51

KOLYA

"Sir?"

I glance at Knox. "Ready. Aim."

A hundred guns cock in unison. It's a ruthless announcement of our arrival, but I haven't come here to play diplomat.

Then I drop my hand and say the word that seals Ravil's fate.

"Fire."

All hell breaks loose. I pull back, surveying the chaos so that I'm better prepared for Ravil's defensive.

As I suspected, Ravil's home is fortified, but his men are unprepared for our visit. This mansion was purchased recently and deeded under an alias. There's no way I would have known about it unless I'd done a deep dive into his dealings the past several months.

Which, of course, I had.

I'm not sure how I feel about Ravil underestimating me, but I'm pretty sure he'll never do it again. Not that I'm going to give him the opportunity.

Milana and half of my men clear a path to the mansion, lined with the bodies of men who chose the wrong don. I follow the path right into the foyer.

Two spiral staircases greet me from either side of the marbled expanse. Overhead, a dome glass ceiling regurgitates refracted rays of sunlight. It's like stepping inside of an uncut diamond.

I look at Milana. "You take the right," I tell her. "Two gunshots in the air when you find her."

"Copy that."

We mount the staircases and end up at opposite ends of the same corridor. She gives me a nod and we head off, our guns drawn, squads of men trailing in our wake.

I kick down one door after another. Empty. Empty. Empty.

But my fourth attempt strikes gold.

The door smashes open to reveal Ravil standing on the other side, holding my fiancée in front of him as a human shield.

She's wearing a flimsy white dress that looks like it belongs to a teenager. Ravil has the side of his face pressed against the locks of her hair. His arm is wrapped around June's waist, and he's holding her so close that she's straining hard against him, nose upturned and jaw clenched tight.

"Cousin," I growl, taking my finger off the trigger as I step gingerly into the room.

I'm just about to fire off the two alert shots that Milana and I had agreed on when Ravil hisses at me, "You alert any of your people and I will shoot her fucking brains out." He's holding a gun to June's temple.

She flinches against the cold mouth of the weapon, but her jaw tightens and she keeps her eyes squarely on mine.

I feel like I'm about to explode out of my skin. All I want to do is close the distance between us and beat Ravil to death with my bare hands.

Instead, I force myself to stay in place.

"You found me fast," Ravil observes.

"I didn't have to find you at all. I knew you purchased this property hours after you signed on the dotted line. I didn't expect you to bring the fight here, though." I sigh and let my gun dangle at my side. "Let her go, Ravil."

"Why would I let go of my bargaining chip?"

"Because that's the only way you're going to get out of here alive."

He laughs loudly, making June flinch again. "You're not going to kill me," he says confidently. "Killing your father cost you half your Bratva. Even you wouldn't be so dumb as to do that twice."

"Abolishing the prostitution trade cost me half my Bratva, and it was a cost I was willing to bear."

"That choice gave me everything I have. It gave me money. It gave me power. It gave me an army of men who despise you."

"And yet you're the one who's cornered."

His eyes narrow. "Let me go, and I'll let your little whore live. Do anything else, and I'll show you no mercy."

I have to suppress my laugh. "That'll be hard to do in cuffs, cousin."

My eyes flit to June's. She looks like a woman who's put her trust in me. "But fine," I tell Ravil. "Let's make a deal. I'll let you leave, with your life and your freedom alike. Just let June go."

Ravil's eyes lock on mine, trying to measure out how far his trust in me extends. He wants to believe me, but he's not sure. Then he pushes June forward suddenly. She stumbles, but manages to stay on her feet, right between Ravil and me.

Ravil raises his gun at the same time I do.

"How good is your word, cousin?" Ravil growls.

I think about it for a moment, and then I jerk my head towards the door. "Go now," I order. "Before I change my mind."

June inches towards me, but I keep my eyes on Ravil as he moves towards the door. We're locked in a dance, matching each other step for step. Him toward freedom. Me toward her.

And then Ravil decides to improvise.

He's about to disappear through the door when his hand lifts. "NO!" June screams, a split second before two shots fire.

My gun and his.

I feel her slam into my side in an effort to take the bullet that was meant for me. I hear her scream in my ear, and the next thing I know, I'm on the floor, with June's body half covering mine. The wet heat of blood blooms between us.

I release my gun and wrap my arms around June, gripping her tightly. From the heavy sound of her breathing, I know she's in pain.

"June," I breathe. "June."

"It's okay," she says, but her voice is weak. "I'm okay."

I twist our bodies around, placing her gently on the carpet. Her eyes are wide and fixed on me. She's conscious and alert. I scan her body and notice the blood on her right arm.

The bullet has sliced past the inside of her bicep. It's a flesh wound, nothing more. I exhale with relief.

"What the hell were you thinking?" I demand, relief giving way to anger. "You could have been killed!"

I can see Ravil's body in my peripheral vision, but I ignore him. He's not moving, and his gun is lying on the floor out of his reach.

She smiles faintly at me from the ground. "Is that your way of saying thank you?"

"Ravil's always been a lousy shot. I was never in any danger." I bend down and kiss her hard on the lips. When I pull back, I cup her face. "I need to stop the bleeding. Can you sit up for me?"

"What about Ravil?"

I glance back over my shoulder at his body. I got him through the chest. His frozen eyes are fixed on me with vindictive malice that he'll never be able to act on now.

"Dead."

That seems to give her the strength she needs. She grips my arm and I pull her to a sitting position. Then I hoist her into my arms and carry her over to the bed.

"Does it hurt?"

"Only a little," she says bravely.

I've never been more proud of her. Maybe that's why I don't think as I tear off my shirt to make a tourniquet for her. I wrap it tightly around her wound, and when I'm done, she sags with relief.

"Don't worry," I say. "Sara will take care of that wound properly the moment we're back home."

The door opens abruptly and thumps into Ravil's body in the process. Then Milana steps through, her eyes going straight to Ravil before she finds June and me.

"Guess I came to the party late." She jumps over Ravil's corpse and is followed inside by another dozen of my men, all armed to the teeth. "June? Are you okay?"

"Got my first bullet wound," June says, sounding surprisingly chipper. "Does that conclude my initiation? Am I Bratva now?"

Milana smiles and shakes her head. "As good as." She turns to face me. "Orders, Don Uvarov?"

I stand tall to survey my men. "Get his body out of here. He'll get a funeral for the sake of his last name. The other dead will be cremated. Bring a car around immediately. I need to get June home to see Dr. Calloway."

Milana nods and heads out to see to things, while two of my men grab hold of Ravil's body and haul him out. I turn to June, ready to carry her downstairs, but one look at the expression on her face has me freezing.

"What's wrong?" I ask.

"Your torso," she says, her face pale. "T-the… scars…"

Fuck.

I stare at my shirt that's now wrapped around her arm. I took it off willingly, without thinking. "I… they're not…"

For the first time in as long as I can remember, I'm faltering for words. At the crucial fucking moment.

"That's why you never took your shirt off around me," she whispers. "You were trying to hide the scars."

I had made the decision to lie about this. I thought I'd settled on it. But now, staring at her trusting face, knowing that she jumped in front of a bullet for me, out of *love* for me… I know I can't lie to her.

She deserves better.

She deserves what Adrian never gave her.

She deserves the truth.

"Yes."

Unease starts to edge into the corners of her eyes. "Why?" she asks, sitting up a little. She winces and grips her injured arm with the other. She shakes off the pain and fixes me with a piercing gaze. "Kolya. Answer me."

And even though I'd vowed never to break her heart, I know I have to. If there's to be any hope of our relationship being different from what she shared with Adrian—I have to tell her the truth.

What happens after that is anyone's guess.

52

JUNE

He isn't speaking.

Why isn't he speaking?

The look on his face says I won't like what he has to tell me. And that realization alone makes me want to forget about the scars and pretend like I don't see them. Like they never even existed.

But I've spent too much of my life burying my head in the sand. It feels like the easier option in the moment, but it's the kind of sacrifice that feeds away at your soul.

I love Kolya Uvarov.

But I refuse to love him at the cost of myself.

"Kolya, please," I say, my voice coming out raspy and fearful. "Just tell me."

I can smell blood and sweat. I can smell the stench of death despite the fact that Ravil's body has been removed from the room. My nose seeks out the scent of vanilla beneath like a security blanket. It's there, but it's masked. Stowed away on the other side of the thing I least want to hear.

"I was there the night of your accident, June," he rumbles.

His words don't immediately register. I frown and repeat them again in my head. "Wait… what accident?"

His eyes dip down and land on the scar on my leg. That's all the answer I need.

The night your dancing was taken from you.

The night your baby was taken from you.

The night your world was taken from you.

"Y-you were there?" I stammer. "I… I don't understand."

He moves to the side of the bed and sits down, facing me. His weight feels comforting, but his words have my heart spinning in painful ways.

"Do you remember where you were before The Accident? That night, where were you?"

I've tried hard these past two years not to think about it, but I couldn't truly forget if I tried. "I, um… I was out with some work colleagues," I tell him. "We decided to get drinks after rehearsal. Adrian said he'd meet me at the bar, but he was late."

"He was late because he came to see me," Kolya explains. "More specifically, he came to threaten me."

I frown, but I can't talk. I can only listen.

"He walked into my office unannounced. I could smell the alcohol on him. He was just drunk enough to speak freely, to behave rashly without any regard for the consequences."

Consequences. Like a warning signal, my injured arm starts to ping with pain every few seconds. Almost as if to distract me.

"He told me that he was done being pushed around. He wanted his pound of flesh. He told me to cede control of the Bratva to Ravil."

My breathing hitches up. "Why would Adrian want that?"

Kolya shakes his head. "I can only guess. Maybe he thought Ravil could legitimize him in a way I couldn't. Maybe he just believed that I didn't want him redeemed at all."

"I feel like I'm going to throw up," I blurt.

"We don't have to talk about—"

"I want to know," I say fiercely, meeting his eyes so that he knows how serious I am. "How was he threatening you?"

Kolya sighs. "He knew secrets about the Bratva. Certain deals, certain alliances. He threatened to tell Ravil everything if I didn't agree to his terms. It would have been catastrophic."

"What did you do?" I ask, even though I think I already know.

"I stopped tolerating him," Kolya says, his voice practically a growl. "I promised Adrian a long time ago that I would always protect him. But I never thought I'd have to protect him from himself." He strokes his chin, lost in memories. "That was the first night I realized that I might not be able to save him. That maybe what he needed was a reality check. I grabbed him and threatened him right back. I told him that if he moved against me, then I would no longer grant him my tolerance or my protection. In response, he tried to take a shot at me… and then he ran."

My heart is hammering so hard that I'm worried I'll miss the rest of this story. "H-he came to me…"

Kolya nods. "He picked you up believing that I wouldn't pursue him if you were in the car."

"You were in the black Hummer," I murmur. "That was you."

I can hear the haunting screech of tires that haunted my dreams for months after The Accident.

"I wasn't going to hurt him—"

"He was driving like a maniac that night. Like he was scared—like something was chasing us. Like something wanted to kill—"

"He was paranoid. I would never have killed him."

"You killed your father!" I cry out.

Kolya's jaw snaps shut, and I feel the invisible wedge drive between us. When he reaches for my hand, I pull it away, pushing the wedge in deeper.

I can see his composure set in as he gets to his feet. "I need to get you to Sara," he says, his tone relapsing back into that stone-cold apathy he does so well.

I muster up my remaining strength and stand. My bicep aches, but I support it with my good arm and start walking. "I'm not going anywhere with you."

"June—"

I twist around, my fury taking hold of my body. "Do you know what I lost that night!?" I demand, choking on my sobs. "It wasn't just my career, Kolya. I… I was pregnant. I lost my baby!"

He stands where he is, watching me warily. He doesn't inch closer.

"You were hiding this from me."

"Hear me out."

"NO!" I scream. "I'm done hearing you out. You, Ravil, Adrian—you're all the same. Men who think that the world is their fucking sandbox. Just… just leave me alone."

And then I run the hell out of that room, away from him, away from all the lies. I expect him to follow me, but I don't hear his footsteps. Not a single sound of pursuit.

When I get to the foyer of the house, I notice two cars parked out front through the glass windows. I change direction and head to the back of the mansion.

I'm not really paying attention to anything. I have no sense of direction and no plan. I just want to get away.

I run through the gardens, my breath coming in painful gasps. An unmanned gate lets me out onto a deserted road. At the end of it, the city looms, tall and foreboding.

I pause to glance at my arm. Kolya's tourniquet is doing a good job of managing the bleeding, but I doubt it'll work for much longer.

So I grit my teeth and start the painful march to the city.

∽

I walk for a while. My knee hurts. My arm hurts. My heart hurts. The world is silent for most of it, aside from the shuffling of my feet and the rasping of my exhales.

Then I register the sound of an approaching vehicle. What are the chances a kind stranger will offer me a lift anywhere? Slim to none, considering my current state. Most people don't make it a habit to pick up blood-soaked nobodies off the side of the road.

And where would I even go? It's not like I can go back to my house. That'll be the first place he looks. My whole past is dead and barred to me now.

No, I'll have to run. Somewhere new. Somewhere he won't expect.

The car screeches to a stop right beside me. The passenger side window slides down. I'm halfway to asking for help when I realize that the driver is masked…

And pointing a gun right at me.

"Get in now," the masked man growls urgently. "He'll be looking for you."

I freeze. *Why does that voice sound so familiar?*

"Hurry."

The moment I'm inside the car and the child locks click into place, he tucks the gun away.

"Sorry about the gun, Junepenny. I just needed you to get in without a fight."

"Who are you?" I demand. "Who…"

"What's the matter, baby?" the man asks, reaching for his mask. "Can't recognize me?"

He pulls it off in one swift move, and I catch a mess of dark, overgrown hair and brown eyes that leave me feeling nauseous all over again.

Adrian smiles, as though he's picking me up from work like he used to. Back when I thought I loved him. Back when I trusted him.

And the gold ring on his finger glimmers in the dying sun.

TO BE CONTINUED

June and Kolya's story continues in Book 2 of the Uvarov Bratva duet, SAPPHIRE TEARS.
Click here to keep reading!

Printed in Great Britain
by Amazon